The Cave of Healing

The Cave of Healing

Adventures in the Worlds of In and Out

WILLIAM HAPONSKI
Illustrations by Mary Barrows

ISBN 1523471859
ISBN 13: 9781523471850
Library of Congress Control Number: 2016900948
CreateSpace Independent Publishing Platform
North Charleston, South Carolina

Caves and Kids Books
8284 SE 176th Lawson Loop
The Villages, FL 32162

info@cavesandkids.com
http://cavesandkids.com

In our mailbox we found this note from Mr. and Mrs. Squires:

Dear Reader,

We cordially invite you to use your imagination and visit us in our wonderful world of In. You will find our cave life fascinating and come to know why we love living here.

Squatty, our son the scientist, says, "All cave formations you will see are real as are the creatures you will meet--some friendly and some terrifying."

Henry and his granddaughter Peggy, our new dear friends from your world of Out, add, "During your journey you may wish to visit Internet and see photos and descriptions of cave formations and creatures we encountered such as

cave stalagmites, stalactites, soda straws, pearls, helictites, flowstone, draperies

blind cave fish, wolf spiders, salamanders, centipedes crayfish, crickets, pseudoscorpions

and many, many more."

Mugs agrees and says "Whoof!"

Your friends always,

Squiggly, Squeally, Squatty, Squishy, Squeezy, and S.Q. Squires

The strange boy said he came from In. At first Henry was thoroughly confused. He was sure he was hallucinating. But with time he would come to know that In was a place of healing.

Part 1

SQUIGGLY SQUIRES, HENRY, AND MUGS: THE GIFT?

One

A Boy from Squiresville

It was not a good day for Henry, almost worse than his most terrible days in the war. He had made his way into the upward-sloping woods behind his house and, panting from the climb, slumped down on the huge rock. An old dented army canteen cup was upside down at his feet. Next to it clear cool water came out of the ground. In the springtime when the water table was high the water made a small stream, but in the summer it slowed to not much more than a trickle. When he had built the house years ago, in those good years, he piped some of the water inside. The rest he had diverted into the large stream near the road. His wife Laurel had helped, shovel in hand.

Mugs was still in the yard below, sniffing his way along slowly. The small dog had once been white as new-fallen snow but was now arthritic and yellowed with age.

Dear Mugs--squashed-in face, teeth out of line--the reason Laurel had picked him several years ago from among the three at the animal shelter. The other two were so cute they would get adopted right away and this dog would get euthanized. She liked him and his crooked smile, and thought the dog might help Henry.

"Who are you, Sir?"

Startled, Henry whipped his head around and saw a young boy standing close to him.

"Don't *do* that!" he scolded.

"Do what?"

"Sneak up on people!"

"But Sir, I didn't. I just formed, and there you were."

"Formed? Formed what?"

"Just formed, Sir."

This was a very strange boy who spoke nonsense. He was maybe a little younger than Peggy, his granddaughter, Melanie's girl. His appearance was extraordinarily strange. Not much of his skin was showing, but what Henry could see was almost translucent, similar to thin, white alabaster that was sometimes used for small windows in medieval churches.

The boy was dressed like those in pictures he had seen of kids from maybe a century or so ago. He wore a light-colored, long-sleeved shirt and long trousers, tucked around the

4

wrists and ankles. On his head was a similarly light-colored broad-brimmed hat from which a shock of such light hair poked out on his forehead that it seemed white. Covering much of his delicately pale face, he wore very large, very dark sunglasses. He should have been in school instead of standing here in the woods.

"Do your parents know where you are?"

"Of course. They sent me here, Sir."

This was getting more weird. Henry had never seen this kid. He knew several of the farm boys along the road, but not this one. Hoping to be able to get him home again safely, Henry asked, "Where are you from? Where do you live?"

"Squiresville, Sir."

"Squiresville? I know all the towns around here and I never heard of it. Where is it?"

"It's in In, Sir."

"Look, you're a very nice boy, and you don't have to call me Sir. You can call me just Henry."

"Thank you Mr. Just Henry."

"No, only Henry."

"I'm sorry Mr. Only Henry."

"No. No!" Henry stopped just short of swearing. "I'm just Henry!"

"Yes, I heard you, Mr. Just Henry."

Henry gave up. This whole thing was so absurd, seeing things, talking to himself. But hallucinations were nothing new. He had had plenty. At VA, Doctor Shepherd told him his drinking didn't help any.

At least this delusion was not terrifying. The kid was polite, and his face had a sweet look, what was not hidden by the glasses.

"What's that?" the boy asked.

"What's what?"

"That thing," he said, pointing.

Henry looked and saw Mugs making his way painfully up the hill toward him.

"That's just Mugs."

"Will Just Mugs hurt me"?

Henry sighed. "No. You have to tell me where you're from. Your parents will be worried."

"Are you sure it won't hurt me?"

"Mugs won't hurt you. He's just an old dog. He likes children."

"A dog? What's that?"

Henry ignored the question and said again, "Where are you from?"

"I'm from In."

"Yes, you said that, now tell me where you're from."

The boy dropped his head in exasperation. It was so hard to get grownups to understand anything. He said one more time, emphatically, "I'm from *In*!"

"In where?"

"Don't you *know*," the boy impatiently responded, stomping his foot. "There!"

He pointed at the hole next to the rock. It was about the size of a fist. Water trickled out of the bottom of the hole.

"Where?" Henry had raised his voice.

"There!" the boy repeated, pointing again, raising his voice even higher.

By this time Henry too was exasperated. He shook his head, trying to figure it out. Despairing, he slowly sat down on the rock. His head ached.

Two

In and Out

For a moment they were silent. "Okay," Henry said. "Let's start over. What's your name?"

"Squiggly."

Henry smiled a little despite himself. This was a rather pleasant delusion. "Squiggly. That's a nice nickname. What's your real name?"

"Mr. Just Henry, why don't you believe anything I say? My real name's Squiggly."

"Okay. What's your last name?"

"Squires. Squiggly Squires."

This kid knew how to tease. It was not going to be easy to send him on his way.

"Okay, Squiggly Squires, now tell me where you're *really* from."

Sighing, Squiggly Squires looked through the very large, very dark sunglasses at the very dim figure in front of him and replied, "If I tell you, will you tell me?"

"Tell you what?"

"What's a dog."

"Oh, that." Henry looked at Mugs who was panting heavily, putting one paw ahead of the other, coming closer.

"Yes," he said finally. "I'll tell you." Somehow he had to find out where this kid was from.

"It's a deal," said Squiggly. "I'm really from Squiresville which is in In," said Squiggly. "Don't you know where that is?"

"No."

"I live in In, you live in Out. Simple."

The boy pointed again at where the water was coming out of the hillside. "Squiresville is in In. And In is in there. It's nice. I like living there--well, almost always. Sometimes it's difficult. Then I have to go to Squabblesville."

"Oh, I see," said Henry, not understanding, though not quite giving up. "But how did you get here?"

Hanging his head in frustration, the boy said, "I told you. I formed."

This was getting difficult. As difficult as some of the early sessions Henry had had with mental health counselors. He had not wanted to go, but finally gave in to Laurel's pleadings. The first one, a psychiatrist, needed more help than Henry did, a real nut case. The second, a psychologist, discretely picked his nose during the sessions. So it was not until years later and the third one, a psychologist, a good one--Doctor Shepherd--that he had begun to open up. Henry understood frustration. He was an expert in frustration. So he said, "Tell me how you form."

Startled, the boy said, "How? You just do."

"Oh, I see."

This might take a long time, Henry thought, and by now Mugs was getting closer. The boy, though, was so rapt in his explanation he seemed not to notice the little old dog, panting up the hill.

"And where is Out?" Henry asked.

"I told you. You're *in* Out."

"Of course," Henry replied. "I'm in Out. I know that."

The boy seemed more relaxed now that he was being understood so thoroughly.

Patiently, like an older child instructing a younger in the mysterious ways of the world, Squiggly went on, "When my parents told me to go to Out, I thought of Water. It would take me there. Simple. Water goes right past Squiresville."

"And so here you are," Henry said. "Simple."

Three

JUST MUGS AND SQUIGGLY MEET

Deeply in thought, the boy was about to add something when Mugs came up behind him and made a soft "Whoof."

The boy screamed and jumped at Henry and clung terrified to him.

"It's okay. It's okay, it's just Mugs. He won't hurt you. He loves everybody, especially children."

Squiggly was sobbing and clinging to Henry. His hat had come off and his very large, very dark sunglasses had gone askew. The boy's hair was all white. Henry had only a second to glimpse the irises of his eyes before Squiggly frantically straightened the sunglasses so Henry could barely see his eyes. Henry had never seen anything like these eyes. They were a pale gray. Not brown, blue, light green, hazel, or darker gray such as most eyes are, but pale gray with perhaps a touch of pink. For that instant the boy had looked like--like what? Not a ghost, not an angel. Perhaps a figurine, one made of almost translucent alabaster. Strange.

"Are you sure Just Mugs won't hurt me?"

Henry grinned despite himself. He had been depressed when he climbed the slope into the woods, but this was a very funny hallucination. In a way it was like the night terrors he had started having a few years after the war when things had gone from bad to worse between

Laurel and him and everybody and everything. There had been nothing funny, though, about those times when he had hurtled out of bed, drenched with sweat, thrashing about, screaming in the dark. He could imagine that this imagined boy must have been terrified to see a very dim frightening shape of Mugs suddenly behind him. The boy was nice, and Henry was having a very pleasant hallucination, not like the terrifying ones he had had, so he might just as well play along with it

"No, he won't hurt you," Henry said. "He likes boys."

Somewhat calmed, but still clinging, Squiggly lifted his sweet face and asked, "You said Just Mugs is a dog?"

Straightening the boy's hat, Henry wiped away the tears on his cheeks. Henry replied gently, "Don't you see he's a dog?"

"A dog?"

Pause.

"And a dog doesn't bite?" the boy asked.

"Well, yes, a dog bites," Henry acknowledged. "Dogs bite to eat food, and sometimes they bite other dogs or cats or people who bother them, but mostly, dogs love people and don't bite. Mugs loves everybody. And besides, his mouth is small, and he can't open it very well, so he would hardly be able to bite you. Here, you can pet him."

Henry took the boy's hand and gently put it on Mugs' head. The hand, tense at first, slowly relaxed and began to rub. In a minute or two the once-terrified boy was squatting beside the dog, smiling and patting Mugs' head, and the dog responded with a big wet tongue against his face. Squiggly pulled back and giggled.

"He kissed you," Henry said. "See, I told you he loves boys. Nice boys."

By now Squiggly had his arms around Mugs' neck and was hugging him. "He smells good,"

Squiggly said.

"Yeah, doggy good," Henry nodded.

"And Just Mugs is soft and warm, Mr. Just Henry."

Henry decided to relax and play along with this hallucination. He sometimes talked to himself. Even before the war. Lots of people sometimes talk to themselves. Nothing weird about that. He might as well talk with this imagined boy.

"Squiggly," Henry said, "you can call him Mugs. He likes to be called Mugs."

Squiggly smiled and softly said, "'Mugs'--I like that--------------------- 'Mugs,'" he repeated, softly.

Henry could see that Mugs liked it too. He had what looked like a crooked teeth grin on his face.

"And you can call me Henry."

Squiggly said, "Sure, if that's what you want, Mr. Henry."

Henry nodded. At least that was better. Maybe there would be no more "Just Henry."

"Squiggly, may I ask how you got that name?"

"Oh, sure. You see, in In, parents don't name their children when they're born, of course. They wait usually until a child can walk and talk and has a more developed personality. Before that, parents just say 'sweetheart' or 'my little honey' or something like that. My mother and father loved to hug and hold me, and I liked that but they say I wanted to be down, running around, so I wiggled and slid down out of their arms. And since our name was Squires-----

"You became Squiggly Squires."

"Exactly," said Squiggly with a big smile.

"Squiggly, how old are you?" Will you tell me how old you are?"

"That's easy. Kind of. I'm a lot older than my baby brother Squishy and a little younger than my sister Squeally and quite a bit younger than my older brother Squatty. Even though he's young, he's a scientist, he really is—and he's only somewhat over--let's see--I'm not very good at this--Squatty, he is so much better at calculating--but I think Squatty is about--well, I guess I have to use Out time so you can understand it. Squatty is about five million, six hundred thousand years old. I'm three million, eight hundred thousand fourteen years old--actually a little more than that since I recently had a birthday. Actually, right now, three million, eight hundred thousand fourteen years, two months, two weeks, five days, seven hours, eight hours, nine hours, ten hours-oh, I can't go on. It's hard to count so fast."

"Hmm, Three million and some years old. Well, that's quite old. You don't look that old. You don't look a day over two million."

Squiggly tried hard not to be annoyed, and said as gently as possible, "You don't believe me again. If you're not going to believe me, why do you ask questions?"

Squiggly had a point, but before Henry could answer, Squiggly asked, "Why are you sad?"

"I'm not sad."

"Yes you are. I watched you."

"Why? Because I was a soldier, *that's why!* I was in a war. They depended on me. They needed me. I -----"

Henry was almost crying.

Now it was the boy who had his arms around the man. Squiggly said, "Don't feel sad, Mr. Henry."

Squiggly didn't know what those words meant--soldier, war-- but they were upsetting Mr. Henry.

"I'm sorry for asking bad questions. I'll go away now and come back when you're feeling better. I'll unform. Goodbye. Goodbye Mugs." Squiggly gave Mugs a pat on the head, and the dog looked up at him.

In a second or two, the boy that had been Squiggly shrunk into a tiny vapor and disappeared back into the small hole where the cold spring water trickled out of the hillside. Henry, watching the wisp disappear, was seeing things. It was a hallucination. Nothing more. But Mugs struggled to his feet and looked sadly at the spot.

For a long time, until the sun began to set, Henry sat on the rock.
Seeing nothing.
Hearing nothing.
Thinking nothing.

Finally he made his way down to the house. Mugs slowly, looking one last time at the small hole, put one foot after another and painfully followed.

Inside his house, Henry poured himself a drink. The place was a mess. Sink full of dirty dishes. Clothes here and there. Floor dirty.

But what did it matter?

What did anything matter?

It was dark in the house now. Mugs had curled up on his rug and was snoring, lightly yipping, chasing a rabbit probably, legs twitching, once again a young dog full of the joy of life.

Henry poured himself another drink.

Four

IMAGINING THINGS AGAIN

It must have been noon before Henry stirred, and some time longer before he was able to get out of bed. He was sick to his stomach. Still in his clothes from yesterday, his armpits smelled bad, and the bedcover had dirt on it where his boots had been.

After awhile he managed to get to his feet.

Coffee. He fumbled around, fixed the coffee pot, and sat there somewhere between alive and not as the coffee perked.

All this time Mugs had been standing forlornly at the door, waiting. When Henry finally noticed and opened it, Mugs tried to ignore the pain from his arthritis and bladder, barely made it to the closest bush and lifted his leg for a very long time.

"Sorry, old boy," Henry mumbled.

He drank some coffee. His head hurt,

He sat for awhile, and when he could think, he found himself wondering if the kid would come back.

"I'm a crazy fool," he said to himself. "There's no kid."

"Squiggly," he said and smiled.

After a few minutes of silence, he spoke. "I'm an old fool."

Later, though, he headed up the hillside to the rock. Mugs slowly sniffed his way behind him. The water as it came out of the ground made soft gurgling sounds, and Henry watched it trickle down toward his house.

"I don't mean to ask bad questions."

Henry didn't even jump this time. Squiggly suddenly was back, sitting on the rock by the little stream.

Henry's head felt somewhat better. So why not play this game?

Mugs had made a kind of contented whine and was rubbing up against the boy who knelt and hugged him around the neck, getting a good lick on his face in return. Then the boy helped Mugs get up on the rock.

Henry said, "Mugs is saying 'Hello Squiggly Squires from Squiresville.'"

The boy responded, "Hello, Mugs. Hello Mr. Henry. You're making fun again, aren't you, Mr. Henry. But that's okay. I'll try hard not to ask bad questions, just nice ones. I don't want you to be sad again."

"You're a good boy, Squiggly, but are you sure your mother knows where you are?"

"Certainly she does. I told you, Sir, my parents sent me."

Mugs had curled up on the rock and put his head in the boy's lap.

"I see. Well, you can ask any questions you want. There are no bad questions. Only bad answers. You ask me some, and I'll ask you some."

"Okay. How old are you?" Squiggly asked.

Henry tried to be funny, the way the kid had been funny about his age the day before. He answered, "Older than fifty and younger than a hundred."

"Fifty what, and a hundred what?"

"Well, I guess I would say years."

The boy burst out laughing, laughing so hard he seemed in danger of falling off the rock. Mugs looked at him as if to ask what was going on.

"Oh, Mr. Henry, you are so funny."

"What's funny?"

"If you are between fifty and a hundred years old, you are hardly past being born. I don't think you would even be home from the hospital yet. You would be wetting your diapers like my baby brother Squishy."

Squiggly laughed and laughed, rocking back and forth. He had to stop petting Mugs so as to hold onto his very large, very dark sunglasses to keep them on his face. "My father is over sixteen million years old and you're older than my father. Come on, now, tell me how old you are."

Henry, bemused, played along and said, "All right. I'm fifty-seven squintillian years old."

This set off more peals of laughter. Squiggly responded, "We learned in school that life on Earth began about three and a half billion years ago. You're just kidding me, aren't you."

"Well, maybe. Okay, ask another question."

Five

THE HENRYVILLE FAMILY

Henry was feeling better. He had no right to be feeling anything, he thought, but he seemed to be feeling better.

"Mr. Henry, do you have a wife and children? And grandchildren?"

"Yes," he answered slowly. "My wife is Laurel, my daughter is Melanie, and my granddaughter is Peggy."

"What about your other sons and daughters and grandchildren?"

"I don't have any. That's it."

"Wow, you have a little family. I have a great great grandfather, great grandfathers and mothers, grandfathers and mothers, a mother and father, an older brother and sister--they pick on me sometimes, but sometimes they're okay--and a little brother. Squishy, he's the baby. He's only a little over sixty-six thousand six hundred sixty-seven years. And I have lots of aunts and uncles and cousins."

"That's nice. Large families are nice."

"Well, usually, but not always," Squiggly allowed. "What's Mrs. Henry like? Is she nice like you?"

"I'm hardly nice," Henry replied, "but yes, she's nice. A lot nicer than I am."

"Where is she? I've only seen you and Mugs. Where's Mrs. Henry?"

The question cut like a knife, but he responded, "Well, she's away."

"Oh, gone shopping? My mother's always going shopping. After work. My father says if she buys one more pair of shoes he's going to start a shoe store."

They both laughed and Henry nodded, again kind of fibbing, implying that Laurel had gone shopping.

Squiggly added, "But then if he started a shoe store, my mother'd have to keep the shoes instead of giving them away."

Henry had no idea what that meant but let it pass.

"What's it like living in Henryville?" Squiggly continued.

"Henryville? You mean down there?" Henry pointed toward his house, only part of which was visible through the trees.

"Yes, that's in Henryville, isn't it? And the house I can see a little of across the stream in front of the house. That's in Henryville too, of course."

"Of course. The other house too. They're both in Henryville," he fibbed. The other house with the small horse barn behind it belonged to Flint Myser. Henry took care of Flint's Breeze, the very old former race horse. He said that Myser was away on business out of state.

The boy had no idea what 'out of state' meant, but asked, "Is that where Mrs. Melanie lives?"

"Well, no." This was getting too complicated and he decided to come clean. "Melanie and Peggy live kind of far away. That property belongs to Mr. Myser."

Squiggly's brow creased. He was confused. "Mr. Henry, then that is Myserville? So close? It can't be. Can it?"

"Yes, I'm afraid so. That's Myserville."

"Wow, you people in Out are crowded! You live just about on top of one another. We have a lot more room in In. Why, it must be twenty-five

21

hundred soda straw lengths from Squiresville to Squabblesville and twice that far to Squalidsville."

Henry hesitated to ask, but then said, "How long is a soda straw?"

Squiggly burst out laughing again. "Oh, you're teasing me. You know. It was standardized millions of years ago. It's the length of the broken soda straw placed in the Weights and Measures Room of Measurements Cave, an SL--Straw Length. We learned that in our science lesson when I was only about two and a half million years old or so. You're just teasing."

"Well, maybe a little. Okay, now I have some questions for you," Henry said.

This was getting more like the night terrors without the terror. The result of drinking too much? The war? Both? Many times across the years Laurel had begged him to quit drinking, had tried every way she could to help him quit. Doctor Shepherd, the last psychologist, the good one, had helped him, and it had worked for awhile. But nothing worked for very long. He was drinking hard again and knew he was going insane, but so what. *So what!* It did not matter. This, being with Squiggly, at least was fun.

So don't sink into the terrors now, he told himself and forced himself back to the matter at hand: Questions.

Six

The Gift

"You said your parents know where you are."

"Yes, they sent me."

"So you said. What did they send you for?"

"Well, I'm not sure I should tell you. But I like you. You're funny. You promise not to tell anyone?"

"I promise."

"All right. They sent me to bring back The Gift."

"What's the gift?"

"I don't know. At least not yet."

"You don't know, but you're going to take back the gift."

"Yes."

"And your parents didn't tell you what the gift was?"

"How could they? They don't know. Oh, Mr. Henry, you are droll." Squiggly's older brother Squatty had used that word, and Squiggly liked it. Squatty, short for his age of over five million, six hundred thousand, and quite thick around the middle, as Henry was to find out later, was always collecting information. He was a scientist, a philosopher, a thinker. He knew a little about almost everything, and a lot about some things, and he would hold forth at great length to anybody who would listen. Squiggly liked to listen. He admired his older brother. Except when Squatty picked on him and teased him. Which was a lot.

Henry said, "Yeah, I'm a real droll guy. They really don't know what the gift is? They didn't tell you? Your parents?"

"They said I'd know when I found it. You see, The Council on Gifts chose me. It's a very great honor which comes to Squiresville only rarely, and I was chosen," he said proudly.

"Well, I should think your parents would be proud of you."

"They are. I had to undergo a rigorous exam. You see, the last time it came around, they chose Studious Stick from Sticksville in Squatter County. He transported to Out and found foot guards at the gate of the queen's palace. He thought the uniforms were spectacular--dark blue trousers, scarlet tunic with wh ite belt around the middle, shoulder straps, big black bearskin fur hat, and he chose the uniform as The Gift. You understand that once The Gift is brought back to In it is replicated into as many as are needed. The Squatter County Sheriff liked the trousers and tunics but found out his deputies weren't too pleased to have to wear those big hats. They may look snazzy in those things, but it gets hot under them, and they're heavy. The hats slide down over their eyes, and they can hardly see who's coming or going, and the fur makes them sneeze. It's difficult to enforce the law when you can't see much and you're sneezing all the time. The Council warned me to do much better than that. They are counting on me."

He added modestly, "There were lots of children considered, but I was the one they picked. My parents had signs made and hung a large fancy one on our front door, and stuck a small one on Koloa's rump, 'Proud Parents of the Chosen Student.'"

Without asking who or what Koloa was because you don't need to know everything there is to know in a hallucination, Henry replied, "Yes, I can see why they would."

Squiggly said, "Our house is nice. I'll bet your house is nice too." He got up to search for a spot among the trees where, through his very large, very dark glasses, he could get a better, though dim, view. Mugs raised his head and looked at Squiggly. Henry noticed that Squiggly moved carefully, with his arms out in front as if to touch things before they could become a problem. Suddenly the boy stumbled. He didn't fall but his sunglasses came off his face and landed on the ground. Squiggly clapped his hands over his eyes and shrieked.

Henry bounded the few steps toward him. Mugs also lurched toward the boy and stood there, in pain from the sudden exertion, looking concerned as Henry held Squiggly in his arms and said, "What's wrong? It's all right. You're not hurt. It's just your sunglasses."

The boy whimpered, "It hurts. Are they broken? Are they broken?" he pleaded frantically.

Henry bent to pick up the glasses. "No, they're not broken. They're fine. Take your hands away from your eyes and I will put them back on you."

Squiggly was slow in removing his hands. When he did, Henry saw that he was holding his eyes shut so hard his face was contorted. Henry put the glasses back on the trembling boy and told him he could open his eyes.

"It won't hurt? My eyes hurt terribly without the glasses."

"No, it's okay. You can open your eyes now. It won't hurt."

Little by little Squiggly opened his eyes and the twisted, frightened face turned back into the pale sweet face of this strange boy. Squiggly carefully moved back to the rock and sat down. Mugs eased his way back onto Squiggly's lap, and in a moment Squiggly was petting him and getting loving looks in return.

Seven

SEEING

"We're going to be honest with one another now, aren't we?" Henry asked.

The reply was hesitant. "Yes."

"All right, then. Tell me about the glasses. Why do you wear sunglasses, such very large, very dark sunglasses?"

The boy had been shaken badly and he was slow in responding. "You don't know?"

Henry shook his head.

Squiggly looked as if he were trying to understand Henry, but said, "Promise you won't tell anyone?"

"I promise."

"The sunglasses are very precious."

"Really? They look quite ordinary to me except they're way too big for you and they're extremely dark. It's no wonder you stumbled. Here in the woods it's shady anyway, and with those things on I'm surprised you could see anything."

"Mr. Henry, I thought you would know."

"Know what?"

Pause -----------------------------------

"Know more than that--oh, I didn't mean to say that. It's not nice for a person to talk that way just because he's upset. Especially a boy to a grownup. I'm sorry."

"It's quite all right, Squiggly."

"You must be sure not to tell."

"I promised didn't I?"

"Yes. Well-----You see, they're not mine. The Head of Council gave them to me with a strict warning to take care of them. If I ever broke or lost them in Out, I might never find my way back to In. The glasses have to go to the next boy or girl chosen from Squiresville to go to Out. Anyone chosen to go to Out has to get back to In."

"That stands to reason well enough," Henry allowed, though he did not fathom why Squiggly or another Chosen Student would need them. Then it occurred to him to ask about Squiggly's eyes, about the irises. Perhaps Squiggly was nearly blind, and his eyes had taken on that unusual color.

"Would you mind, Squiggly, if I asked you a very personal question?"

"No. Not at all."

"Your eyes. Are you-----are you nearly blind?"

The boy who had been so upset and hesitant, now giggled. "Blind? Nearly blind?" he laughed. "That is a good one. My Nature Club leader says I can spot a wart on a salamander at a thousand SLs when it's light, such as when you approach an exit to Out. Not very light, but a little light."

"Don't you mean when it's almost dark? You can spot a wart when it's dark?"

"No, silly!--Oh, I don't mean to sound rude. Mr. Henry, *anybody* could do that. I mean when it's *light*. A little light. A few of the other club members can see a little bit when it's light, but I am much better. You see that, don't you? Grownups can see that, can't they? It's simple."

27

"Of course, simple," Henry agreed. "Anybody can see well when it's dark, but you see well when it's light, and some club members are okay, but you can see far better than they do when it's a little light, and that's quite an accomplishment. Sure, I see that. Any fool can see that."

And then Henry *did* see it. Could it be? Yes. It could. In In, it must be very dark, totally dark, down inside the earth, and somehow Squiggly's pale gray irises react to the darkness to make it-----Was it possible? In In, Squiggly saw well, and in Out he needed protection from the light. Henry realized the preposterousness of what he was thinking. Must be the drinking. Surely the drinking. But to test his theory he asked, "Now if you were to stay here after dark--that is, after our sun goes down, could you see? Without your sunglasses?"

"Of course I could see. Any of my friends even with poor eyesight could see. I don't like the sun. It scares me. It's horrifying. It hurts. It's the worst thing about coming here to Out for The Gift. I can see at night anywhere. I sat on the rock and watched you the night before you came up here."

"You watched me? You were up here watching me? But I was in the house, and you couldn't ---- It was dark." Then he remembered. It would be different for Squiggly.

"Yes, I watched you. You came out and just stood. Don't you re-member? Your head was down, and you stood there a long time, and then you went back in. You looked sad. I didn't want you to be sad."

Henry had been more than sad. He had stood long, then gone back in, shut the door, and poured himself another drink.

Now Henry sat on the rock, thinking. The boy sat quietly beside him.

It was late. Dark was coming on, and Squiggly was saying he needed to go, there would be many things he had to do in In. "Goodbye, Mr. Henry. You'll come to see me tomorrow won't you?"

"Sure."

Henry thought how preposterous it was, making promises to an illusion, but he said, "Sure. I'll come to see you."

Squiggly hugged Mugs who gave him a parting, especially slobbery kiss.

"Promise?"

"I promise."

Henry watched as Squiggly unformed into a wisp and, waving good-bye, disappeared into the little stream where it trickled out of the hillside. Mugs looked dejected, and as his made his slow way down toward the house, he often stopped and looked back.

"It's okay, Mugs," Henry said as they reached the house.

Henry was hungry. For the first time in a long time he was hungry and, instead of opening a can of something, he rummaged in the freezer and pulled out a large steak that had heavy frost all over the wrapping from having been in there so long. He unwrapped it, stuck it in the microwave on defrost, and waited as the microwave worked. He washed his hands, poured himself a drink and emptied the dishwasher of the clean dishes and then began rinsing and stacking dirty ones in the washer. Then he found a tomato which had white mold only on one small spot on the side, cut it off, then sliced it, put some Miracle Whip on it, put it on a saucer and stuck it in the refrigerator to keep until supper.

An hour or so later he had showered, shaved, dressed in clean clothes and finished washing the pots and pans in the sink. He checked the steak on the broiler--almost done--remembered the drink and drank some of it. Mugs was watching the steak intently. Wiping the table clean and setting it properly for one--fork on the left, knife and spoon on the right, tomato salad to the left--he got the steak and sat down.

"What are you looking at, old boy?" he asked Mugs, as if he didn't know. Slicing off a generous piece of meat, Henry cut it up and set the dog dish down for Mugs. The dog gulped down the pieces, and before Henry had barely tasted his steak, Mugs was looking up mournfully for more. Henry ignored him as he ate a few bites, but then, not able to withstand the plaintive look, sliced off another big piece and cut it up, leaving himself only a little. While Mugs dug in and finished the steak, Henry finished his piece, got out some rather stale bread, wiped the drippings from his plate and ate the bread and tomato slices to satisfy his hunger.

It was a good feeling. To be hungry and want to eat something. To have it taste good.

When he cleared the table he saw he had not finished his drink, and instead of downing it, he poured the remainder down the drain. He went to bed and within seconds fell asleep.

Eight

An Icemaker in Henrysville

Henry got up earlier than usual, some time before noon. His head wasn't hurting much, so after coffee he began picking up clothes scattered here and there and hanging them in closets. Then he tackled his disgusting bathroom. After making his bed--the first time in weeks--he was pooped. Way out of shape. He had not exercised in years. He felt old.

Henry slumped into a lounge chair and closed his eyes. He'd keep going on the cleanup after he rested. He tried not to think, and fell asleep.

When he awakened he was not sure where he was. Then he realized, and it was late. He was hungry. Finding stale bread he made a peanut butter sandwich, put it in a bag and started up the hill, Mugs behind him.

Absurd.

Totally preposterous.

He was going up the hill into the woods to meet a figment of his imagination. A boy named Squiggly who formed and unformed and came to Out but lived in In.

Worse, he talked to this apparition, and it asked questions. Interminable questions.

Absurd.

At the rock, he picked up the dented canteen cup, rinsed it clean from its long disuse, filled it at the hole where the water came out, and had a cold drink. Mugs finally joined him, panting heavily. Henry gave Mugs a drink out of the cup and when his dog no longer wanted any, dumped the rest out and filled the cup again. He and Mugs ate the sandwich. Henry washed down his half sandwich with gulps of the clear, cool water. Delicious. The water. The stale sandwich.

But he was disappointed.

Disappointed at what?

That Squiggly had not come? Disappointed in the non-recurrence of a hallucination?

More than absurd.

"Mr. Henry, I'm sorry I'm late."

The boy had climbed silently up onto the rock beside Henry, and already Mugs was shifting to put his head in Squiggly's lap, eyes rolling up adoringly, looking into the boy's face.

The relief Henry felt was even more crazy than the disappointment. He said, "It's okay, Squiggly. What have you been up to?"

"Up to? I didn't go up to anywhere, I just went to see The Council on Gifts."

Strange how the boy took some things so literally. It was this naïveté that made him at once so funny and so charming. He was a refreshing contrast from the two kids up the road who delighted in riding bikes by his house and calling out swear words or taunting him with "Hey, Bonkers, catch us if you can. Yeah, yeah, yeah, Nutsy Fagin."

Henry could tell by the boy's withdrawn demeanor that he was upset.

"Do you want to tell me about it?"

Squiggly was silent. It must have been a minute or so before he raised his head and said, "No, Mr. Henry."

"That's okay, but it might do you good to talk about it."

Squiggly thought, and thought some more. "I like to visit you, but-----No, I don't think so."

"Did you talk to your parents about it? Children should talk to their parents when there is a problem."

He was a fine one to be giving advice. His daughter Melanie had talked to him several times across the years, pleaded with him, then shouted and sworn at him, and it just got worse.

Henry said, "You don't have to tell me." Then, to make the boy feel better, Henry asked, "How would you like to visit Henryville? Would you like that?"

Henry thought that a half-smile had appeared on the boy's face but couldn't be sure because of his very large, very dark sunglasses. In a moment, though, any trace of a smile had gone away.

"No, I don't think so."

"Why? It would do you good."

"Mr. Henry, no. Because the last time when I tried to get a better view of Henryville through the trees I tripped and my glasses fell off."

Behind the glasses the boy seemed close to living the terror all over again. Henry saw his mouth contort.

"It's okay," Henry said, trying to temper the frightening experience. "I'll help you, and I promise I won't let you fall. I'll hold onto you so you don't lose your glasses."

The lines around the boy's mouth slowly went away, and he said, "Promise?"

"I promise."

Brightening, Squiggly added, "If we go, may I see some of the other houses in Henryville?"

"Well, it's getting kind of late, so maybe we should just visit my house--this time."

Henry was on shaky ground with the implication there were other houses in Henryville, and this, likely as not, would set off another round of questions.

But it did not. Squiggly carefully got to his feet and Henry helped him down off the rock. Squiggly helped Mugs down and the three of them slowly, cautiously, made their way out of the woods. Henry had his arm around Squiggly, steadying him at each step.

Inside the kitchen, Henry had the boy sit in a chair. Mugs sat on the floor beside him. From what Henry could imagine, based on what happened when Squiggly lost his glasses, the scene in front of the boy must have been quite dim. The sunglasses were very dark.

Squiggly surveyed the kitchen slowly, moving his head, shifting in his chair, taking in the entire room.

"Kitchens in Henryville are different from ones in Squiresville," the boy said.

"I should imagine they are," Henry acknowledged.

"Do you know what all these things in here are," Squiggly asked.

"Oh, yes," Henry assured him.

"Do you use all of them to get dinner?"

"Well, not all of them, but sometimes a lot of them."

"Wow!" Squiggly said in astonishment. "We don't have so many things. Where's Mrs. Henry?"

"Well-----she's away."

"Still away? You're going to have a late dinner when she gets home. It'll take some time to prepare."

"That's true," Henry said. "Would you like a coke? You have cokes in Squiresville I take it?" Henry got a can and held it up.

Squiggly shook his head.

"Too bad. Won't you have a coke? They taste good."

"Yes, please. I'll try it."

Henry got a glass, went to the refrigerator and pushed the lever on the icemaker. The racket made the boy jump violently.

"What's wrong!" Henry said and went over to settle him down.

The shaken boy asked, "What was that awful noise?"

"Just the icemaker in the refrigerator. It won't hurt you." He got another glass and said, "Here, take this glass and we'll go over there and you can operate it."

Squiggly wasn't too sure about that, but he let Henry lead him across the floor.

Henry wondered how much the boy could really see. What was clear and what was dim? Henryville, he supposed, could be a frightening experience to a boy from Squiresville.

"Look. See the thing that sticks out there?"

Henry guided the boy's hand to the lever just to make sure. "Do you see it?"

"Yes."

Henry stepped back. "Well, put the glass against it and push and ice cubes will come out."

"What are ice cubes?"

Henry sighed. "Just push it and see."

The boy pushed and jumped again at the sudden racket. Fortunately he also yanked his hand back from it, which shut it off. A few cubes had fallen into the glass and some onto the floor. Mugs sniffed at them.

"There. You did it. That wasn't so bad was it?"

But Squiggly was looking into the glass he was holding. Apparently he could see well enough because he said in amazement, "They're all the same shape. A perfectly symmetrical shape."

"Certainly they are," Henry assured him.

"All the *same*," Squiggly repeated in a tone of no less amazement.

"What do your ice cubes in Squiresville look like?"

"Not like this. We just take the awl to a block of ice and poke off some pieces. They're jagged. There is no way I could get even one piece to look like these."

"I suppose not," Henry agreed without fully understanding.

The boy drank and smiled. "It tastes good."

Squiggly finished his coke and said, "I should go now, Mr. Henry. I have already had a most tiring day."

"Yes. At The Council, you mean?"

"Yes."

"Well, it is getting dark," Henry said, and carefully helped the boy out the door, down the steps, and across the back yard into the edge of the woods. Dusk soon would be turning into night. Just after they entered the tree line, a car rushed up the driveway and came to an abrupt, loud squealing halt. The boy shrieked and clung desperately to Henry.

"That fool Myser," Henry said to himself, but was also heard by the boy.

"Shh!" he said to the petrified youngster. Squiggly's face was pressed against Henry's chest. Squiggly had taken off his glasses and was holding them in his hand so he could see better.

"Shh!!"

Flint Myser was out of the car and calling loudly, "Henry!"

He waited.

Louder, "Henry, I'm back!"

Henry could well see that Myser had returned, and he needed to get the boy up the hill. "Shh!!" he said to Squiggly.

"Drunk. He's drunk again," Myser said loudly to himself.

Myser got back into his car, roared it backward out of the driveway, slammed it forward for the fifty yards or so down the road, and screeched it to a stop in front of his own garage.

The boy had collapsed in Henry's arms. Henry patted his head and told him over and over it was all right.

Finally Squiggly asked, "Is it gone?"

"Yes. It's gone."

"How can Mr. Myser still be alive?"

"What do you mean?"

"That awful beast ate him but he came out of the side of it alive. He called to you and he wasn't even hurt, at least I don't think so. I could see quite well--it's what you call getting dark, so I was seeing better--and I saw him climb out of the side of that horrible beast. I *saw* him!"

"It's okay. They've gone away. I have to get you back up the hill."

"That's all right. I can see quite well now," said Squiggly. He added, "I'll help you back to your house so you don't stumble in the dark, Mr. Henry, and then I'll go home."

Henry replied quizzically, "You'll help me back? To my house? So I won't stumble? "Are you sure you can make it home okay?"

"I'm sure, Mr. Henry. But don't you want me to help you back to your house?"

"No, I'll be fine."

"Well, okay then, Mr. Henry. Be careful you don't stumble. Good night, Mr. Henry. Good night, Mugs."

The boy bent down, kissed Mugs and got his usual big wet kiss in return, then disappeared in the dark near the big rock.

Nine

THE SECRET WORD

The next morning, Henry thoroughly cleaned the kitchen and ran the steam mop on the floor. It was exhausting, and every so often he had to go out onto the deck and sit. He heard the large stream in front of the house near the road gurgling, and he saw a woodpecker hard at work on a tree. When had he last noticed such things?

In the afternoon, Henry climbed the slope slowly enough that struggling Mugs could keep up with him. As they approached the rock, Squiggly, wearing his very large, very dark sunglasses, was waiting with a surprise.

"Mr. Henry," Squiggly said breathlessly, "I told my parents about my visit to Henryville, and they would like you to come see them. They think you are a nice man."

Oh, great! For days he had not only been talking with an imaginary boy, but now was getting an invitation from his imaginary parents to visit them in the imaginary Land of In.

"Thank you, Squiggly."

In earlier years, on those times when he had felt somewhat better he would let Laurel make an appointment with Doctor Shepherd. He never would go while in the depths of despair no matter what Laurel did. He would only get angrier and drink more. Now, for a moment he thought he should go back down the hill and call Doctor Shepherd. In the next moment he knew he wouldn't call him, but he would walk away from this hallucination.

He turned and started down toward the house. Mugs was confused, standing and looking first at Squiggly, then at Henry.

"Mr. Henry," Squiggly called. "Please don't go. They would like very much to meet you. Please?"

Henry stopped momentarily, turned and said, "Squiggly, this is nuts. I'm talking to myself. Seeing things. Seeing you. It's the drinking."

Why was he telling a boy such things?

"But Mr. Henry, you haven't been drinking-----as much."

"No-----No," he replied slowly, without stopping to think how the boy knew that, much less knew what drinking meant. "I haven't been drinking as much. "And that's the problem. I'll fix that."

No way he would call Doctor Shepherd now.

"Please, Mr. Henry."

Henry saw the boy wiping tears from his cheeks, his head lowered in despondency.

He couldn't stand to see it. He thought for a minute.

"All right. I'll go. Tell your parents I will go see them."

What did it matter? It was a hallucination. He had been on terrible trips, and at least this one might prove interesting. Even pleasant.

"Oh, wonderful! You'll go," the boy cried in delight. "You'll like it. I know you will. Let's go right away."

"I have to take Mugs back home first," Henry said. He thought that maybe when he got back down the hill with Mugs he would come to his senses.

"No! No, please! Mugs has to come with us!"

"Mugs? He could never keep up on a long journey. It would be too much for him. In fact, my old bones ache. Arthritis. Kind of creaky, and it would be too much for me too."

"No it won't Mr. Henry. You'll see. And Mugs has to come. He has to. Please?"

Crazy. This was nuts. Never before had he gone with anyone on one of his wild trips. He went alone. Always alone.

Finally he said, "All right."

"Oh, thank you!" the boy gushed. "Thank you! Now don't be afraid. We're just going to unform and we'll be off."

"Unform? How do we do that?"

"Well, I just do it, but you have to put your hand on Mugs and hold my hand and then make a wish for you and Mugs to go with me."

"Nonsense! Kids say 'Abracadabra' and nothing happens."

"That's not true," Squiggly protested as gently as he could so as not to appear rude. "They often get their wish."

"Oh, sure! Nothing ever happens."

"Yes it does. They have wonderful things happen to them. They go on marvelous journeys and see fantastic things and get other kids to go with them. The girls get to be a princess and the boys get to be a prince. They play fantastic games and get to talk about beautifully strange things when they say 'Abracadabra.' You just have to believe. Just say 'unform', and add these secret words and believe."

Squiggly stretched up and whispered the secret words into Henry's ear.

"Oh, all right. I believe. I'm nuts, but I believe. "Unform," Henry said, and he added the secret words.

And he believed.

He must have actually believed because the three of them instantly turned into tiny wisps and were sucked into the little hole where the stream emerged from the hillside.

Ten

Henry looked around, confused, amazed. He was on the bank of a river in a large cave. Squiggly and Mugs were beside him. Mugs looked bewildered. Squiggly had taken off his hat and was holding it in his hand. Henry looked behind him at the entrance to the cave where the river flowed out into the light.

"Yes, Mr. Henry," Squiggly said, but didn't look into the light. "That is where we were a moment ago, outside the cave entrance. We were in Out."

Henry objected, "But there was no cave, only a hole the size of my fist, and there was no river, hardly more than a trickle."

"Mr. Henry, you are in In now," Squiggly said as if that explained everything.

But it explained nothing. How could a small hole in a hillside become a large cave and a trickle of water become a river? In fact by the light coming in from the mouth of the cave Henry saw that they were in a cave connected to a tunnel with a lot of water running through it. Crazier and crazier. This was the weirdest pipedream Henry had ever had.

Squiggly said, "Squatty told me when I was little, only about two million years old, that people accommodate to an environment. When you wished and believed and said the words, that's what happened. You are in the environment of In. Simple."

"Simple," Henry agreed. What use was there to question such a simple explanation?

"Squatty is much better than I at understanding these things," Squiggly said, "but let's go along. We need to get around the big bend in the tunnel to catch our ride."

Without questioning any more, Henry fell in behind the boy on the narrow path along the river and they walked upstream as Mugs sniffed his way along. Henry knew something of caves, having been in a few as a youngster. He remembered one in which the guide said at the entrance that some very extensive caves had significant fauna--animals--in them. Here near the entrance would be the trogloxenes--frogs, bats, and other animals which sometimes sought shelter or even lived there, but got their food from outside the cave.

As they walked, it became increasingly dark. The air was still, cooler, and very humid. Mugs gamely hobbled along as fast as he could.

When they turned the bend, Henry had to slow down considerably. Behind him was faint light, but ahead of them, darkness, and he could see virtually nothing. He stopped. Squiggly also stopped.

"Sorry, Mr. Henry. I'm beginning to see much better."

"Great," Henry thought. Squiggly was seeing better now that it was getting darker.

"Here," Squiggly said. "Put these on." He reached out to hand Henry his very large, very dark sunglasses.

"Yeah, sure. They'll be a big help," Henry said sarcastically.

But he groped and got hold of them and put them on. Miraculously he could see. Not very well and not very far, but he could see. Everything appeared to be in shades of gray which trailed off into black in the distant darkness.

"There, now you have moonglasses. That's better for you. And for me," the boy said.

"How can you tell in this dark?"

"How? Because you have them on, and I don't. Both of us can see. In fact I see very well. When we get to my house, I'll get some moonglasses for Mugs too. He'll like that. You probably aren't seeing very well with them, but they are better than nothing. I couldn't see much through my sunglasses when I was with you in Out."

"Why are they called moonglasses?"

"Simple. You can see somewhat like you'd see on a moonlit night. I don't like the moon. It's not as bad as that horrid sun, but bad enough."

They started walking again upstream. Squiggly held onto Mugs' collar to guide him along, bending to pat him soothingly. This was quite a hallucination. Henry could see the path more or less okay and some distance off it on either side before objects began to melt into darkness. Only now and then could he see the roof of the tunnel. It was too high over them in darkness. He could see and hear the river beside them. It made rushing, swirling sounds as it flowed quickly downstream.

After a few minutes' walk they came to a dock sticking out into the river. A fish that looked to be twenty feet long was tied up to a stalagmite next to it. To Henry, the fish seemed to be alabaster white, somewhat like Squiggly. Where its eyes should have been, there were just two slight mounds, an opaque chalky white. Strapped on its back was a platform with bucket seats fastened to it. Henry briefly lifted the glasses from his eyes and saw what he guessed he would see. Nothing. Total blackness. No fish, no Mugs, no Squiggly. It was disconcerting, and he readjusted the glasses on his nose so he could see objects in shades of gray again.

"Here, I'll help you up, Mugs," Squiggly said as he guided the dog onto the fish's platform and put him in a seat. "Now, you're not going to like this, but I have to fasten your seat belt. Be a good doggie, okay?"

Mugs was good, not only when he got strapped in but when Squiggly put a helmet over his head and wrestled a life jacket around him. "We're not taking any chances with such a good boy now, are we."

Apparently not, with Mugs or with Henry. Squiggly handed Henry a helmet and life jacket but put none on himself.

"Aren't you going to wear some?" Henry asked.

"Well, Mr. Henry, of course not."

"Why not?'

In his instructional tone, Squiggly said, "There is Earth, Air, Fire, and Water. That's what there is. Or at least that's what people thought long, long ago. Squatty--he's a scientist, or at least is going to be one--he says that's not true, that modern thought is different. But I kind of like the old way. In In we're at one with all of them. How can they hurt us? When I come to Out from Squiresville I use Water. I just swim down the river. I love to swim. Most kids do. So there we are."

Squiggly untied the rope from the stalagmite, climbed back up to take his seat, and made a strange clucking sound which came out in spurts, causing vibrations the cave fish could sense. He said, for Henry's benefit since blind cavefish presumably couldn't hear, "Okay, Silver, take us home."

Silver set out with a vigorous lurch.

Henry cried out, "Heigh ho Silver!" followed by a "Get >em up Scout."

Squiggly looked inquisitively at this funny old man who said the strangest things.

"You'll like this ride, Mr. Henry. Most of it. Some of it, though, will be a bit exciting. Silver is well trained, so you have nothing to fear. He's a waterfall climbing cave fish. My parents got him, oh, I guess three or four million years ago--not very long ago--but he has been completely capable and trustworthy."

The ride would be a bit exciting? The understatement of the century--or should it be mega-millennia Henry wondered when they came to the first fast water.

Silver plunged ahead upstream as if it were child's play. Waves and whitecaps surged and washed up onto the platform and got Henry's feet wet. The cool spray against his face, though, felt good, and only then did he realize it had been humid, somewhat warm and stuffy since they had been in In.

Mugs, unable to see a thing in the utter darkness and not pleased with all the rocking back and forth and the noise of water sloshing around him, was not thrilled. Now and then he expressed his displeasure with a whine.

Squiggly, though, was thoroughly enjoying the ride, grasping his hat on its broad brim and waving it like a rodeo rider having the ride of his life and wanting to let the crowd know he was the best.

After several minutes of tossing about, they suddenly emerged from the tunnel into a small lake in a large cave. So far as Henry could tell in his limited range of vision, it was hauntingly beautiful. Huge cream-colored limestone stalactites reached down out of the darkness overhead, some almost touching the cream and gray stalagmites exposed above the perfectly still surface. Some of the stalactites and stalagmites sparkled like diamonds. Silver, seemingly on autopilot, went into slow cruise mode and Squiggly and Henry took in the beauty. Only small rippling waves went out from the fish and made delightful tinkling sounds in the vast stillness as the little waves lapped against stalagmites.

Henry could not entirely enjoy the dainty sounds. His ears constantly rang with tinnitus, the result of too much small arms and machinegun fire, too many tank guns, too many helicopters, too many explosions erupting close to him. The high-pitched screech was always there, often unbearable, and there was no option other than to bear it. But for now he enjoyed hearing his own breathing, and Squiggly's. This was a great comfort in the eerie vastness of the cave.

"Squiggly," he said, "this is a magical place."

"I know. And alive. The cave is always growing. Every drip of water makes the cave formations grow a little. I love it here."

"Yes," said Henry slowly. "I can see why."

Silver seemed to know exactly where he was going and he avoided obstacles. Although Henry saw only white bulges where Silver's eyes should have been, the huge fish swam around the large stalagmites without bumping into them and resumed his course on their far side.

Squiggly must have anticipated Henry's s question, so he provided the answer. "Blind cave fish have rows of sensory papillae on their head and sides. They use them to help navigate in total darkness. The fish feed primarily on microscopic organisms, as well as small crustaceans and salamander larvae. We learned this in science class."

"Of course. Simple," said Henry.

"Simple," agreed Squiggly.

If the first fast water had been a test of Henry's courage, the next obstacles--a stretch of fast water leading to a series of stair-like waterfalls, then another stretch of foaming, churning water around stumps of broken-off stalagmites, and then a huge vertical waterfall looming ahead--Big Falls--were terrifying.

"Oh!!!" gushed Henry.

As Silver went into high gear, the sound of the wild river was deafening as waves of cool water crashed against them. Henry hung onto his glasses with one clenched fist and onto Mugs' collar with the other. The first low stair-like waterfall had been relatively easy, and the next ones, but Big Falls loomed ahead.

At the base of Big Falls, Silver lurched, swishing his tail and fins violently. Henry was thrust back hard into his seat as Silver jumped almost vertically, nearly gained the crest, and crashed back into the pool at the bottom of the falls. The seat belts were all that saved them from being thrown off. Squiggly was squealing with delight, leaning over and clapping Silver on his side, and letting forth loud whoops of approval, but Henry and Mugs thought it was no fun. Mugs growled his disapproval.

Apparently taking strength from his little rider, Silver lurched upward again in a mighty leap to conquer Big Falls, and strained as he teetered on the crest. He had landed just where the river went over the falls, and his thrashing tail did no good, sticking out in the air over the edge. Squiggly was whooping delightedly, "Heigh ho Silver!" accompanied now by Mugs' frantic barking and howling.

Squiggly shouted, "Waterfall climbing cave fish can actually climb the walls and make their way up river with no need for jumping over falls, but Silver likes the challenge."

Henry feared they could not possibly survive, but in an instant, Silver made a huge thrust forward with his powerful fins and suddenly all was calm ahead of them, the precipice of the waterfall safely at their rear.

"There!" Squiggly gushed with satisfaction. "Wasn't that great, Mr. Henry? Not bad at all, was it!"

Henry wasn't sure he would ever be able to talk again. "No," he croaked. The moonglasses, though somewhat crooked and spattered with water, he still held on his nose. "Piece of cake."

Directly ahead, standing on a perfectly placid surface of what appeared to be a limitless lake, was a huge, long-legged creature with an elongated thin body perched atop its legs, and a head that looked somewhat like that of a caribou with projecting antlers. It too had an alabaster color similar to that of Silver, the courageous waterfall climbing cave fish.

"Good Geraldine, right where she should be," Squiggly remarked. "We really don't need a water scooter since Silver could take us up to the dock, but Geraldine is faster. She's young and loves to race across the surface."

Silver slid up beside the creature and Squiggly clucked and said, "Down, Geraldine." Squiggly explained that Geraldine, like Silver, could not hear or understand what he said, but was trained to sense and obey the vibrations of the clucks.

The water scooter bent her long legs, anxiously lowered her whitish body to the water alongside Silver, and fidgeted until her passengers were aboard and buckled in their seats. Squiggly had hardly gotten out his clucks and words of thanks to Silver for a good job before Geraldine bolted off like a racehorse out of the gate. Henry's head snapped back and Mugs disapprovingly went, "Whoof!"

The distance of the race was considerable since this was a huge cavern containing an expansive lake. When Henry could get his senses together he saw that they were high off the water over those long legs and getting a very smooth ride. Astonishingly, behind them a pattern of circles marked Geraldine's footprints on the water surface, a trace of only slight ripples.

"They can scoot across the surface because they have a multitude of tiny hairs on their feet," Squiggly said.

"You learned this in science class," Henry offered.

"Yes, and from my older brother. He loves to tell what he knows."

By the time they got to the distant shore, a duration of several minutes in Out time despite the speed of their trip, Henry found that his clothes which had been wet from the splashing at Big Falls were now nearly dry.

They docked, Geraldine lowered herself, and Squiggly's clucks, a soft, soothing sound this time, thanked her for such a nice trip. He then removed Mugs' seat belt, life jacket, and helmet. The dog stood up but remained still, afraid to take a step in the total dark. Apparently surprised and pleased that he was alive, though, Mugs gave himself a good shake, scattering water droplets everywhere, and said, "Whoof."

Henry held Mugs in his arms, and in stepping onto the dock, he put his dog down, leaned over and saw a reflection of himself in the water. He did not have very large, very dark sunglasses on his nose. They were very large, yes, but the lenses were white.

Squiggly explained, "The lenses are made of a particular kind of crystal which is hard to find in In, and I don't know how they got their name since we have no moon here. Horrible thing, a moon. Probably got the name from the Science Committee studying reports about Out. I'll have to ask Squatty. They aren't perfect, but they're better than nothing," he assured Henry, "just like when they were my sunglasses in Out, better than nothing."

How the glasses had changed from sunglasses into moonglasses Henry had no idea. He hoped Squatty would know.

Ridiculous. This hallucination seemed to lead from here to there and go on endlessly.

He would come out of it soon.

He always did.

Eleven

SQUIRESVILLE

The large sign at dockside read, "Welcome to Squiresville, Friendliest Town in In."

Squiggly softly clucked, thanking Geraldine, who instantly sped off across the lake.

"Ah, faithful Koloa," Squiggly said as he walked up to a dark-colored creature which looked like a huge spider. "I'll give you some nice fresh amphipods when we get home."

Mugs was terrified. Since he could not see, he was probably upset at what he sensed and smelled. Henry at first was not much braver. Through his moonglasses Henry could see that Koloa had maybe eight legs that each looked to be ten feet tall, on top of which was a stocky body. On the creature's rump was a sign, "Proud Parents of the Chosen Student."

"Nice bumper sticker," said Henry. Squiggly raised his eyebrows, questioning.

"Just a little joke," Henry said, and Squiggly nodded without understanding, then smiled.

"Bumper sticker," the boy repeated, pleased. "Bumper sticker," he giggled. "I like that."

"Down, Koloa," Squiggly clucked in a high-pitched manner, and the timid creature obediently bent its knees and lowered itself so the underside of its body was flat on the ground.

"Mugs," Squiggly said, patting the dog's head to comfort him, "Koloa is just a blind wolf spider. He has a venom sac that doesn't work much because he's descended from many generations of tame spiders, and he wouldn't hurt anybody anyway, especially a nice doggy like you. Let's all get on."

Squiggly scampered up happily and asked Henry to lift the dog aboard. Henry lifted, then pushed from below, and couldn't help but laugh at Mugs. The trembling dog, although he could see nothing in the blackness, had closed his eyes tightly against this frightful experience. Henry, though, after the wild trip up river, was gaining confidence they could survive anything, and he climbed up.

Koloa ambled off in a rolling, somewhat limping motion not unlike that of a lame camel. Their path soon was very steep uphill, and Koloa was breathing heavily, making snorting sounds as he exhaled. "Easy, Koloa," Squiggly called and clucked, and the creature slowed his pace. Henry looked back at the lake, and in a few Out minutes they reached a point where a natural indentation in the wall of the cavern allowed them to pull over so Koloa could rest a bit.

Henry looked behind, but now they were so far above the surface of the lake he was not sure if he any longer saw the water through the glasses. Squiggly said they still had a lot of uphill ahead of them because Squiresville had to be built well above the historic high water line for floods. When Koloa's breathing returned more to normal they set out again and after a few more rest halts emerged onto a plateau.

Squiggly acted as guide, describing this section of Squiresville. Although Henry could see only dimly beyond a hundred yards or so through his moonglasses, he could make out some of the huge cave. Along the crest of the hill overlooking the lake were handsome houses of cut stone in what appeared to be different subtle colors. Squiggly confirmed that there were shades of gray, light orange, brown, white. The roofs were of cut or rough gray slate. All in all, these were impressive, expensive houses surrounded by what seemed to be large lawns. But of course in the total darkness of the cave, no grass was growing on them. Instead, on some patches of the lawn's stone surface were small, beautiful round objects that Squiggly called cave pearls. And in place of shrubs and trees, pieces of small and medium-size broken stalagmites and stalactites had been placed to line the long, curving driveways. It was a breathtaking scene.

Although he could not trust his eyesight in this extremely dim atmosphere, Henry heard children's voices and thought he saw them at play among the houses. Also, some very large, new-looking, blind wolf spiders were parked under elegant porticos. They seemed to range in color from very white to quite dark. Poor Koloa looked quite shabby compared to those shiny wolf spiders. One of them appeared to be undergoing a careful polishing at the hands of what Henry took to be a chauffeur.

"This is what we call Low Meadows," Henry's little guide proudly pointed out. "People of very modest means live here. They perform all sorts of useful work, and quite well. They are janitors, tool operators, spider drivers, you name it."

"My goodness," Henry said, "I would have expected this to be the best section of town. I see nice big houses with lake view, large--uh--spiders under the porticos." The spiders were much larger than Koloa who was not shiny at all but exceedingly drab.

"This *is* the best part of town," Squiggly confirmed, "if you're talking about nice houses, shiny spiders and such things."

Mugs still had his eyes closed, maybe snoozing as an escape from strange smells, abrupt motions, and all sorts of frightening things.

After entering a broad road and slowly passing along the scenic outlook in front of the houses, Koloa turned onto a narrow side road leading sharply upward. Ahead, Henry vaguely could see that the road was a natural cut into the side of the cave. The houses now were smaller, the yards not so big, and the blind cave spiders in the driveways not so large or well shined. But most of them were still bigger and looked to be in better shape than Koloa. Against the cave wall behind the back yards were formations of stone draperies and veils, beautiful indeed, some nearly translucent showing what might be brown and yellow stripes running through them, similar to bacon. The children must have great fun playing hide and seek among them, Henry thought.

"This is Middle Manors," announced Squiggly with measured pride. "Don't you think it's very nice?"

Actually, Henry thought it not half so nice as Low Meadows, but not bad. The Manors name was probably dreamed up by some real estate agency wanting to put a more elegant touch on their listings. At first, as they proceeded, there was room behind the houses for backyards, though small. Then as panting Koloa took them higher, the rear of the houses now seemed to be set almost against the wall of the cave. There not only were tiny back yards, but hardly any front yards, and the edge of the road seemed to be dropping off into the darkness as they climbed. The road now was very narrow and close to the brink of a cliff. Most frightening! Henry hoped that swaying Koloa was sure-footed, and he was glad that Mugs seemed fast asleep.

"Yes," Henry said to be polite, "Middle Manors is very nice."

His guide continued, "Most of what we call mid-level employees live here--foreladies, bookkeepers, skilled craftsmen, plumbers, people like that."

"Well, that makes good sense," Henry said, although of course it made no sense at all. Why would a janitor live in such a beautiful large house in Low Meadows with a big lawn and lake view, and his supervisor, a forelady, live up here, rather precariously at that?

He thought about it and then smiled. "Forelady?"

Middle Manors was a fairly steep climb, and it took a few minutes and a lot of Koloa's panting before they passed through and reached its outskirts.

"The Scenic Heights section of Squiresville is coming up," Squiggly announced excitedly.

Henry certainly hoped so. In the dimness of his view, the road was now a most strange, narrow, and frightening one. It went sharply upward. The wall of the cave was rounding over their heads.

"You're going to like Scenic Heights. This is where the heads of companies and other organizations of Squiresville live, and the doctors, lawyers, scientists, people like that. This is where I live," he said proudly.

Henry was greatly relieved he could see so little and so dimly. These houses were small and haphazardly crowded together. He looked at the closest one. The cut stones were certainly rejects with uneven surfaces and odd angles. The construction appeared to be that of apprentices who had learned very little of their trade. The stone colors were drab grays, and the slate roofs seemed in danger of sliding off. With miniscule front yards and no back yards at all, lots of dreary houses appeared to be here in Scenic Heights. The wolf spiders in the driveways looked as if they had seen better days. Several of them had scrapes in their sides like Koloa's, and now and then a leg was missing. Almost all needed a good wash and polish. There were a few large old clunkers, but most were quite small.

Squiggly proudly said, "Isn't it beautiful? The best place to live in Squiresville."

Scenic Heights, where the professional and ranking business people lived in small, decrepit houses, quite certainly was the least desirable section of Squiresville Henry thought, but he said, "Sure is. The very best place."

Looking at the small, scruffy spiders, Henry thought, wryly, "Maybe they get good mileage." But he had to admit to himself that the many stalactites and limestone needles and soda straws hanging from the cave roof gave the place a boost from its overall shabby look. That aspect of Squiresville indeed was beautiful, and he said so.

Squiggly didn't respond. He was clearly so excited he was nearly speechless.

After a few seconds he said, "We're *here!*"

Koloa, heaving, head down, turned into a driveway and stopped. Only then did Henry notice that Koloa, in addition to having some bad scrapes and dents, had a missing leg--seven instead of eight. And that accounted for his limping, swaying motion.

Squiggly clucked and said, "Good Koloa. Good boy. I'll get your amphipods shortly."

Koloa was dutifully lowering himself to the driveway. Squiggly told Henry to be sure to hold onto Mugs' collar when he helped the dog down. That warning was unnecessary. Henry hung tightly to the collar and, bending over and on shaking legs, followed Squiggly up the narrow sidewalk to the front door.

Henry looked behind. "Oh!" He could see nothing except blackness, not even the surface of the lake, well below, much beyond his range of sight.

"Look, Mr. Henry," Squiggly cried out excitedly, pointing at the front door.

There was the sign, much bigger than the bumper sticker on Koloa's rear, "Proud Parents of the Chosen Student." It glittered, but not so much as to hurt the eyes of anyone passing by. They would surely see it.

"Mother had it done in glowworm paint. Don't you think it looks nice?" the boy asked, head held high.

"I certainly do."

Mugs, eyes still closed, went "Whoof," as if in agreement, but more likely was just pleased to be down off that thing that smelled so strange and gave him such a rolling, rocking ride.

Twelve

HOME AT LAST

Henry was greeted at the door with a big hug from a rather large woman dressed in very old-fashioned clothes. She wore a high-necked dress and long-sleeved vest. Under her dress which came to just below her knees were bloomers reaching down and clasping her ankles. Momentarily Henry glanced over her shoulder at the small family room with old furniture. Everything smelled and looked spic and span clean.

"Mr. Henry," the dark-skinned woman gushed, unwrapping Henry from the folds of her arms and holding him now at arms' length and studying him, "I'm Squiggly's mother you don't mind I hope if I hug you I've heard so much about you Squiggly says you're a wonderful man we're most pleased to have you and please call me Squeezy," she said before she was caught with the necessity of pausing for a breath and squeezing him again.

Her eyes seemed to be pale gray, almost translucent like Squiggly's. Henry couldn't be sure because what he saw through the glasses were mostly differing shades of gray.

"Mrs. Squires, uh, Squeezy, please call me Henry."

"Mr. Henry's my friend," the boy said to his mother, bursting with pride.

"And Mugs," Mrs. Squires said warmly. "Welcome." She bent, picked him up and wrapped him in her arms.

Mugs, sensing that the bad times of jumping up waterfalls and riding on smelly, rocking creatures were behind him, and much better times lay ahead, snuggled against her and quietly thanked her with a big lick and a Whoof.

Before Henry had a chance to compose himself, she was calling up the stairs for the children to come down, and then out the back door for her husband to come into the house. He arrived first, a very small man with a tiny paint roller in his hand, the kind used for small touch-up areas. Through Henry's moonglasses he appeared to be of medium brown color, perhaps like some Latinos. Paint, wet and dried, was spattered here and there on his face and work clothes of the old fashioned sort like Squiggly's.

"It's very nice of you to want me to visit," Henry said to him.

The man nodded politely at Henry and extended his hand, but before her husband could say anything, Squeezy, smiling broadly, said, "We wouldn't have missed it for anything."

"Dad, he's my friend," the boy added, bursting with pride.

"This is my husband, S.Q.," Mrs. Squires said with a loving, proud smile, hugging him.

S.Q. was hardly taller than Squiggly. He almost disappeared into the large woman's hug.

"He has just finished painting the fence now he's going to do the house you did finish it didn't you dear?"

"With *that* paint roller?" Henry blurted out before he could catch himself.

"Yes isn't he a dear it's taken him let's see only a few thousand years or a little more and it is such a nice job a very nice job he always does wonderful work."

S.Q., which sounded like "askew," extended a paint-spotted hand and said, "Pleased to meet you."

"Children hurry up you mustn't keep Mr. Henry waiting," she called up the stairs again.

In a moment, down they tumbled, pushing and shoving.

Pulling Squiggly to join the other two and putting her arms around her children, Mrs. Squires said, "This plus the baby is our squad Mr. Henry now you two politely introduce yourselves to our very special guest isn't it nice he came to see us came all the way from Out to see us?"

"I'm Squatty, the oldest," the short, plump boy said, squinting through thick clear glasses. His facial features and skin pigmentation seemed to be Asian.

"And he thinks he's the smartest," squealed the girl, giving him the hip.

"Squeally my goodness," Mrs. Squires admonished her. "Now get the baby and introduce him to Mr. Henry my goodness such manners-----

Squeally, very light-skinned like Squiggly, quickly disappeared and almost immediately reentered the room holding a bundle. The baby let out a yowl and screwed up his face, straining.

"This is my baby brother Squishy," Squeally squeaked, then all of a sudden turned up her nose at the incredibly foul odor.

"Mo - *ther*-----!!!"

She hastily handed the dark-skinned baby to her mother who went off quickly with him.

"Squatty," Henry said, "I understand you're a scientist. Squiggly says you're over five million years old. How is that possible? The dinosaurs were killed off sixty-five million years ago along with just about every other form of life in some kind of catastrophe, and Homo Sapiens didn't-----"

"Ha!" Squatty snorted, disapprovingly. "Homo Sapiens. Wise man! Huh!"

Ignoring the rude retort, Henry continued, "He didn't even appear until about two hundred fifty thousand years ago, so how can you-----

"Just goes to show that In is the best place to live," Squatty said in his superior way. "Always was, always will be." Squatty began lecturing Henry on why In was superior to Out.

Mrs. Squires hurried back into the room, saying, "My goodness Squatty don't be so know-it-all this is a guest he-----"

"No, Mrs. Squires, it's okay," Henry assured her. "Squatty, what do you mean it's the best place to live?" he asked.

"You don't know? Being underground, pretty much protected, when Out was being ravaged, wiping out the dinosaurs, sounds like a pretty good deal to me. We're way ahead of you in Out. We may develop slowly, but we've had three and a half billion years to do it. We're way ahead. Simple."

"Yeah, simple," Henry acknowledged, without mentioning that the clothes everyone wore were a century and a half behind times.

Squatty said, "I have an experiment perking," and rushed to the stairs.

"Oh, yeah," Squiggly said, "Squinchy always has something perking."

"I'll get you later, Squirty," Squatty called back down to Squiggly.

Even before Mr. or Mrs. Squires could say anything, if they were going to, Squiggly was apologizing. "I'm sorry, Mr. Henry, but sometimes he gets on my nerves."

"Older brothers can do that," Henry agreed.

What was going on here, Henry wondered. Their skin, so different, all in one family. Their eyes, all the same pale gray, so far as he could tell, looking through the moonglasses.

And the clothes? Everybody's clothes were from a long bygone era. If In was so advanced, why were they so far behind in clothes?

But why should he be surprised? At anything? This was just another hallucination. An interesting one. So ride it out, he told himself. He had always ridden them out.

Thirteen

An Ice Box in Squiresville

Mrs. Squires left to finish changing Squishy and putting him back into his crib. In the interim, S.Q. showed Henry his latest completed patch-up chore in the living room, a section of ceiling that had been stained with a water leak from an earlier repair attempt in the upstairs bathroom. Being generous, Henry gave him credit for trying, but the patched area was quite noticeably rough and discolored. S.Q., though, was quite pleased with the results.

"Not bad, wouldn't you say, Mr. Henry?"

That depended on your definition of bad, Henry thought, and replied, "Not bad at all, Mr. Squires. Quite good in fact."

Mrs. Squires was calling from the kitchen to come in and have a cup of What'siss.

Henry found the kitchen to be like the living room, small, clean, and simple: stone stove and oven like a kiln, stone sink, stone table and chairs, a piece of wooden furniture he could not identify, and not much else.

Squeezy motioned for him and S.Q. to have a seat at the table while she poured steaming cups of What'siss for the three of them.

Henry looked at the brown liquid--through moonglasses it looked as if it could be brown--then took a sip. Not bad. Not good either. Strange taste.

Squeezy launched into, "Oh yes you must wonder about it I thought we'd try it it's not new on the market been around a long time but we never tried it you know and we found we like it so I'll get more next time I go shopping."

"Yeah, get it and another pair of shoes," S.Q. offered and got a dirty look from Squeezy in return.

She did not shut up, though, and added, "It's a distillate of organic particulate matter they get from one of the streams up river I don't understand these things but Squatty our oldest boy will be glad to tell you all about it he knows the origin and process and distribution he knows everything about it he-----"

"Yes," S.Q. agreed, "He'll be glad to tell you."

Squeezy gave S.Q. another disapproving look, then smiled and said, "It's not really called What'siss by the manufacturer but Squiggly when he was a little boy only a million years old and just beginning to talk asked >What'siss' and we laughed so hard I thought I'd-----"

"And she actually did," S.Q. said with what might pass for a twinkle in his pale gray eyes.

For this most unwelcome comment he got hands planted on hips and a stare from Squeezy.

"May I ask," Henry interrupted before things could deteriorate further, "what is that piece of wooden furniture?" pointing at it.

Looking surprised, Squeezy replied."It's not furniture it's a kitchen appliance why I'm surprised you don't know it's just an ice box not top of the line and not new but quite functional the wood floated in from Out and our cabinet makers shaped it so beautifully don't you think-----

She opened the door to display a block of ice in the top compartment on the left and what must have been food on the slate shelves to the right side of the ice. "We get ice from the very edge of Out in what you call winter at least that's what Squatty calls it and keep it packed in dried algae to keep it from melting it's quite nice to have cool food the workers don't like going to the edge of Out they don't mind the cold so much but even with very dark sunglasses their eyes hurt don't you think snow is terribly hard on the eyes it's a wonder the gatherers do as well as they do in harvesting the ice-----

"Yes of course," Henry broke in. In fact, Henry remembered his father telling him about growing up on the farm, and one day at the State Fair they had come upon an exhibit of what life was like in the old days. His father had pointed out each item and described it.

Some of the Squires' kitchen was quite similar to the one in the exhibit, ice box, ice and all.

With eyes lowered now and in a modest tone, almost wistfully, she said, "Of course we don't have a refrigerator with an icemaker as you do-----

For the first time, Henry realized he had seen no evidence of electricity anywhere in the house. No lamps or ceiling lights. In fact, he had seen no electric lights anywhere on his journey through In.

But of course. People who could see in darkness had no need for electric lights. Quite certainly, light would hurt their eyes.

"Whew!" he said to himself. "This one is a doozy." But he knew that this illusion too would pass. He would come out of it with little or no memory of what had happened.

"We're having grilled Mexican tetra for dinner along with wolf spider eggs and fried algae all fresh from the market this morning," Mrs. Squires said, pointing in the ice box to a platter full of alabaster-white small fish, then into the hot oven at a metal pan full of what looked like roe but was probably the spider eggs, and another pan of what may have been a greenish slime that was baking.

"Looks real good," Henry said, although his stomach was disagreeing with him. "But you needn't have gone to such trouble."

"No trouble at all we're so pleased to have such a special guest aren't we S.Q. it's just wonderful wonderful-----

"Real pleased," S.Q. replied.

Just then, Squeally came flouncing into the kitchen in a dress which seemed to have come from a thrift store, clean and well pressed but certainly not purchased at an upscale boutique, and her lips were dark, seemingly tinted with something that might have passed for lipstick.

Her mother scolded, "Now stop that! you're much too young for that we're going to have a talk later-----

"Oh, *mothers!*" Squeally protested.

"Please set the table dear."

With that, Squeally went to a cupboard and pulled out dinnerware and silverware. She began placing it around the table as her mother checked in the icebox for something. Henry picked up one of the plates--gold! And the eating utensils were sterling silver! Although he was not entirely sure because of the moonglasses, the weight was right and he could think of nothing else.

"Beautiful!" he said, staring.

Mrs. Squires turned around and said, astonished, "Squeally don't use our everyday things dear we have a guest please get out our good set."

"Everyday!!" Henry said.

"Oh I'm so sorry you had to see that -----" She gushed out many other things which were lost on Henry in his astonishment.

"Children can be such a trial don't you think Mr. Henry you think they know what to do and ohhhhh I'm not sure what happens to them sometimes ohhhh everyday things for an honored guest ohhhh but you'll have a word with them won't you dear," she said to S.Q.

S.Q. nodded sternly.

Henry said, "They were gold and silver, weren't they. Where do they come from?"

"Well Goldville and Silverville but the townspeople there build their houses and streets out of those and if you want my opinion it's terribly monotonous everything gold or silver so in Squiresville and I'm quite sure everywhere else we use them for everyday things like plates and bowls but I'm sorry you had to see it-----"

Squeally put away the glistening gold and silver items and got out plain-looking dark-colored stoneware and what looked like plastic eating utensils but in reality, as he later learned, were some kind of composite.

Mrs. Squires helped Squeally set the table, saying, "There that is so much more beautiful don't you think Mr. Henry?"

Henry thought otherwise but nodded in agreement. Mugs, having had a hard day, was sound asleep.

The images in Henry's mind jostled one another for priority as to which to consider first, that of the icebox, of S.Q. taking charge, of gold and silver houses and streets or any one of many other things for which he had no answer.

Mrs. Squires continued, "I suppose I should be home more and with the children when they get home from school but I'm so busy at the plant I'm afraid I neglect them but S.Q. does a marvelous job raising them so I don't worry too much and in the evenings and on weekends I try to forget work and just spend quality time with them and my husband." She gave S.Q. an adoring look and bent over behind his chair and hugged him.

Mrs. Squires added, "You can tell them over and over what you expect them to do and how they should act because they're children and-----do have a word with them S.Q. please."

S.Q. replied gravely, "I certainly will."

"Oh my it's getting late," she said, "Time for Great Great Grandfather to come down for dinner and it's not ready please grill the fish now dear."

S.Q. nodded, got a platter of fish from the ice box and went out onto the very small back patio which, Henry could see through the door, was really just a few flat stones on the limestone right up against the cave wall.

"What does the plant produce, Mrs. Squires?" Henry asked to make conversation while she--call me Squeezy please, she admonished him again--was bustling around, moving a fork slightly, placing a cup a bit more to the side.

"Oh we make paper products--tissues, towels, writing paper, other things, mostly from seaweed." she replied.

"That's nice. What do you do there? What's your job?"

"Oh I own the plant."

"Well, that's impressive."

"The business is growing nicely I started from scratch not too long ago about four million years I think, not very long after Squiggly was born--'scratch'--that's an inside joke at the plant," she said and giggled, rolling her eyes.

"My first tissue and towel products really were scratchy but then Squatty developed a formula can you imagine a mere boy he invented a formula that made them fluffy soft and my marketing manager came up with the brand name 'Squeezy Soft.'"

She laughed again and said, "It really took off we now have over sixty percent market share and we're producing night and day to keep up and we just roll out the orders of Squeezy Soft just roll them out," she said, tickled with her metaphor. "One time a tissue machine malfunctioned and they rolled right out the door and kept on going down the street with us chasing after them."

"Well, paper products keep you busy. It must be very lucrative."

"Oh it is," she said modestly. "I'm able to pay my employees well most of them live in Low Meadows and the others in Middle Manors they need the bigger houses for growing families you see."

Henry didn't see. "Do any of them live here in Scenic Heights?"

"Oh yes several they're my executives in charge of divisions of course I have other executives and managers around In who also live in upscale developments like ours of Scenic Heights we also have owners of other corporations living here one of them is our next door neighbor Mrs. Scoot she has a blind wolf spider leasing business that supports a huge area of In and she supplies small fast spiders to the Squat Squad."

Henry had no idea what that meant, but it could wait. In a hallucination you don't need to know everything at once.

Henry could see Mrs. Scoot's house out the kitchen window, very close to the Squires' house. It was even smaller and more unimpressive looking than the Squires' house, shabby even. In their driveway was what looked like a wolf spider on its last legs, in a manner of speaking. The legs, what there were of them, obviously had a lot of miles on them. Or rather, straw lengths? Henry wondered why the neighbor who did such a thriving business didn't drive a more impressive spider. Certainly she could afford what she wanted. After all, she lived in Scenic Heights.

"Nuts. I'm going totally nuts in this crazy place," he told himself.

But he didn't have to ponder the problem any longer since an old man came shuffling into the kitchen. Rather, a very old man. As a matter of fact, an ancient man. So ancient that Henry thought if there were a wisp of air--which there wasn't, so deep inside In--the man would collapse into a small pile of dust.

"Oh Great Great Grandfather," Squeezy said cheerfully.

He was so old and thin and white, very white, that it seemed one could see his bones through the nearly translucent crinkled flesh.

"Great Great Grandfather Squires this is Mr. Henry Mr. Henry this is Great Great Grandfather Squires Mr. Squinty Squires."

The frail man's eyes were closed to the degree that only slits remained.

"How do you do, young man," Mr. Squinty Squires croaked pleasantly, head angled forward on his scrawny neck, which, incidentally, gave his extremely pale eyes--what little there was to see of them through his squint--an even more unusual appearance.

"How do you do, Sir," Henry responded. Young man? To a great great grandfather who must be at least forty million years old in In years--if Henry's hasty proportional calculations were anywhere near correct--Henry, a grandfather himself, must appear to be a mere youth. Maybe even an infant. But if an infant, the great great grandfather would not have called him a young man. Would he?

S.Q. came in with what looked like charcoal but in actuality was a platter full of the formerly alabaster-like fish.

"May have gotten them a touch overdone," S.Q. said simply.

"Oh no dear they are perfect just perfect don't you worry a bit about them just perfect," his wife effused.

Dinner was an experience, all the children at the table, all excited about one thing or another and all talking at once. Baby Squishy threw up on the table, himself, and one or two others. Henry was so taken up in the commotion he hardly noticed what he ate, which was much for the better. Mugs was offered a plate of some kind of food but sniffed, flopped down on the floor, and eased himself back away from it.

After dinner while she was clearing away the dishes, Mrs. Squires asked Henry about his icemaker and refrigerator. He explained, and she had a lot of questions, raising her eyebrows with each new description, as if she were a child listening to a grownup reading a particularly enchanting fairy tale.

"Really?" she would say. Over and over. "Really?"

Great Great Grandfather Squinty Squires sat through it all, saying nothing.

Henry was tired. He felt ill at ease, anxious. When Mrs. Squires served a cup of hot What'siss, Henry could see his hand tremble as he reached for the cup. He had been through a lot in these past days and hours. Too much.

He wanted to get out of there. He wanted for this hallucination to come to an end. He wanted a drink.

It had been what? Two days, he thought. What he was experiencing now, hands trembling, he had gone through before. Those times when he had quit drinking. Or tried. Quit for awhile.

Great Great Grandfather must have noticed, because he asked Henry to step out onto the patio with him. Henry followed the wizened man who led the way slowly outside.

The ancient man said, "Son, you are troubled."

For a long time they sat, saying nothing. Henry could hear Mrs. Squires doing the dishes, Squiggly and Squatty helping her with the drying.

"Stop that!" Henry heard her say, and he saw Squiggly peeking around the door frame at him. Squiggly's head disappeared instantly, and Henry heard the soft rumble of conversation in the house and the sound of slate cabinet doors being opened and closed.

After some more time passed, Great Great Grandfather Squires said, "Son, there's help."

Pause.

"But you must want to get it."

Pause again.

"Do you?" the ancient man croaked.

Henry didn't answer.

"If you do, take Koloa to Squabblesville tomorrow. Good night."

With that, the old man creakily rose, went into the house and out of sight.

In a few minutes, after Henry had time to mull over these strange happenings, Mrs. Squires stuck her head out and quietly said, "Mr. Henry your room is ready you must be tired it's been a very long day for you a long trip up river and meeting all of us and-----

Henry wasn't listening as she endlessly added instances of what a long day it had been for him.

She was right. He was very tired.

Squiggly said, "I'll get Mugs his glasses tomorrow. They're not ready yet. But he can sleep in my room. He's tired, aren't you, Mugs," who agreed with a whoof. " Good night, Mr. Henry."

"Good night, Squiggly."

In the tiny upstairs bedroom--Squeally's by the looks of it-Bgirl's things on the wall--Henry wanted a drink. He got undressed and with shaking hands slipped on a pair of old-fashioned pajamas that were laid out on the bed. They were some kind of cloth, maybe made from kelp. He took off his moonglasses, groped and put them on an end table. He was in total darkness. Absolute darkness. He could vaguely hear Squeally who seemed to have been temporarily exiled to the living room to sleep. The baby cried and then was quiet.

Henry lay down and tossed and turned and tried to sleep in the dark.

Total dark.

Absolute, total dark.

His head hurt. He wanted a drink. He was confused.

And he was afraid.

Fourteen

A Visit to Squabblesville

Henry had not slept well, and when he awoke he fumbled about for his moonglasses. When he got them on he went to the bathroom, then downstairs to find it quiet. The children had gone to school he supposed, and he could hear Mr. Squires puttering around somewhere, no doubt keeping his ear out for any cry from Squishy. Henry found the baby in his crib in the tiny bedroom off the living room, sound asleep.

Mrs. Squires had left a note. It read, 'In haste guidebook on table lunch and water bottle in icebox tote bag to carry them help yourself to What'siss fried eggs on stove Koloa fed and ready to go he will take you he knows the way just climb on and he will go S.Q. and Squiggly have Mugs see you this evening take care.'

She was a love, this charming, funny, big-hearted lady who, he had learned, gave much more to her employees than she took for herself. But then, this seemed to be the case in In. He understood. Except maybe for the shoes that she bought, enough for a shoe store? He would ask S.Q. about them later. And where in this little house would there be room for a closet full of shoes?

Henry sat drinking his What'siss and feeling worse, not better. He needed a drink, not this strange stuff. He would not go. Not to Squabblesville, not to anywhere. He might just step out the front door and take a couple more steps off into the darkness above the lake. That would stop his hallucination.

Ridiculous. The idea of a hallucination was a hallucination.

But since he had met Squiggly he did want to get better. He did very much want to get better. He had tried so many times.

Might as well go to Squabblesville.

In a kind of daze he gathered the guidebook, lunch, and water bottle and stuck them in the tote bag. Koloa, faithful Koloa, was waiting in the driveway, belly to the ground. Henry climbed up to a seat and felt the beast rise and begin its limping, ambling walk. Henry sank into himself.

By the time he was aware of what was going on, Koloa was in Low Meadows, turning onto a side road that had a sign pointing to Squabblesville. He was vaguely aware of going past large houses, one by one, and finally none at all. They were in open country, in a manner of speaking. They were still in the cave, but after some time they began coming to fissures in the cave wall which had roads or paths leading into them from the main road, all marked with signs giving the names of the villages and distances: Endless Cavern 1,734 SLs, Highville 2,673 SLs, Squallville 3,623 SLs; Squeamishville 5,944 SLs, Goldville 6,783 SLs, Silverville 7342 SLs and so on.

SLs? Straw Lengths, no doubt. Just as Squiggly had learned in science class.

As they were going along as fast as Koloa could go, which was not too fast, a large wolf spider came up behind them and slowed down, then hung back at a steady interval. On its back was a small figure wrapped in cloak and hood so that the face was almost totally hidden. Probably some kind of monk. Henry forgot about it.

Now he was becoming more aware of the landscape through which they passed. The road wound in and out around giant stalagmites whose tops he could not fathom because they were beyond his range of vision through the moonglasses. And they bypassed what appeared to be huge slabs of rock which had spalled off the side of the cave and fallen to the floor. It was a rough country, one of rugged beauty.

After some time they came to a large sign:

Squatter County

County Seat--Squabblesville

Do Not Litter

And shortly thereafter, a signpost directing them off the main road: Squabblesville 2,987 SLs.

In a few minutes they were at the cave wall where a fissure loomed up into the darkness. Ahead of him, the road to Squabblesville entered the opening. At first there was plenty of distance on either side for two way traffic. Then the road got steeper and narrower. At some points, Koloa was obviously laboring as he gamely made the climb. Then the fissure got so close on both sides there was barely room for one way traffic. This was quite frightening. What would happen, Henry wondered, if there was an earthquake? Rocks would come crashing down where there was no room to escape, and the walls might even press in and squash them.

Shaking such thoughts from mind, Henry slowly traveled on. Every now and then in the narrowest strictures they would encounter a traffic signal which was a glowworm. The sign beside it would read, One Blink Stop: Two Blinks Go.

This system worked well. On one blink Koloa would halt in the pull-off to let oncoming traffic pass, heading toward Squiresville. The drivers were the only ones aboard each carrier, most of which were blind wolf spiders, but some were other creatures, so far unknown to Henry. The drivers invariably seemed to be deep in thought and gave no notice to Henry or Koloa. Then after a few minutes Henry would see the two blinks from the signal, and they could resume their journey. There were not many wolf spiders on the road today, so Koloa made reasonably good time.

Finally the fissure opened into another cave, a large one, and ahead of them was the sign:

A Hearty Welcome

SQUABBLESVILLE

Population 0

Our Motto:

Squabble Out Your Problems

Leave Your Burdens Here Behind You

Embrace What Lies Ahead of You

Henry screwed up his face and wondered, population *zero*?

He had not had to use the guidebook because Koloa obviously knew the way. But now he dug it out of his tote bag. It was a very thick and heavy book, the kind scholars produce and is called a tome. It probably should be called a tomb since often the information in such books, so meticulously collected and categorized and edited and reedited and argued back and forth across entire scholarly careers, had found a final resting place almost surely to be undisturbed for eternity.

The first few pages were not bad. He found the answer to population zero on Page 3 where it said that Squabblesville was somewhat of a misnomer in that it was more like a business park than a village. People did not live here. They only came here to work or as clients. The sole purpose of the place, according to the book, was to adjust squabbles and consequently to make every client happier and more productive as an individual, member of a family, business or other organization, or society as a whole.

The book explained on Page 4 that clients could get two kinds of treatment, depending on what they needed. Since life would be exceedingly dull without squabbles of some kind to liven things up, you could either go to the Ensquabble section of town to learn techniques for becoming more squabbly, or to the Desquabble section to learn how to tone it down so you wouldn't be driving everyone nuts. The goal was never to achieve an exact balance. Only a complete boor would want to be in that condition. Consequently, the counselors at Squabblesville did a lucrative business since, within a short time of having returned home, most people managed to squabble too little or too much. Many would turn right around and head back to Squabblesville for another treatment.

Obviously there were more roads leading to Squabblesville than just the one from Squiresville. Few wolf spiders had passed them on the road, and yet the parking lots were almost full, row upon row, with only a few open parking places left. This was partially explained by the discovery that each new arrival of a wolf spider or other conveyance revealed only one person aboard. Page 5 clarified this observation. Only an individual can come to the decision to seek help. The book advised that it does no good to have someone else make the ultimate decision, or to bring a crowd along. Henry skipped the Ensquabble section on Page 6 and went right to Desquabble on Page 8. Here in the subsection on serious squabble problems he found that deciding to seek help is a courageous step to be taken alone by a person who has not otherwise been able to resolve his or her problems. This was courageous especially for men because of how they view themselves, macho, in charge. No man wants to be perceived as weak.

The rest of the 1187 pages seemed to be devoted to success and failure stories which at this moment were of no interest to Henry. He had business of his own to attend to.

Koloa seemed to know what section of town was their destination and he headed toward the big sign, Desquabble, Left Lane. He narrowly beat another wolf spider into what seemed to be the only vacant parking spot, and the rider shouted a profanity and gave Henry the finger.

"Get a life!" Henry shouted back.

Dismounting, Henry came to the gate of a courtyard that was further sectioned beyond it, as indicated by two huge signs he could see as he peered inside. One read ENTRANCE. The other read EXIT. ENTRANCE was packed with three lines of people. EXIT stood vacant.

Henry thought that maybe the clients go out the back door when they finish their session instead of exiting through EXIT. Made sense. He knew from his visits to mental health counselors how it felt to walk back out through a waiting room. He was never quite able to convince himself that those people were there for the same reason he was, and he felt conspicuous, especially on those times when his eyes were red and his cheeks were still wet from wiped away tears.

Standing stiffly at the ENTRANCE gate was a deputy sheriff, nattily attired in full dress foot guard uniform. Henry could see no eyes under the black bearskin headdress, but a bead of sweat ran down her nose, and her mouth recited in a monotone, "Line 1 Whines, Line 2

Gripes, Line 3 Trouble Big Time." She punctuated the litany with a hearty sneeze, Ah--CHOO!

He went to Line 3 at ENTRANCE. The person ahead of him turned and said, "Don't waste your time," and pointed to EXIT.

Henry raised his eyebrows, and the man pointed again, more vigorously this time.

Henry asked, "I'm supposed to go in EXIT?"

The man pointed again.

Henry said, "Who's on first?"

His blank look told Henry he didn't get it. Henry shrugged his

shoulders, looked at the sneezing guard, then took the man's advice. He began walking through the spacious empty section, watched by all the people waiting in Line 3.

The sign on the clinic door read, Welcome, Come in EXIT. So he entered EXIT.

The waiting room was full, and he felt self-conscious. There were three doors, marked, of course, Whines, Gripes, and Trouble Big Time. On the latter was a nameplate: Doctor de Squawk, Squabbler-In-Chief. French, no doubt. Henry sat down and tried to remember a few words in French which he thought might come in handy but did not even have time to get to the kind of nervous stage one can work up while waiting to see a counselor, especially a new one. The door marked Squabbler-In-Chief opened and the doctor stuck her head out. "Entrez," she said pleasantly to Henry.

Dr. de Squawk? Maybe French Canadian with perhaps some Indian blood mixed in. "Oh, oh, I'm in trouble," Henry thought, wishing he had worked harder in French class.

Fifteen

RESPONSIBILITY

B ut there was no problem.

In English the doctor asked him to sit, introduced herself, and told him to please be comfortable while she reviewed the files that had been prepared by his three previous counselors. How she had gotten those files Henry had no clue. Could she call him Henry? She could.

She opened the first folder, read the first page and said, "Hmm." She repeated the "hmm" as she read the next page. "Yes," she said, read some more and closed the file. She looked up at Henry and said, "This guy needed more help than you did. "A real nut case."

"Exactly!" Henry agreed.

Doctor de Squawk started to read the second file, also short. At the first page her brow wrinkled and she reached into her drawer. Out came a pair of tweezers with which she carefully grasped the page, read it, and said, "Hmm." She delicately turned the page, grasped the second with the tweezers, quickly read it and said, "Picked his nose."

"Exactly!" Henry agreed.

The third file was a long one. She read intently, turning page after page. Finally, she said, "Doctor

Shepherd was a good one."

"I agree," said Henry.

"I've already taken several minutes of your time, so if you don't mind, let's see if I have this right." Doctor de Squawk said, "You thought the war was not one in which America should have engaged, both for moral and practical reasons, right?"

"Correct."

"You and Laurel were deeply in love and cherished your baby. Yet you left college and enlisted because you felt that you had an obligation to do what you could to bring the war quickly to an end. Although you were preparing to be a teacher, after basic training you went into Medical Services and got excellent training as a medic at Fort Sam Houston."

"Right."

"And you found that you couldn't help all of your buddies. Sometimes several of them were wounded at the same time, and you had to treat them, but you couldn't do all of them at once, and some of them didn't make it."

He didn't answer.

She said gently, "Henry, I don't want you to relive any of this. I'm trying to go over it quickly so you can be helped. It's necessary, though, to confirm some basic findings."

Henry was fighting against the tears. And losing.

Doctor de Squawk handed him a tissue and said, "It's okay."

She continued, "This kind of thing happened several times. Why couldn't you do more, you asked yourself over and over."

Henry was sobbing.

"I'm sorry, but we're almost there. Stateside, you went back to college and managed to finish your degree and get hired to teach. You tried hard, and the kids liked and respected you, but your anger at higher-ups was always a problem. They didn't seem to really care about the students, and you did not get tenure. You got another teaching job but it lasted only a year. You and Laurel had problems. You tried, but life was a mess. You were withdrawn, argumentative, overbearing, had no real friends because you didn't want any close relationships. They were too easily the source of heartbreak. You tried counseling sessions twice and it didn't get you where you wanted to go, and your drinking became more and more of a problem. Do I have the essence of it about right?"

"Yes!"

"*YES!*"

Doctor de Squawk said, compassionately and sincerely, "Then finally you tried Doctor Shepherd. He helped you a lot, didn't he." It was a statement, not a question.

He blubbered the answer, "Yes."

"Doctor Shepherd asked you if you would want to be the kind of person who would not be deeply affected by all this, and you said you would not. He told you that your reactions were perfectly normal and predictable, and that you were far from alone in struggling with PTSD. Many veterans had it. You found Doctor Shepherd to be not just a good counselor but a fine man, and you made some progress as you proceeded with the counseling and with trying to put your family and professional life back together."

"Yes," Henry breathed. He was exhausted.

"At your last meeting with Doctor Shepherd, he told you that you feel responsible for everything. He said that no one is responsible for everything that happens or fails to happen. Some things just happen, and they have consequences. You cannot control them. You can only work to gain control over how you react to these things. And you can succeed in this effort. He told you that, right?"

"Yes."

"And he suggested some group counseling for awhile so you could see how others had similar problems, and you went to some of those sessions and got something out of them."

"Yes."

"But instead of going back to counseling, you stopped, lost another teaching job, drank more heavily, and Laurel finally had to leave. Also your daughter Melanie could not get through to you any more than Laurel could. And Peggy, your granddaughter, pulls back from any close relationship."

All true.

Doctor de Squawk let the silence extend into what seemed like several minutes. Henry was slumped in his chair, hands limply at his sides, tears rolling down his cheeks.

Suddenly there was what sounded like a command: "Soldier, sit up straight! Look me in the eye!"

Henry was so shocked he did just that, wiping away tears with the backs of his hands.

Doctor de Squawk said firmly, "You are not responsible for everything, but you *are* responsible for Laurel, and you *are* responsible for Melanie, and you *are* responsible for Peggy--responsible to love and be loved by them. It was not your fault, not entirely, but the fact is you have made their lives a mess. Laurel is in living hell. You hardly ever see Melanie, and Peggy doesn't know her grandfather. You can do something about that. It won't be easy, but you *can* do it! You did a wonderful job in the war, you did a wonderful job with many of your students, and you can do a wonderful job for your family and for yourself. *You are responsible for them and for yourself!* Do I make myself clear?"

He almost said, "Yes Sir," but instead muttered, "Thank you, doctor."

She said, "Go back to Doctor Shepherd. He is good. As good as you will get. Goodbye, Henry, and good luck." She rose and shook his hand.

84

Henry was in a stupor, and he found himself outside the back door, bewildered. He stood there until he saw a sign, To Parking Lot. He moved numbly along the path, somehow found the right spot, climbed up on Koloa, and was out of Squabblesville before he realized fully what had happened.

A small hooded figure on a large wolf spider hurried past him and disappeared in the distance on the road back to Squiresville.

Sixteen

A Romp with Mugs

Henry was hardly aware of the return journey on the road through the narrow fissure. He was in the same kind of exhausted state he had experienced numerous times in combat. But in combat he was always clear-headed. Now he was in a fog. He became vaguely aware of the sign welcoming travelers to Low Meadows. Koloa turned off onto a path and came up to the edge of what one might call a field, an open area where there were only a few small stalagmites and not much of any loose cave pearls. Several small blind wolf spiders were parked rather haphazardly next to a large one, the way kids ditch their bicycles when they're in a hurry to join in some fun. The large one, breathing quite hard, lowered itself to the ground.

"Hello, Mr. Henry. I hope you had a good trip. Come join us. Mugs is having a good romp with us."

It was Squiggly.

"He's a little out of shape," Squiggly explained, pointing at the large wolf spider. "We rode our spiders here to give Mugs a chance to run and play."

Henry started to say, "Run and play?" In the first place, Mugs was old and arthritic. In the second place Mugs couldn't see anything in the total darkness of In.

But there was Mugs amid a small crowd of laughing boys and girls of various skin colors, light to dark. Mugs was running and fetching a bone the kids would grab and throw. He was barking and jumping joyfully. Strapped on his face was a pair of very large, very white-lensed moonglasses. On his mouth was a wide grin, revealing his crooked teeth. He grinned like that back home when he was pleased, just as he frowned and planted his feet firmly when he was not.

The sight brought Henry fully awake. Mugs looking younger, running and playing? Shocked, Henry said, "I think I'll just sit and watch a minute."

"Oh, sure. You must be tired from your long day. I'll have Mugs rest too for a bit. I don't want him to overdo."

Henry made his way to a stump of a stalagmite and sat while Squiggly turned toward the crowd of kids and called to Mugs to come and sit. Mugs

wanted to play some more but obediently broke loose and came over to the boy. Seeing Henry he rubbed up against him and turned his eyes up in that look of happy pride at having done something special. He was panting hard from his exertion, and Squiggly went over to an ice chest to get a bottle of water for the dog.

Mugs must have thought Squiggly wanted something else too, so he trotted over to the large wolf spider, pulled something off its back and came trotting back to Henry, dragging it. It was a cloak with a hood.

As Squiggly returned with the water he saw the dog standing there proudly with the cloak in his mouth waiting for approval.

Instead, Squiggly said, "Oh oh."

Henry looked at Squiggly.

"You followed me."

The boy hung his head and was quiet. Then he raised it a little and said, "But Mr. Henry, I wanted so much for you to go to Squabblesville."

Henry said, "You knew that Koloa would take me there without getting lost. He knew all the turns."

Silence.

Henry waited.

Nothing.

Finally, Henry said, "If I wouldn't go in to see a counselor, you were going to be there to convince me."

More silence.

Henry said, "Come here, Squiggly."

The boy came hesitantly to him and Henry took him in his arms. "It's okay. But you see, it doesn't do any good for someone else to force a decision like that on you. You have to make it all alone. I've at least learned that."

"I'm sorry, Mr. Henry."

Those pale gray eyes were tearing up.

"Oh, come on now, it's okay. It's okay. You were just being my friend."

Henry pulled out his handkerchief and wiped away the tears. "Smile now for me, won't you?"

With difficulty, Squiggly smiled, and in a moment all was right again.

Mugs was ready for another round of play. He trotted off toward the kids who were calling him. Squiggly turned away to follow, but Henry stopped him for a moment by saying, "He looks the same, kind of yellowed, but he seems not to be in pain. How did you do it?"

Squiggly turned and called back, "I didn't. Squatty did. He made up a potion. Simple."

Yeah, real simple. Henry had tried several medicines that the vet suggested and nothing seemed to work. The fact was, Mugs was well along in years, and nothing could prevent what was happening to him. But look at him now.

The kids finished playing, came over to say hello to Henry and to pet Mugs, and then they hopped on their small spiders for return home. Henry asked another question.

"Squiggly, you were terrified when you first saw Mugs. How come the kids weren't?"

"Well, they were at first. But I showed them how tame he was and what a good boy, and I finally got them to try petting him. Pretty soon he was kissing them and then we started throwing the bone. After just a few minutes some of them were trying to trade me their pet wolf spiders for Mugs. I told them I didn't own him, and besides, they wouldn't be able to give me enough spiders even if they gave me all of them in the whole world of In for Mugs."

"Well, you have a point there."

"Come on, Mr. Henry, mother is fixing cave crickets for dinner. They're imported. We don't get to have that very often. The best ones come from a place called Mammoth Cave. Squatty makes fun of the name because he says that cave is not so mammoth compared to some caves in In. It's the longest cave, true, he says, but he thinks that the size of the chamber is more important, and the Sarawak Chamber in a place called Malaysia is more impressive. Of course he's an authority even though he's never been to either one. But Squatty does know a lot. Sometimes, though, I just wish he wasn't such a know-it-all. Father wanted to grill the crickets on the patio, but mother said she didn't want him to have to go to such trouble and she would stir-fry them on the stove.

Wondering how in the world one could grill crickets, and remembering S.Q.'s grilled fish of last evening, Henry thought that Squiggly's mother was a wise woman.

But crickets?

Henry climbed up wearily onto Koloa. Going to the shrink was always exhausting. It truly had been a long day.

Stir-fried crickets?

Seventeen

ICE BOXES AND LIGHT BULBS

Henry didn't remember much of the dinner. During his unit's pacification mission in the war he had always managed to get down whatever was served to him and later thank his hostess profusely for it. And there had been some weird things.

Stir-fried crickets, he discovered, were best washed down with What'siss, trying not to be conspicuous about it. When a plate of crickets was put down for Mugs, he looked at it with curious eyes through the moonglasses, and surprisingly he ate some. Henry wondered what his motivation was, to please his hostess? Or was he just awfully hungry?

Afterward they sat in the kitchen, he and Mugs and Mr. and Mrs. Squires and Squiggly.

"It really is a nice ice box don't you think Mr. Henry?" Mrs. Squires asked.

"Yes, I do. Really nice."

"Of course it's old but really quite adequate."

"Yes, I should imagine quite adequate."

"The people down in Low Meadows have large new ice boxes but then they have large families ours is old and small but quite adequate don't you think dear?"

"Yes," S.Q. replied. "Quite adequate."

While his wife went to the ice box to give it a hug, S.Q. quietly said to Henry, "She'd probably bring home ice boxes instead of shoes if they weren't so big and heavy."

"What's that about ice boxes dear?" Mrs. Squires said.

"I was saying to Mr. Henry that some ice boxes are too big and heavy."

"Yes that's the truth but ours although old and small is quite adequate."

S.Q., having gotten himself out of hot water by the narrowest of margins, agreed again, "Quite adequate."

"But," she said wistfully, "a refrigerator with an icemaker would be nice wouldn't it dear?"

"Yes, it would be nice," said S.Q.

"But really the people down in Low Meadows would need a refrigerator with icemaker much more than we do many of them have such large families you know."

Henry was just awake enough to suggest, "It wouldn't be much use without electricity."

Mugs had fallen asleep but opened one eye as if he might join in, but then thought better of it and closed it again.

Squiggly, though, jumped into the conversation. "But we have electricity. Or at least we could."

"How so? I haven't seen any evidence of it," Henry said.

"That doesn't mean we don't have it," Squiggly countered in as respectful a tone as possible. "In fact, it was one of the Chosen Ones selected by our very own Council of Gifts who happened to emerge through a faucet into the laboratory of a Mr. Edison and found out about electricity. After Mr. Edison got a trip to In, he gave him the plans for producing it."

"Really?" said Henry. "Edison had hallucinations too? He thought he came to In?"

Not understanding, Squiggly continued "That was lots of millions of years ago. We learned that-----

"In science class," Henry said, finishing the sentence.

"Yes, and in addition to the plans for electricity the Chosen One also brought back what is called a light bulb."

"I haven't seen any here."

"No, but, "Squiggly replied, "once a Chosen One is selected by The Committee, the choice of The Gift is left entirely to her or him. That's why the procedure for being chosen is so thorough. It's a great responsibility to make a good choice. The Chosen One was severely rebuked by The Council for coming back with a light bulb and the plans to make electricity. Waste of a perfectly good trip to Out, and those trips don't just grow on stalagmites, they said. Electricity, they cautiously came to agree, might prove useful in some way some day, but what could anyone do with a light bulb? Nobody is sure what electricity would be used for. But our scientists have been working on an explanation-----

"For lots of millions of years," Henry interrupted again.

"Yes, but Squatty has some ideas on what to do about electricity, and he'll probably beat the grown-up scientists to an answer. Of course we'll never hear the end of it. But a light bulb? What in the world good is a light bulb"

"A light bulb is used to produce light," Henry said, solving the problem right then and there.

"Why would anyone want to do that?" Squiggly said, quite offended.

"To see at night, of course. When it's dark, you just flick a switch and the light bulb turns dark into light."

"How awful!" Squiggly nearly shouted. "That's *ghastly*."

"Oh, sorry," Henry apologized when he saw the horrified look on the faces of everyone in the room. All except Mugs who slept on as if turning on a light wasn't worth waking up for.

"I get it. You're just being funny again, Mr. Henry," said Squiggly, and laughed.

Henry came close to reminding Squiggly of the visit to his kitchen in Henryville, but then remembered that the inset lighting in his house didn't at all resemble the pictures Squiggly had probably seen of Edison's bulb. Besides, Henry was very tired, punchy, and wanted to go to bed.

He asked Squiggly if he could go back to Out after breakfast.

Squiggly, crestfallen, looked at him, then at Mugs, and kept his eyes on the dog for several seconds. Slowly, and with his eyes misting up, he said, "Yes, Mr. Henry, if you have to go."

All of the Squires family looked sad but tried to act naturally by making small talk. The last thing Henry remembered before he went up the stairs to the bedroom was Mrs. Squires saying one more time, "A refrigerator with icemaker wouldn't that be unusual and quite nice don't you think dear," and S.Q. agreeing, "Quite nice."

Eighteen

SHOES

At breakfast Henry found Mrs. Squires hustling about the kitchen, setting out a meal for him of cave fungi that tasted something like shredded wheat, and fried spider eggs that tasted like – fried spider eggs. She interrupted herself to give him a big squeeze, saying, "Oh we wish you didn't have to go it was so nice to have you and Mugs with us you must come visit us again I hope you will forgive me for running off but there's a problem at the plant one of the machines won't stop running it did this before but we thought we had it fixed and it's spewing out rolls of paper and they're going out the door and rolling down the street again oh dear I've packed you a nice lunch and put some iced What'siss in it but of course my little chunks of ice are not perfect forms such as you get from an icemaker so you will have to forgive how they look goodbye and please please visit us again." She hugged Henry, then held him at arm's length, looked at him, and pulled him close and squeezed him again. "Oh dear," she said, dabbing her eyes and hurrying out the front door.

Squiggly said that his father was out pushing the baby in the stroller, and both Squatty and Squeally had already gone to school but, as the

Chosen One still on his quest, he did not have to go today. Then he noticed that his mother, in her rush to get to the plant, had forgotten to take a bag with boxes in it.

"The shoes," he said, and hurried to the door with the bag, only to discover that Koloa with his mother driving had disappeared down the road.

"Oh well, she can take them tomorrow. I'll put them back in her closet. Mr. Henry, I don't think you've seen the rest of the house, just the downstairs and Squeally's upstairs bedroom and the bathroom. Come up, please, and I'll show you Squatty's and my room."

Henry followed him up the narrow stairs.

"This is our room," Squiggly said, walking into a very small room with two bunks, a desk and a work table. "This is my side," he said, pointing to a neat area opposite to a mess--bed unmade, shoes and clothes dropped here and there, and a table that looked like a mad scientist had just vacated it, leaving steaming pots and vials of experiments behind. "Squatty calls his side The Lab and forbids me to disturb anything. Who would want to," he said, twisting his face. "Actually," he added proudly, "Squatty is very intelligent, and even if he drives me nuts sometimes, he's my big brother. His teacher says he's going to be the head of the Science Committee one day. That would be a fantastic honor, don't you think?"

Henry replied that indeed, it would be an extraordinary honor, and he followed Squiggly out of the room into another bedroom, a somewhat larger one, but still very small.

"This is my parents' bedroom. Mother keeps her shoes in here," Squiggly said, opening the closet door.

From what he had heard thus far, Henry expected to see dozens of pairs of shoes. Instead, there was just one pair of what looked to be very expensive, beautiful shoes. Squiggly pulled two shoe boxes from the bag his mother had forgotten and placed them neatly on a shelf. "She can take them tomorrow," he said.

"Squiggly, I thought your father was going to start a shoe store if she bought any more, but I don't think that three pairs of shoes is a lot."

"You haven't seen what she buys. She has been taking shoes to give them to the thrift shop. I bet she's taken four dozen already."

"I'm sorry to ask, but that pair of shoes looks to be very expensive," Henry said, pointing.

"Oh, they all are. She buys nothing but the best."

"Hmm," Henry exclaimed, pulling at his chin, thinking he had seen Mrs. Squires in only a well worn, rather old, obviously not expensive pair of shoes.

Squiggly must have known what he was thinking, and laughed. "She only puts a new pair on once and wears them around the house for awhile. She preens in front of the mirror and almost always asks my father if he doesn't think that her new shoes are nice. He always says they are nice, indeed."

"And then she takes them to the thrift store?" Henry asked, completely befuddled.

"Of course," Squiggly replied, as if nothing could be more natural. "She wants the ladies in Low Meadows to have nice things, and they couldn't afford them if they went to the shoe store to buy them."

"Yes, I see," said Henry, but wasn't at all sure he understood. The people who earn little money get expensive shoes that had been worn only once, and at thrift store prices. They live in the nicest, largest houses with big yards because they are the working class and need the room for growing families and can't afford to live up here in the expensive district of Scenic Heights where the executives live in houses that are small, often dilapidated, and close together.

"Yes, makes perfectly good sense," he repeated.

It was a minor concession to reason. After all, this whole thing was a hallucination.

Then it was time to go. Squiggly carried his broad-brimmed hat and the lunch, and he opened the door for Henry and Mugs.

Nineteen

RETURN TO OUT

Koloa, faithful old Koloa, had pulled back into the driveway, panting heavily from his quick trip down to the factory and back. After giving Koloa a chance to rest, Squiggly, Henry, and Mugs got aboard, and this time Mugs seemed not to mind the wolf spider so much now that he was sporting very large, very white moonglasses similar to Henry's. Maybe this was because it's not so much the thing one sees that's scary, but the things one can't see. Or maybe just because Squatty's potion had some lasting effect and Mugs was in a good mood because he did not feel the arthritis so much.

As they pulled out of the driveway and Henry looked down into the vast darkness rising from the surface of the lake so far below that he couldn't even see it through his moonglasses, he was not as queasy as he had been on the trip up the hill. He seemed to have accustomed himself to this strange environment to the point that he was no longer expecting disaster to be always just ahead, waiting.

Koloa took it easy going down, and Henry had a chance to look leisurely at Middle Manors and admire again the beautiful draperies of translucent limestone behind the houses. Soon they were passing through Low Meadows, and then after a long downhill ride they were at dockside. Geraldine, their water scooter, was tensing for the thrill of the start. Once again they were hardly in their seats when she took off, thrusting them backward. Squiggly grabbed his hat to keep it from flying off.

Henry enjoyed the smooth ride high above the water. Apparently Mugs did too because he leaned forward into the wind and had a lopsided grin on his face. Henry thought he looked like Snoopy piloting his Sopwith Camel fighter plane, off to shoot down the Red Baron. Squiggly smiled and patted Mugs, then leaned his head into the dog's neck and kept it there. Henry thought Squiggly was crying. After awhile, Squiggly lifted his head and looked straight ahead.

Again, although it was a considerable distance across the lake, because of their speed, it seemed like a quick trip.

Silver, the blind waterfall climbing cave fish, was waiting at the dock on the far side of the lake. They went aboard and were off with no 'Heigh Ho Silver' this time from Henry, who was feeling the pain of a very subdued Squiggly.

It was only a short trip in this calm section of the river, and very soon Henry heard the enormous waterfall ahead, Big Falls. Silver sensed it too and suddenly thrust forward, now racing at full speed. Before Henry knew it they were at the brink of the falls and sailing out into space.

Silver kept perfectly balanced, head just slightly higher than his tail. Squiggly was holding onto Mugs, calming him. The boy felt none of the thrill that had marked the earlier trip upriver, and uttered nothing as they pancaked to a perfect landing and continued downriver as if no gigantic waterfall had ever existed.

Henry, watching Squiggly and Mugs, was hardly aware of the much smaller waterfalls ahead and their easy passage of them. Mugs was the only person--not person--the only one in the world who was totally forgiving of Henry. Mugs never criticized. Mugs never cajoled. He never tried to help and end up causing him pain. When one night Henry came home drunk and stumbled over Mugs in the dark and kicked him and instantly was horrified at what he had done, Mugs just gathered himself and came and rubbed against his legs. Mugs was pure love. Unquestioning, unshakeable unadulterated love. He only gave, never expecting anything in return.

Well, maybe a pat on the head. Or a hug.

For the rest of the ride down the long tunnel, sometimes through whitewater, sometimes through calm pools, Henry had his hand on Mugs' head, patting it gently, while Squiggly hugged the dog around his neck.

They reached the final dock on river's edge uneventfully, lunch uneaten, and said goodbye to Silver who turned and swam off slowly upstream. Without really wanting to talk, Henry asked Squiggly why they didn't just take Silver all the way to the cave's mouth instead of having to walk the rest of the way.

Quietly, head lowered, Squiggly replied, "It would be cruel to bring a fish who lives far upriver out into that awful light."

Henry nodded.

Henry and Squiggly were silent as they walked along the narrow path, heading downriver. As they came to the bend in the tunnel Henry first sensed, then saw, the very faint light on the walls and ceiling ahead of them. As they progressed toward the mouth of the cave the light became more noticeable.

A few more steps and Squiggly said, "I think you should give me the glasses now, Mr. Henry."

Henry said, "I believe so," and removed them. He could faintly see in the dim light, but not as well as he had seen while wearing the glasses in the darkness. As he was handing them to Squiggly, Henry heard a faint clicking sound.

Squiggly stopped, and was now standing rigidly still, listening intently.

"Oh no!" Squiggly breathed.

The clicking became a clacking and shuffling and was getting closer, as if many somethings were moving across the floor of the channel, approaching them.

Mugs, still with his moonglasses on, growled. Henry thought that even in the faint light the dog might still be able to see something through them. Henry said, "Squiggly, let me have the glasses back!"

The boy's hand trembled so much he lost hold and the glasses fell onto the pathway. As Henry fumbled at his feet, trying to find them, and then clapped them back over his eyes, Mugs barked.

Loudly once, then again, louder Mugs barked. Henry had difficulty in holding the little dog back by his collar as Mugs strained frantically forward against the now horrifying noise.

Twenty

Gigantic Threats and Diminutive Heroes

"Pseudoscorpions!" Squiggly screeched. "Oh!"

The boy was terrified.

Henry grabbed Squiggly's arm and, holding tightly to Mugs' collar, turned to hustle them back up the path to the rear.

"No!" Squiggly shouted. "We have to be sure which way. The channel echoes. They might really be behind us."

The terrified boy clung to Henry.

"They have terrible claws," he said, "and they will poison us and eat us."

This was a bad spot on the path for seeing anything well. The dim light coming from the cave entrance down river was impairing Squiggly's vision, and the moonglasses were of only limited help to Henry. Mugs was straining, thrashing, trying to attack whatever it was.

Suddenly, around the corner in front of them a huge claw like that of a crab reached to snatch them, and a stream of awful-smelling poison spurted out of the claw and sprayed the path almost at their feet. Missing its prey on the first grab, an enormous pseudoscorpion, twice as tall as Henry, thrust his head and the other claw around the corner.

Behind and to the sides of the leader were more of them jostling for position to strike.

Henry shoved Squiggly behind him and in doing so slipped, falling hard on the path, stunning himself and causing him to lose his grip on Mugs' collar.

Two huge claws waved in the air on the ends of extended arms, and as one of the massive pincers darted down to grab Henry, Mugs rushed inside the arms and leapt with all this strength at the head of the beast, barking and trying to bite at the same time.

Just as quickly, Squiggly jumped and grabbed Mugs before the stream of venom could hit him. This instantaneous reaction by the dog and boy must have startled the creature because the grasping, clutching claw struck the ground beside Henry with a thunderous CLACK!! instead of snatching up the momentarily defenseless Henry and thrusting him into its hideous mouth.

Henry, his thigh hurting from the fall, was now on his feet and he swept up both boy and dog in his arms and quickly hobbled back along the path to the river's edge. Rushing after them was a horde of pseudo-scorpions spitting venom at them and crashing their huge claws down perilously close, but not hitting their targets--the man, boy, and dog who were now in the river and swimming desperately out to midstream to get away from the awful beasts.

Henry--chest heaving from exertion, shocked by the coldness of the water, and choking from having gotten some of it in his lungs--looked back over his shoulder at the mass of huge waving claws, stabbing in frustration out toward them. Some of the pseudoscorpions in the front rank had been pushed into the water by the onrushing ones behind them, and they were scrambling to get back on the bank, making an awful clacking and sloshing.

"You okay?" Henry gasped to Squiggly who called back, "Yes. Are you all right, Mr. Henry?"

Henry said, "Yes" although his thigh hurt, and he could not help but grin as he looked at Mugs whose head was held high, moonglasses still on his face despite the fray, and front paws churning and propelling him downstream. Mugs too had a lopsided grin on his mouth, as if to say that pseudoscorpions aren't as tough as they think they are.

They were safe. The beasts were now out of sight. Henry, Squiggly, and Mugs were good swimmers and, still swimming, Henry removed his glasses and passed them to Squiggly who with one hand put them on and said, "That's better. The awful light is getting closer. I think we can swim back to the path now. We're way down river from those horrible stinking things."

Soon they were ashore. With his breath still coming heavily, Henry put his arms around the boy in a big hug and said, "Squiggly, you saved my life. Thank you." He kissed the boy's wet forehead and hugged him tighter.

"No, it was Mugs, Mr. Henry. He's the one who attacked the pseudoscorpion. Wasn't he wonderful?"

"Yes, you're right. You are both heroes."

Squiggly beamed at the compliment and save Henry a high five.

"Where'd you learn that?" Henry asked, grinning.

"Oh, I just learned it. Here, Mugs," he said to the dog and got down on his knees. Mugs, probably thinking that Squiggly wanted to shake hands, raised his paw and grinned as Squiggly gave him a high five too.

They started walking toward the light, the limping man and the boy with arms around one another. Mugs, either still feeling the effects of the potion Squabbly had given him, or more likely so proud of himself that a little arthritis wasn't going to slow him, trotted happily ahead of them, head held high.

When Mugs stopped and turned to be sure the others were behind him, Squiggly stooped and removed Mugs' moonglasses. "You won't need those now, Mugs."

Squiggly said, quietly, with his head down, hidden under the broad brim of his hat, "You're going to be in Out in a minute of your time. Now Mr. Henry, when you see that you and Mugs are outside the cavern--be certain you are outside--say 'Form.'"

"Okay." Henry stopped and kissed the boy's forehead. Squiggly knelt, held Mugs and kissed him several times, getting slobbery licks in return.

Crying, Squiggly turned and ran back up the path. Mugs whined and lay down, looking back at the vanishing boy.

In a daze, Henry took Mugs by the collar and led him toward the cave exit. Before Henry could fully grasp the consequences, and thinking of how much he loved this boy, he found that they were outside. The large cavern was at his rear, and the river was rushing down the hillside to his right. He said, "Form."

Bewildered, feeling strange, he looked down at the trickle beside his right foot and the big rock beside him. He saw his house through the trees down the hill. Mugs also looked dazed. The dog raised his eyes to him in a questioning look, and then looked left. And right. He turned around, and around again.

There was no Squiggly.

Henry sank down on the rock and tears began to roll down his cheeks. Mugs wandered around the little opening where the water came out, and he poked a paw at it, then dug and scratched at it for a long time. Finally, head drooping, he just lay down at Henry's feet and whimpered.

They stayed there until almost dark when Henry finally rose and said, "Come on, old boy. It was nothing. It didn't happen."

The man, pressed under the weight of so many difficult years, and the dog, yellowed with age and again limping from arthritis, slowly made their way down and out of the woods.

Twenty-One

EMPTINESS

Henry entered the still house and Mugs slowly, painfully entered behind him. Moving like an automaton, Henry went to the liquor cabinet, pulled out a bottle and set it on the table. He slumped into a kitchen chair.

After some time he said to Mugs, "Want some supper?"

The dog just lay there, chin lowered on the floor, eyes staring up mournfully.

"I'll get you a hotdog." This was a treat Mugs loved. Henry got out a pan, filled it with water, put it on the stove, pulled the hotdogs from the freezer compartment and put one in the pan. He took a saucer from the cupboard.

Henry sat back down. In front of him was the bottle. It remained there, untouched, as if the effort to reach for it would be too much. The water began boiling, and as he pulled out the hotdog, cooled it, cut it into pieces, and put it down on the saucer in front of Mugs' nose, he said dejectedly, "Here you go, old boy."

The dog never moved.

They remained there until it was completely dark, Henry sitting at the table, immobile, the dog at his feet, not eating. Finally Henry got up and made his way to bed.

For a long time he lay in the dark, warm tears rolling down his cheeks until the pillow was wet. The last thing he remembered was saying to himself, "It was nothing. A hallucination."

When Henry awoke it was midmorning. His hip hurt. Strange. Why was that? He started the coffee and opened the door for Mugs. For a long time the dog didn't move, but finally he got up and painfully made his way outside where he lifted his leg. Then he started slowly up the hill, limping. Henry watched him go until he could no longer see him through the trees. He went inside, got a cup of coffee and came back out onto the deck. In a few minutes, from the direction of the rock, he heard a mournful wailing.

Heartsick, Henry went back into the kitchen. There in front of him was the bottle. He picked it up, looked at it, set it back down, returned it to the liquor cabinet, went back to his chair and slumped in it.

Why was he tortured with such a hallucination? None of the others, what he could remember of them, had been so painful, bad as they were. He couldn't remember ever feeling so bad.

"Soldier, sit up straight!"

Startled at what he thought he heard, he sat up. He was imagining a voice. Surely there was no voice.

"You are responsible for them and for yourself!"

He could almost *see* Doctor de Squawk here in front of him. He sat for many minutes, listening to the emptiness of the house. Finally he made his way to the phone and dialed the number he knew without thinking.

Doctor Shepherd said he had a full schedule for the day but would stay late and see him if he needed it right away. Henry said no, he would take the next available appointment.

He went outside, walked slowly into the woods, and went up the hill. He had his head down, seeing nothing, and was almost at the rock when he looked up.

There was Mugs wrapped happily in Squiggly's arms!

Joy at seeing the boy left him speechless.

Squiggly, wearing his old-fashioned shirt and trousers, broad-brimmed hat, and the very large, very dark sunglasses, jumped up, hurried to him and hugged him. "Mr. Henry, I'm so glad to see you!" Squiggly buried his head against Henry's chest.

Twenty-Two

CHOICE OF THE GIFT

"Squiggly," Henry said, "I didn't think-----

"Oh, Mr. Henry, I hadn't abandoned you. But I had to go back home."

"Why? How did you get there? How did you get by the pseudoscorpions?

"I'm pretty sure they weren't even there any longer, but I swam way out in the middle of the river then upstream until I got back to the dock above them just to be certain."

"Swam? Against that current? You must be some swimmer."

"I swim well," he said modestly. "And then I took Silver back up river, just like before."

"But why didn't you come out to Out with Mugs and me?" Henry listened to what he just said and began to realize how silly this hallucination was becoming again. He remembered a time or two of waking from a dream, then falling back asleep and having the dream more or less continue, but he had never had a hallucination to match this long tale. Not by a long shot.

"I was-----I was confused. It was hard. I-----I needed to talk with Mother and Father. And with Great Great Grandfather."

"And did you?"

"Yes."

"I bet that helped a lot."

Squiggly was having trouble now, and was looking past Henry, as if thinking the whole thing through once again.

Henry suggested, "Why don't we go down to the house and have a nice cold coke and you can tell me, if you want to. Or we can talk about something else. You don't have to share it with anyone. I'll hold onto you so you don't stumble and lose your glasses. Okay?"

After several long seconds, Squiggly nodded his head.

Henry saw the lines in Squiggly's face. Whatever it was, it was bothering him terribly. Mugs made a whimpering, sympathetic sound, no doubt sensing how troubled his little friend was. Squiggly bent down and hugged him and patted his head. Mugs thanked him with a big slobbery kiss.

Henry kept quiet on the trip down the hill, feeling that Squiggly would talk if he wanted to. Mugs closely limped along behind them.

In the kitchen Squiggly sat at the table and Mugs pushed himself up against the boy's legs and lay down at his feet. Henry got some glasses, went to the refrigerator and pushed the icemaker lever, dropping cubes into a glass. This time Squiggly did not jump at the noise. He just watched, still with the troubled look on his face.

"Mr. Henry, grownups make lots of decisions, don't they." It was a statement.

"Yes, Squiggly, they do. But children have to make decisions too."

"But grownups know a lot more than children and it must be a lot easier for them to make decisions."

"Well, I'm not at all sure that's true."

Silence.

Henry thought it was not easy for adults to make difficult decisions. Often it was painfully difficult. And it couldn't be easy for children either.

"It's The Gift," Squiggly said. "It's hard."

"I kind of thought it might be that."

"Mother told me again how proud of me she was that I was The Chosen One. You know, she works very hard."

"I could see that," agreed Henry.

"She gets up early and lays out breakfast so it's easy for us to fix it and eat it, and she has long hours at the factory but she makes time for all of us too. When she gets home, sometimes father says he has finished a project and she says, 'What a nice job you have done dear it's all fixed is it?' and most often whatever he was fixing is not fixed and there's a mess for her to clean up. And sometimes Squatty's experiments go wrong and there's another mess for her. And she has dinner to prepare, and our clothes to-----Oh, Mr. Henry, she works hard."

"Squiggly, you are a sweet boy for recognizing that. You must love her very much."

"I do. She's the best mother in the whole world. She deserves more than I can ever give her."

"I'm sure she is happy to have such a nice boy to love her."

"And Great Great Grandfather-----

Squiggly wrinkled his brow, thinking.

Henry waited and then asked gently, "Do you want to tell me?

"Great Great Grandfather I think knows almost everything and he could tell me how to decide but he just said I have to do it. It's not fair. He could tell me and then I would know."

"Well, maybe Great Great Grandfather does know just about every-thing, and maybe he has a good reason."

"Mr. Henry, you sound exactly like him," Squiggly said in a hurt tone. Then he said, "I think it's good to do something for someone else, don't you?"

"Very good. It's probably the best thing you could do, to do something for someone else. In fact you have a responsibility to do good things, especially for someone else."

Henry stiffened when he realized how close to the mark this came to Doctor de Squawk's counseling.

Squiggly thought for a moment. He was looking at the refrigerator. "I've decided," he said.

Henry knew what Squiggly was thinking. The icemaker. The nice refrigerator with icemaker in place of the ice box. Squiggly could transport it back somehow, probably unform it, and the Committee could have it replicated to make a nice contribution to the standard of living in In. They could figure out Edison's plan to supply electricity. Well, Squiggly could have it. This boy deserved to have what he wished.

Squiggly said, "Mugs. I would like The Gift to be Mugs."

Twenty-Three

SAYING GOODBYE

Henry was struck speechless. His mouth was so dry he could not talk.

"Are you-----are you all right, Mr. Henry?"

Only once had Henry been so instantly and thoroughly confounded, and it was when the RPGs struck three of his platoon vehicles at once, killing and wounding the others.

Now he himself was the casualty. Mugs was the one constant in his life. In his troubled travels, Laurel had not been able to make it with him to the end. Melanie had dropped out along the way, seeing the futility of it. And Peggy never had a proper chance to start. And through it all he had Mugs. He got the same love and attention and--yes, concern--from Mugs whether he was drunk or sober, manic or depressed, or somewhere in between.

"Mr. Henry, you look awful. You should sit down. Here, I'll help you," Squiggly said.

"I-----I'm all right."

The boy helped him to a chair. "Here, Mr. Henry, have some of my drink."

"No. No. I'm fine."

"My decision was bad, " Squiggly said. "Very bad, and I'm sorry." Tears ran down Squiggly's cheeks.

Henry tried to think and nothing was happening.

Squiggly got the words out, "When you said that people have a responsibility to do good things, especially for someone else, I thought you would approve. I misunderstood, and I'm sorry."

Now Squiggly was sobbing heavily. "I take back what I said. I'll go home and talk with Mother and Father and Great Great Grandfather and tell them I was bad. I'm sorry," he blubbered.

Mugs had struggled to his feet and was looking up at the boy, helplessly.

Henry heard himself say, as if it came from deep within him as something profound and entirely beyond his control, something that was his essential self, "Squiggly, don't cry. You made a good decision. It was the right decision."

But the boy cried still, sobbing out, "I wasn't trying to be selfish. I wanted to bring back the best Gift in the whole world, and for every child in In to have a pet like Mugs-----

He couldn't go on, and Henry wrapped him in his arms and rocked him. "It's okay, Squiggly. I understand, and you are right. There could be no greater gift than for every child in In to have a pet like Mugs. And Mugs--don't you remember how well he felt when he got the potion, how he played with all of you, and how he attacked the pseudoscorpion? It's all right, Squiggly. Mugs is a wonderful Gift. The Committee can replicate him. Mugs, you want to go with Squiggly and be his doggie, don't you."

Mugs looked at Henry, then at Squiggly, and rubbed up against both of them.

"Come on, Mugs," Henry said, "we'll go up in the woods. We'll go now."

Squiggly was still wiping away at tears but he went outside with Henry, and Mugs followed them. How long it took them to get to the rock and the little stream of water coming out beside it Henry had no means of determining. It was as if it was all in a dream. But they were there, and Henry bent down and took the dog in his arms and said, "Good old Mugs. You'll feel better. You'll be able to play again. You be a good doggie, okay?" He kissed Mugs' head and squeezed him one more time and said, "Please Squiggly, go now. Take Mugs and go now. Goodbye."

Henry gave the boy a hug and a kiss on his cheek.

Squiggly said, "I love you, Mr. Henry."

Henry said, "I love you too, Squiggly."

And in a moment two wisps of vapor disappeared into the little mouth of the opening where the tiny stream emerged from the hillside.

Henry sat down on the rock and cried harder than he had ever cried, in huge, body-shaking gasps. He stumbled back down the hill, staggering from tree to tree and holding on to keep from falling down, wracked with sobs that only someone who has had long trials and unfathomable loss-----eternal, never healing loss-----could understand.

Twenty-Four

JUST A DREAM?

The rest of the day was as if it didn't exist. Henry had made his way to the back yard and then onto the old logging trail that wound through the woods, and he started walking. The trail looped for three miles and came back on itself. He made a loop without even being aware he had done so, seeing no one, and no one seeing him in the woods. He must have made two or three more loops before walking became difficult in the fading light. At dark he was back in the house and he had downed one coke, then another, and then gone to bed still dressed, just flopping down on the bedcover. He had not been aware of it during the walk, but now his hip hurt terribly. How could that be? He was only vaguely aware he smelled bad from the sweat that soaked his clothes.

He could not sleep. The loss hurt so much he could only try to take it out of mind. Nothing was in focus. Nothing was sensible. All was just hurt.

A t some point he must have dropped off into that exhausted sleep that comes to people in deep grief. His room was now light. It was morning. One shoe was on his foot, the other tipped on its side on the bedcover. He lay still. Surprisingly, instead of the image of Mugs and Squiggly disappearing, he remembered Mugs running and barking and playing with Squiggly and the other children in the field at Low Meadows. He remembered some of what they said, and how young and happy Mugs looked. Squatty had given him a potion and it had done wonders. If only it would last. But of course it *would* last. Back here with him at home Mugs had been old and arthritic. He would not live much longer. But in In-----was it possible?-----yes it was. Things there were relative, not absolute. In Out years, Mugs was old. But in In, where everybody seemed to have lived millions of years already, why then, Mugs had many more years to live--in fact, probably millions of years. Squatty's potion could keep him feeling well for a long time. A very long time. An unimaginably long time. And maybe the replication process would make a potion unnecessary, and Mugs would live on and on without it for a long time. And he would have Squiggly to love him, and kids to play with, and-----

Squiggly's decision was not selfish, Henry concluded. Squiggly in fact was giving a precious gift to the children and grownups of In. Mugs would be sort of replicated, not really cloned to be exactly the same. Surely the Science Committee would create many kinds of dogs, large, medium, and small, in lots of different breeds--couldn't they? And the people of In would know what it is to love a dog, and be loved in return, unconditionally. What a wonderful Gift!

What an amazing Gift!

This recurring thought, and many more like it, jostled against his pain of loss.

After lying there for a long time, Henry got up, fixed breakfast, ate it. He found he was ravenously hungry, and he toasted some more bread and ate more slowly this time, tasting it. It was good. The coffee was good.

But he was lonesome. The house was quiet, and most of the time he could hear only the screech of tinnitus in his ears. Periodically the loss, the pain, the loneliness would return. Then slowly it would be driven out by the good feeling he had over Mugs' happiness. Each time he thought about it he realized that right now Mugs would be free of his arthritic suffering, loving his Squiggly, and being deeply loved in return.

All of this could not be a dream, a fantasy, a cruel hallucination.

Could it?

Henry would look around, wondering, and Mugs was nowhere to be found.

Twenty-Five

A Visit to Dr. Shepherd, and a Dog at Play

He struggled with it all that day and into the next. Hard. Wondering what he could tell Laurel--what he could tell Doctor Shepherd. He looked at the liquor cabinet. His hands had been shaking ever since his return. At times he had no urge whatsoever, and at others, it was so compelling he felt like grabbing the bottle and downing it.

But he had not.

So far he had not.

That evening he got up the courage to call Laurel. She hadn't wanted to talk with him but he asked her please to listen. He said he had made an appointment with Doctor Shepherd.

"So?"

"Laurel, please, it's different."

No response, then, "It's been different before and it's always the same. Henry, I can't take it. Can't you get that through your head?"

She hung up.

Surprisingly, though, when he called her back, she answered. Maybe it was the tone of his voice, whatever, but when he told her he hadn't been drinking she at least talked to him. "Yes, Henry, we've been all through this."

"No we haven't. Things have changed. Will you come up tomorrow morning, and ask Melanie and Peggy to come see me sometime?"

Silence. Then, miraculously, slowly, "Yes, I suppose so. In fact, they are coming in tomorrow. "

<hr/>

Laurel came just before lunch. In the driveway she let him kiss her on the cheek, pulling back from the hug he tried to give her. When she came into the kitchen she said, "You've been cleaning house."

"All morning," Henry said.

"Looks nice," she said and smiled a little. "Where's Mugs?"

She saw the look on his face

She said, sadly, "It's over?"

Tears came to his eyes, and she got up and came around to the rear of his chair and put her arms around him and kissed his cheek and rocked him gently. "I'm sorry," she said. She was crying, and they both cried.

"Where is he, up in the woods?" They had always said that when it was time, that's where Mugs would want to be, in the woods that he had so loved.

She wouldn't understand. Not now at least, so he just nodded his head. In a sense, Mugs indeed was up in the woods.

Melanie and Peggy arrived just before Henry had to leave for his appointment with Doctor Shepherd. Both were tentative. When

Henry put his arms around Peggy and kissed her cheek he could feel the tenseness. As he drove down the driveway, the three of them raised their hands in what looked like a subdued, hopeful wave of good luck. In the rear view mirror he saw them turn and head back into the house.

In the thirty minute drive he had plenty of time to think. But nothing was clear. What would he tell Doctor Shepherd? That he had been to In and seen a psychologist named Doctor de Squawk?

By the time he pulled into the parking lot at the clinic he had decided. There are some things you don't tell even your shrink, at least not right away. Instead, maybe the two of them could just pick up where they had left off more than a year earlier.

The return drive home seemed to take a long time. The session had been much like some earlier ones, only this time apparently Henry had been more receptive to the Doctor's gentle leading of him into the responsibility issue. Henry had said he thought he now understood better than before that he was responsible to his family and to himself, but not to everybody and everything that involved him. Sometimes things indeed do just happen.

As he pulled into the driveway he saw that their cars were gone. A note was on the table. Laurel had written, "Hope everything went well. Call me." Melanie had added, "You can do it, Dad. Love you." And even Peggy had said, "Hope you can do it, grandpa."

It would be difficult. That much he had learned.

But he had done some difficult things, especially in the war, and maybe he could do this one.

And this time make it last.

As dusk was falling he walked up into the woods, sat down on the rock, and looked at the trickle of water coming out of the hole. All was quiet except for the ringing in his ears and the usual light rustlings of leaves and a squirrel or two and the occasional back and forth calls of birds.

Henry listened. For several minutes he listened. Then he heard it. The faint, far far away sound of a dog at play, happy barks, and of children laughing.

Henry smiled, wiped away his tears, got up to go back down the hill and said to himself, "It's been a good day."

Part 2

SQUEALLY SQUIRES AND PEGGY: FRIENDS?

One

Strange Grandfather, Strange Girl

P eggy was on a visit to her grandfather's house. She and her mother Melanie and grandmother Laurel had not been here in a long time. Just as well. Nothing to do out here in the country.

Bored, missing her gang back home to boss around, Peggy went up the hill in the woods behind Grandfather Henry's house.

It was somewhere here in the woods that both she and Mugs loved that Grandmother said he had buried the little dog. Riding Breeze, Mr. Myser's old horse, the woods, and Mugs were about the only things she had ever liked about coming to her grandparents' home. Grandfather was too embarrassing, especially in the last few years, with his drinking and PTSD. She hadn't understood any of it when she was younger, and now she was just--resentful. He had made a mess of everything. But Mugs--sweet, lovable little Mugs with his crooked teeth, goofy smile, and slobbery kisses--had always made her feel better.

Today, though, she didn't want to feel better. She didn't want to be here. At her grandfather's or in these woods.

"Hmph! This stupid place," she said to a curious squirrel who stuck his head around a tree trunk at her and got a pinecone thrown at him for his nosiness.

"You could come with me."

It was a high voice, very high, like a squeal.

Startled, but for only a moment, Peggy stared at the strange girl sitting on the large rock. She wasn't there, Peggy could have sworn, only a second ago. The girl with the high-pitched voice seemed to be about Peggy's age and was wearing funny old-fashioned clothes, a wide-brimmed hat, and very large, very dark sunglasses. What little skin was showing around the glasses and at her wrists was so light-colored it appeared to be alabaster, almost translucent. Weird.

"You know," Peggy scolded, "you could have said something instead of waiting until I was right on top of you."

"All right. You don't want company? Have it your way," she squealed, and with that, said, "Unform."

Instantly there was only a tiny wisp of vapor that was sucked into a small hole where water trickled out of the hillside next to the big rock.

"Wow!" said Peggy, slapping her forehead. "Must in fact be catching."

Not one to be shaken by much of anything, Peggy sat down on the rock to think. PTSD was not a disease she would catch from her grandfather, her mother Melanie had assured her.

The first time she knew about PTSD was a few years ago as a small girl. She had been sound asleep in the upstairs bedroom of her grandparents' house, this same house she could see through the trees, down below her. She had bolted up in bed and stared at the apparition in her doorway.

"Get the dustoff in here!" her grandfather had shouted at her. The lights in the hallway were on, and he was in his pajamas, drenched with sweat, and he had a wild look in his eyes. Then he swore at her and shouted, "I said get the dustoff in here. Now!"

Most kids would have been terrified, but even at that tender age Peggy had learned to stand her ground. She had shouted back, "Get it in here yourself!" and slammed herself back down on the bed and pulled the covers up over her head.

Whatever a dustoff was, she had no idea. Then she heard Grandmother Laurel intervening, and in a few minutes, her grandfather Henry was downstairs with Grandma, and she could hear him. Crying, she thought. She later learned that this type of thing had been going on for a long time. Grownups think that children don't know about things, but they do. It was embarrassing, and she was determined to have nothing to do with it.

Peggy looked at the hole where the water trickled out. Anyone with a weaker disposition than Peggy would have been concerned about seeing a strange girl suddenly appear, then turn into a wisp and disappear into a hole in a hillside. Peggy, though, was quite sure she didn't have PTSD and would figure it out.

Two

Puzzles

"Mom," Peggy demanded that evening at the supper table, "Can you inherit PTSD?"

Melanie, her mother, replied, "Why no, honey. It's just something your Grandpa has."

"When are they coming back?" Her grandparents had left to go back to Grandmother Laurel's house, leaving her and her mother at Grandfather Henry's house in the clearing in the woods.

"They'll be back a little later."

"When is Grandma going to come back here to live?"

"I've told you, not until your Grandpa is better."

"Yeah, like never."

"Stop that! Can't you understand he can't help it?"

"Yeah, like Dad couldn't help leaving us."

"Peggy, honey, please try to understand these things."

"I *do* understand. That's the problem."

Her mother slowly shook her head, as she had done so many times before. Nothing she said or did seemed to get through to her only child.

"Grandma called earlier. She says Grandpa's much better. He likes his counselor at VA and she thinks the program is doing him a lot of good. I think your grandfather may have changed a lot recently."

If Peggy admitted anything, which she didn't, she might have agreed. When she saw her grandfather briefly before he and Grandma had left early in the morning he did seem to have changed. But then, at other times it had seemed that way but it didn't last.

"And when they get back," her mother continued, "soon all of us will go to Disney World."

"Yeah, just like the last two times we were going to do that. I'll be old enough to work there before we go. I can be Minnie Mouse."

"Please, Peggy, honey, I know it hurts, but things just haven't worked out."

Although Peggy hadn't gone there, she knew all about it. Lots of kids had gone and had told her, and she had heard their parents' rather less than enthusiastic descriptions which were always qualified because they were pleased that, through it all, their kids had had a good time. "Disney World is just a big hassle anyway. Crowds. Lines. Can't get the rides you want," Peggy said, dismissing the matter.

With that judgment, their day more or less ended.

Except in the dark upstairs bedroom while Peggy puzzled over the strange girl.

A will o' the wisp, she concluded. A stupid phosphorescent light that flits over swampy ground at night. Just spontaneous combustion of marsh grasses that dupe people into thinking something magical was happening.

Still puzzled, Peggy decided to figure it out tomorrow and fell asleep.

Three

A Very Strange Girl

The next morning Peggy was not at all sure. When she saw the wisp it had not been night, not even dusky, and there was no marsh on the hillside. Just the small outflow of water, which in these early summer days was not much more than a trickle that came from the hole. Her grandfather some time ago had said it was from an artesian well deep in the hillside, and in the spring the surge of water would flood their backyard until he and Grandma had dug a ditch to divert the flow into the large stream in front of their house.

He was a smart man, her grandfather. He had been a soldier. Then a college professor. One who could not get tenure and had to take part-time teaching. One who could not get along at all in the academic world. She admired his stubborn, self-destructive independence. But she would never let him know it. It wasn't that she couldn't like him. It was that he tried too hard to be a good grandfather when all he needed to do was stop drinking.

For most of the morning she tried to figure out this business of the strange girl. Peggy went for a long walk, looked listlessly at Mr. Myser's horse barn but didn't see Breeze, looked at cows in a pasture, watched a farmer drive a tractor back and forth, and then she picked a few wild flowers. As she neared the house she heard her mother call her for lunch, and while eating she was still trying to decide if it was all imagined. It seemed so real.

After lunch, deep in thought, she went outside and climbed the hill in the woods behind the house. She sat down on the large rock next to the trickle of water coming out of the small hole and closed her eyes. Maybe something would begin to make sense.

After a minute or two of listening to the sounds of the woods and the tiny stream, she had the feeling she was not alone.

"You had to find out, didn't you," the strange girl said in that shrill, squeaky voice. It was not a question. The girl was standing near her.

Peggy didn't like it. In games, *she* was the one who created the illusions and the other children played by her instructions. When she was smaller *she* decided who would be the Queen, and who the Maid in Waiting. Now that she was older *she* was the pitcher and the other girls were the fielders, or *she* was the Olympic skating champion and the others were her fans. This had to be a dream. She had not really awakened and had breakfast this morning, and had seen cows and picked flowers. That was just part of the dream. Wasn't it? Of course. Obviously she was still asleep in her bed upstairs in grandfather's house.

But she wasn't. Not wanting to doubt anything, she was positive she wasn't still asleep.

"Why do you wear such strange clothes?" This time it *was* a question and the phantom girl was asking it.

Standing, Peggy retorted, quite annoyed, "*Me*? *You're* the strange one. You and your funny dress, and what are those things – bloomers? – sticking out under it?"

"They're pantalettes, and you really ought not to be exposing so much of yourself. It's not a pretty sight, your skinny legs."

"Well, *really*!!" Peggy retorted. "These are shorts. Nobody wears those things you have on."

Peggy was frustrated, and for once was on the brink of tears. This was a horrid girl with such light hair, what she could see of it, that it seemed white. Most unbecoming. And she wore very large, very dark, very stupid sunglasses.

The apparition said, "You're Peggy, aren't you." It was not a question. "You're Peggy, Mr. Henry's granddaughter."

"How did you know?"

"I know. I'm Squeally. Squeally Squires. I thought you might want to come to In with me. The Regional Youth Games are being held. One of our Squiresville teams made it in fairball and one in hitball. We can watch. And tomorrow we're going to Wiggly World. But I can see you're--yeahh, quite stuck up, and you won't go just to spite yourself."

"I will too!" Peggy scolded. Then she added the necessary qualifier, "If I want to."

"Well, come on then. You have to say 'unform' and-----The phantom girl whispered some words in Peggy's ear.

"You're kidding,' Peggy protested. "Little children play games like that. I'm too old for-----

"How old are you?" Squeally asked.

"Eleven."

"Eleven what?"

"What do you mean, eleven what? I'm eleven years, two months old."

With that, Squeally erupted in laughter, laughing so hard she gasped for air and bent over.

"Well!" Peggy said, offended. "What is so hilarious?"

"You-----you----- eleven years? That means you're-----" She laughed hard again. "You're not even out of diapers."

"Oh, really, and what does that make you?"

"Are you serious? I'm about four million, two hundred thousand years old."

"Oh, sure. You're a nut."

"Just make a wish to go with me, say 'unform,' and believe it will happen and add those secret words."

Squeally bent toward Peggy and whispered the words again into her ear, reached to take her hand and said, "Say it, believe, and we'll be off."

Peggy, still miffed, backed away and said, "I've never heard anything so ridiculous." But for some reason she could not explain, she took Squeally's hand and said "unform" and made her wish and added the secret words. She didn't feel like believing in such silliness but she must have believed because all of a sudden she saw the girl become a wisp and disappear into the hole with the trickle of water coming out, and instantly Peggy felt strange, as if she was being vaporized and sucked in behind her. She closed her eyes. When she opened them she was standing with her back to the entrance of a huge cave with a river running out the mouth of it.

"Good. We're in In. You'll like it," Squeally said, clapping her hands delightedly.

"Whoa!" Peggy said, slapping her forehead, looking around her in bewilderment.

Four

WILD TRIP UP RIVER

"What is going on here?" Peggy was astonished, and stared in awe at the cave and looked at the rapidly rushing river going past the path she was on.

"You wished to go with me to the Games." Squeally said in her high voice. "If you're chicken you can go back out. Back out to Out. I guess you're just all talk."

"I am *not!*" Peggy replied, defiantly. This was a horrid girl. Peggy's friends didn't argue with her and insult her. They didn't dare.

"Okay, then we'll go," Squeally said and let forth a piercing clucking sound. From the dim interior of the cave a huge substance sprang out of the darkness and landed next to them. It was a creature that looked like a cricket with very long hind legs and a mottled whitish-brown body, and extra-long antennas projecting from its head, only it was as large as a horse.

"Holy Jiminy!" Peggy yelped.

But whether it was because of amazement or some response mechanism that had accustomed her to surprises that would frighten anyone else, Peggy did not recoil from the creature. Squeally must have approved because she said, "Most of the kids in school would have been scared. You must be used to blind cave crickets jumping at you."

Peggy swallowed the lump in her throat and said, "Happens all the time. No big deal."

Squeally made a soothing, strange clucking sound which seemed to combine high and low notes, with segments of long duration mixed with short twitters. She then said, "Down, Rhapsody."

The beast sank to its knees and turned its head. Peggy thought its huge, clouded eyes had a soft look, and its mouth was smiling.

"What was that sound you made? That clucking?" Peggy asked.

"Oh, that's just how we communicate with cave creatures. Most of them don't actually hear it, but they sense the vibrations with their extra long antennas or other sensory organs. We learn how to do this kind of naturally, I guess, like we learn to talk. Our parents teach us, and we imitate them. Only the creatures that have been trained and tamed will respond to it, not the wild ones. I just added, 'Down Rhapsody' so you would know what I was doing."

That was a whole lot for Peggy to understand all at once, so she just nodded, hoping it would become clear at some point.

"Come on," Squeally called excitedly as she scrambled far up a very long rear leg and pulled herself onto a bench seat that was strapped onto the back of the creature. Peggy did not much like someone else taking charge, but she gulped and followed her.

Peggy clapped on the helmet Squeally handed her. As Squeally was fastening the seat and shoulder belts that held them in, side by side, she said, "Our next-door neighbor Mrs. Scoot has a whole fleet of them, and blind wolf spiders, scooters, waterfall climbing cave fish--whatever anyone wants for transportation. She has a huge dealership, biggest one in In. She lets us use them whenever we want. We could walk the path up to the dock ahead--it's real pretty along the river--but your grandfather and Squiggly had a pseudoscorpion attack them on their way out, so-----

"My grandfather!' Peggy gasped. "What do you mean, my grand-----

"He didn't tell you he was here? I should have thought he'd tell you something like that."

Peggy closed her eyes, then opened them again slowly, expecting this hallucination to disappear. But Squeally was still there. The dark recess of the cave was still ahead of her, and the river to the cave entrance was still rushing by her.

"Here," Squeally said, "you're going to need these later." She had taken off her very large, very dark sunglasses and handed them to Peggy. "As long as I don't look back at the cave entrance I'm more or less okay in this twilight. On you, these will be moonglasses." For an instant, Peggy glimpsed Squeally's eyes, a strange pale gray, almost translucent like her skin.

Squeally continued, "And hold onto the glasses. Don't let go of them. Later, when you put them on you won't be able to see as well as I will, but it will be better than nothing. Let's get going."

Squeally was about to give the start signal to Rhapsody when Peggy interrupted. "I just thought of something. I can't just go off. My mother wouldn't know where I've gone. I can't do that to her."

"We're only going to be gone three days. You'll be back on the third day."

"*Three* days? She'd think I had been kidnapped or something, I-----

"Three of *my* days, silly. Three *In* days!" Squeally said it emphatically, as if that explained everything.

"I heard you. I can't be gone not even one day. I-----

"Oh, all right. Let's see. What is it in Out time? Your time. I'm not so good at math, but let's see----- Squeally wrinkled her brow, calculating. She made motions with her fingertip as if writing everything down on her wrist, then mumbled, "Three days times twenty-four hours in a day, hmmm, times sixty seconds in an hour, hmmm, divided into-----oh, I can't go on. Squiggly or Squatty could do it in their heads. But three In days couldn't be more than a second or so of Out time. She won't go looking for you if you're only gone a second or two will she?"

Peggy said, haughtily, "Of course not!" This was one complex hallucination, so probably best just to see it through, she thought. Besides, it was interesting.

Squeally made a shrill clucking sound, and as Rhapsody jumped, Peggy's head was snapped back against the headrest. She had the sensation of being thrust into space like an astronaut at liftoff. Rhapsody had leapt toward the dimness ahead of them, and for part of a second, Peggy could vaguely see the ceiling of the huge cavern come perilously close until in the next instant they were dropping away from it.

"Wheee!" Squeally screeched. "I love it, don't you?"

The instant mixture of astonishment, exhilaration, and fear that Peggy felt was like that on the sudden plunge of a roller coaster. "Love it," she managed to say, bravely she hoped.

One more bound took them to a big bend in the river where it was darker, and she was pushed down hard into the seat by the landing and almost instantly thrust back again by another bound upward.

"Wheee!" Squeally chirped again, and this time Peggy joined in with a big "Ahhh!" of thrilled, chilled delight.

Another landing and liftoff took them this time deep into a channel of darkness. On about the third or fourth bound, Peggy realized it was not only dark, it was totally dark--absolutely dark--a kind of dark she had never experienced. And now, despite her usual grit, she was afraid.

Squeally had clucked and Rhapsody had landed. Peggy could see no channel ceiling and no river although she could hear it moving beside her. Rhapsody stayed put and did not take off in another leap. This bounding in utter darkness had unhinged Peggy and she was fighting back tears when Squeally said, "There! We're going to change to Angie here. And put on your moonglasses."

She really must mean sunglasses, Peggy thought, and although it was moronic, she put the very large, very dark sunglasses over her eyes.

"There. Now you have moonglasses," Squeally was saying. "Don't ask me how they got that name because we have no moon here in In--horrid thing, your moon, it's so bright--but you'll be able to see something. They're not perfect, but then, when they are sunglasses in Out they are far from perfect in keeping that atrocious sunlight out of a person's eyes. Can you see okay?"

"Well--not okay, but I can see for some distance at least. It's kind of gray. Then everything fades into darkness."

Through the glasses, which now had white lenses, Peggy thought Squeally's eyes still appeared to be that strange light gray color, but she could not be sure. Peggy scanned the area around her. She could see

141

far enough to discover they were in a large channel, something like an irregular tube with water running through it. They were on what appeared to be a river dock.

"It's better that we get off here," Squeally explained. "Cave spiders have webs up ahead, and we don't want to get caught in one of them with Rhapsody's jumps. It's a wildlife preserve, and those spiders haven't been domesticated. We don't want to get poisoned and eaten by a wild spider."

"I certainly hope not," Peggy agreed, with a shudder she hoped Squeally didn't notice.

Squeally let off another shrill clucking, and in the water alongside the dock, a large, very white shape slowly rose.

"Angie, honey, do you want to take us for a ride?" Squeally squeaked.

Through Peggy's moonglasses the creature looked like a submarine slowly surfacing, shedding water from its silvery-pink, almost translucent back. It was very long creature with a blunt nose and no eyes. Even though Peggy's glasses allowed her to see only in shades of gray, she thought she could detect what could be blood-red projections where its ears might have been. In fact, Squeally explained, they were gills.

"I ask for Angie every time. She's a blind salamander. Squatty--he's my older brother, a scientist--he says that you Outers would classify Angie as a troglobite amphibian. Angie is young but well-trained and dependable. She can go in both water and on the cave walls and ceilings. Squiggly--he's my younger brother--he likes to take Silver upriver--Silver's a blind waterfall-climbing cave fish--but it can be a wild ride. That's okay with me, but last time when Silver couldn't make Big Falls on his first leap and fell back into the pool below I got really dunked. I don't like my head being under water that long."

Peggy, not wanting to show any weakness, said, "Huh, Silver sounds like a lot of fun. I'd like to ride him sometime." She paused, then added,

"But Angie's okay too. It's been awhile since I've ridden on a blind salamander."

There was room enough aboard Angie for several people, but the two girls were the only passengers for this trip. They climbed up, buckled their seat and shoulder belts and put on their helmets. Squeally made a soft clucking sound. Angie moved smoothly away from the dock and lowered into the water so that only part of her head and a bit of her back were showing as her four legs churned and her tail slithered in a propelling motion. Soon they were racing up river, and Peggy dimly saw the walls of the channel slipping by fast, behind her.

"This is great," she called over the rushing noise to Squeally who replied, "You haven't seen anything yet."

All of a sudden a stair-like set of waterfalls loomed ahead and Angie seemed to go in supercharge to meet the challenge. She threw herself into the water that spilled off the first level, and Peggy hung onto the seat as her head whipped and her eyes opened wide behind the lenses of her moonglasses. Maybe this ride hadn't been such a good idea.

Squeally, though, was squeaking with joy. "Isn't this neat!"

"Neat!" Peggy shot back, hoping to sound brave.

Angie crested the first level and bucked her way up the remaining levels. Then, having conquered the final one, she slowed for a moment as if pondering her next course of action. All of a sudden she thrust forward and Squeally said, "Two more little falls like this one and then you're in for a real thrill. Angie loves this part."

"How can she see to steer?" Peggy called loudly over the river noise.

"She doesn't see. She doesn't have eyes. She's blind. We're not sure, but vibrations seem to guide her. She just senses things ahead and around her."

"Hmm," Peggy responded, hoping that Angie's sensors were well tuned for this mad dash over the next two falls.

At this speed it did not take long before Squeally was shouting, excitedly, "Big Falls ahead. Sometimes Silver and Angie race up river to see who can get past Big Falls first. Last time I rode Angie, and Squiggly rode Silver."

"Who won?"

"Angie and I did. Of course. Silver and Squiggly? They're only *boys*. Hang on, now, and hold onto those glasses. Don't lose them."

That warning was unnecessary. With one hand Peggy was gripping the railing around the seat with all her might, and with the other was pushing the glasses hard against her face. They were the only thing between her and absolute darkness, and the idea of losing them was, even for Peggy, frightening.

Five

Big Falls and the Grotto of Tears

Angie ploughed ahead into the current, and soon was in an area of rapids where the river cascaded against partially sunken and broken stalagmites. Broken stalactites and huge stones were strewn about at the edge of the water where they had spalled from the ceiling of the cave, making the area look like a sinister badlands. The girls were tossed about in their seats and splashed with cold water as they peered eagerly ahead.

Peggy could hear a roaring noise, getting louder and louder. Suddenly Angie accelerated and Squeally screeched, "This is it! Big Falls."

Through the dim view provided by her glasses, Peggy got just a glimpse of the torrent pouring over the top of the falls ahead of them before Angie suddenly turned left and she and Squeally were thrust hard right. Now Peggy could see the wall of the cave rather than water rushing in a blur beneath her, and Big Falls was ahead and to her right and Angie was out of the water and shooting up the cave wall, her feet propelling them in an arc. In an instant they were directly over the brink of the Falls and upside down. Peggy fought against the G forces but was powerless to do anything more than try to keep her head from being thrust to the side. She felt like a pilot in a fighter aircraft must feel doing a tight roll. Then they were racing down the wall on the opposite side of the river, and the Falls with its roar of the cascading water was behind them. They had made a loop on the walls and ceiling of the cave.

"How'd you like it?" Squeally asked breathlessly.

"Wonderful. I could do that all day." Actually, Peggy questioned whether she wanted to do it again, ever.

"Me too, all day," Squeally affirmed.

In front of Angie was a huge expanse of lake with a perfectly calm surface. "Squiresville is ahead, but it's quite a distance," Squeally said.

Off to their right, through a narrow opening, Peggy saw a cove that looked interesting.

"There are lots of them on the lake, but this one is the prettiest," Squeally told her. "I call it The Grotto. I'll show you."

She clucked and Angie, now swimming easily, slowly, turned into the entrance. The view ahead of Peggy was breathtaking. She could see only partially into the cavern, but the scene was magical--ivory-colored stalagmites rising out of the crystal-clear, dark water, and from the darkness above, grayish stalactites reaching down. A few broken stalagmites stuck up out of the glassy water like volcanic islands with their tops sheared off.

They went farther into the recess of the cavern, and as they glided along, the little waves from Angie reached out in a V behind them and rippled softly against the stalagmites, making a kind of pleasant tinkling song of where they had been. For the first time, Peggy realized the stillness. In the enormous vastness of the dark beyond her limited range of vision, the noiselessness came almost as a magical sigh, and it enveloped Peggy in an invisible robe of melancholy.

After a few minutes of quiet gliding, Peggy wanted to stop and get out. Often, at home, she had wished to be alone but could only imagine some quiet, deserted place where she could brood and nobody could find her. She had never actually seen such a place. Until now. She became aware that the air was somewhat cool and very humid, and perfectly still. She wished she had worn a sweater.

"Could we stop?" she asked.

"Certainly," squeaked Squeally. She clucked and Angie stopped waggling her tail and paddling her legs. Silently they glided up to the side of the cave where an almost flat shelf of rock stuck out into the water. Squeally unbuckled the seat and shoulder harnesses and she walked down Angie's side and then jumped the rest of the way onto the flat limestone. Peggy was right behind her.

Peggy stood in awe of the sight. Through her moonglasses, the dimly lit scene was like an enchanted room of a stone castle. A magic castle. Gray and white flowstone rippled down toward her, making a kind of terrace which could be easily climbed. As she walked forward to inspect it she saw formations that looked like draperies hanging in folds, reaching out from the wall, and growths that appeared to be beautiful white and silver flowers growing out of cracks. Near her feet was a small pile of pure white stones, round like marbles, and she scooped up some and held them in her hand. What a beautiful necklace and diadem for a princess they would make!

"They are cave pearls," Squeally said.

"This is incredible," Peggy breathed softly.

There was only one problem.

Peggy was not alone.

She would have liked to drink all this in silently, and wander about, looking.

Look at the strange stone formations.

Listen to the water drip from the ceiling onto the water surface below.

Feel the remoteness of this enchanted place.

Let it merge slowly into her loneliness.
Allow the tears to come.
Cry.
All by herself.
Alone.
She wanted to cry where no one could see her.
She would rename this place, so quiet, so personal. It would be The Grotto of Tears. But she would tell no one.

Peggy sat down on a flowstone shelf that came out from the wall. A few seconds must have passed before she realized that Squeally was standing, then sitting beside her.

"You don't have any friends, do you," Squeally stated, quietly.

"Of course I do!" Peggy snapped. "Why would you say such a thing?"

"Because you don't."

"I certainly do! I have friends around me all the time. I'm the one who thinks up things for us to do. I'm the only one with good ideas, and we do them. Everybody knows that."

And everybody did. Peggy was smart in school and the teachers were always praising her for her unique stories, for the way she not just understood many things but could make them come alive for her classmates. When the kids would ask how she knew something she would say she just did. She never lacked for kids around her, mostly girls, but sometimes boys too.

Squeally squeaked, "Having people around you doesn't mean they are your friends."

"It certainly does!"

Squeally was spoiling everything. She had destroyed Peggy's beautiful, sad reverie. She had destroyed the stillness of the grotto. She was a hateful girl.

"They follow you, they do what you want them to do, but they don't like you."

"How do you know! Just goes to show you how much you know."

"Name me one person who would be your friend all the time--even when you aren't taking charge of the group and-----

"You're horrid!" Peggy said, and would have cried if she had been alone, but she wouldn't give this rude girl the satisfaction of seeing her weakness, of knowing that she could not in fact think of any one of the kids she could call a friend, a friend all the time. Not one.

"I could be your friend," Squeally said in a soft squeaky voice.

"You! You my friend? I don't need you. You look weird, and you sound weird, and you wear weird clothes. Be your own friend!"

Six

A KOLOA RIDE TO THE BALLPARK

Peggy wanted this stupid dream to end. Instead, they were back aboard Angie, soon out of the cove and rushing at top speed the considerable distance across the lake. She said nothing, crossing her arms determinedly, and sitting stiffly in her seat. Several minutes later they reached a dock.

"We're here," Squeally piped with a note of keen anticipation. "This is Squiresville. We'll take Koloa right to the park. You'll like the Regional Youth Games," she said, as if nothing had happened between them. "Thanks, Angie," Squeally said, and clucked to the blind salamander who slowly sank out of sight as they stepped onto the dock.

A huge creature was waiting for them.

"Koloa, good boy, down," Squeally said, and the dark-hued creature lowered itself obediently so they could climb up to their seats. "He's our old blind wolf spider. He only has seven legs--lost one in an accident when he was little--but he's very dependable. And lovable."

What there was to love about this awkward beast Peggy was not sure, and, determined not to talk to Squeally, she kept her mouth shut, clambered aboard, and plopped herself in her seat, crossing her arms hard.

For several minutes (at least in Out time) Koloa struggled in climbing the road that led sharply uphill away from the river. Squeally stopped him a few times so he could regain his breath. Finally, a wheezing Koloa brought them to a plateau and the old blind wolf spider slowed while his breathing became easier.

As Koloa now moved along in a rolling motion, Squeally said, "This is Low Meadows. It's the nicest part of Squiresville--if you mean housing and transportation, things like that."

Even in keeping her eyes straight ahead, trying to ignore Squeally, Peggy saw beautifully crafted cut-stone houses with slate roofs. A few large wolf spiders were parked under porticos at the end of long, curved driveways. The creatures looked nice and new, shiny white or gray or brown, most unlike Koloa's old, weathered appearance. The lawns were large and had small broken stalagmites that had been collected and carefully placed as if they were cultivated shrubs.

"This is where most of the workers live--janitors, truck drivers, lawn maintenance people."

Peggy was surprised. These houses appeared to be pricey. How could such workers afford houses like that, with lots of room between them and a nice view of the river below? And she wondered what the lawn people did. The lawns were solid stone. How do you mow a solid stone lawn? This was a stupid place.

"It's quiet here today," Squeally said. "It's a holiday and just about everybody is at the Games."

They rode through the town and after several minutes were on the outskirts where the houses were fewer and farther between. As they went, Peggy could hear a noise in the distance which, upon getting closer, turned out to be the roars of a crowd erupting irregularly.

"Somebody just scored. Or maybe caught one," Squeally said. "Oh, it must be an exciting game."

Peggy condescended to nod coolly but said nothing.

Seven

THE GAMES

The parking lot was filled with blind wolf spiders, blind salamanders, blind crickets, blind centipedes and millipedes and more –
just about every kind of transportation so useful in the absolute darkness
of Squiresville. Koloa had to lower himself into a parking place far out
from the field. The stands ahead of them were descending layers of flowstone packed with people, all roaring, which through her moonglasses
looked to Peggy to be a tumultuous sea of two colors. She could not be
sure, though, since colors through her glasses were just shades of gray.

"Come on," Squeally shouted excitedly above the noise as she ran
forward.

Not forgiving Squeally, but not wanting to be left behind in this
strange land, Peggy ran and caught up. They raced forward together, ran
under a banner that said, Regional Youth Games: Fairball.

They climbed the flowstone layers as Squeally looked for her mother
and father.

Going up and down the aisles were vendors, young men and women
of what appeared to be different skin colors and facial features. They
were hawking what looked like hotdogs, but they were calling out, "Get

your flatworm pods, nice hot flatworm pods," and hands were reaching out for them.

What in the world? Peggy thought. The idea of eating worms was gross, but the vendors had a brisk business.

"We'll get some later," Squeally promised.

"No thanks."

Peggy was trying to remain aloof but found the scene fascinating. She had assumed that all In people would have light, virtually translucent skin like Squeally's, and many did, but the skin colors as seen through her glasses seemed to range from light to very dark.

Squeally said that the school colors of the opposing teams were green or blue and pointed out which was which. Through her glasses, Peggy saw that the green appeared to be a lighter gray than the darker color, blue.

The roaring stands around Peggy were a flood of green shirts, caps, banners intermingled with blue shirts, caps, and banners, all in helter-skelter motion like waves tossed by a swirling wind. Squeally explained loudly over the roar, "The team in green is the Squiresville Squirts. The fans in green in the stands are the Squiresville Squallers. We can make a lot of noise. Our team always knows we're behind them."

The boys and girls on the field were playing baseball. At least that's what it looked like, a baseball diamond with boys and girls from both teams in the usual positions. Except they were strangely dressed. Each player wore a soft cap with a small visor, a loose-sleeved shirt hanging down to the elbows, knickers and knee socks. They resembled teams Peggy had seen in photos from maybe a hundred years ago. The players, like the people in the stands, appeared to have varying skin colors.

"The other team, in blue, is the Watersville Warblers," Squeally squeaked as loudly as she could to be heard, and pointed at the field. "Their supporters are the Watersville Wailers. They sure can make a racket too. When they get wound up they sound like a huge crowd of crybabies."

The team at bat wore blue and the team in the field wore green. Squeally pointed out her short, chubby older brother Squatty sitting on the green bench and said he was the manager of the Squiresville Squirts team.

"He would like to be a coach, but he's best at administration and does an okay job as manager," she said. "Squiggly, my younger brother, is at home with my aunt, watching our baby brother, Squishy. We call him Squishy because he-----well, you know."

"Oh, there they are!" Squeally waved and caught the attention of her mother and father in the stands, a few rows above and to the side of them.

Two seats on the flowstone had been saved for the girls. Not that anyone was seated, of course. Something on the field had caused the Squiresville Squallers, the greens, to spring up from their seats and squall their approval.

In the confusion, Peggy found herself wrapped in a big warm hug of Squeally's mother. "Oh my dear you must be Peggy it is so nice of you to come visit us Squeally was afraid you might not come but we are so pleased you did," she said in a gush.

Mrs. Squires was a large, dark-skinned woman wearing a very old-fashioned green blouse and green skirt, under which were bloomers. She was waving a 'GO GREENS' placard. Although her skin color was different, she had the same pale gray eyes as her daughter. She rocked Peggy back and forth lovingly as she said, "This is my husband S.Q. he's a wonderful man you'll like him a lot when you get to know him oh my goodness----- She was interrupted when the green crowd let out another squalling roar. S.Q., a very small man about as tall as Squeally, nodded his welcome as Mrs. Squires released Peggy to wave the placard and cheer at what had happened on the field.

What *had* happened on the field? Now that Peggy was free from the hug to look, she saw a blue player trotting from third to home base, waving and smiling at the crowd.

Why were the *green* fans cheering? It looked as if the player on the *blue* team had scored a home run.

Now another blue player was up to bat. The green pitcher wound up and delivered the slowest pitch across the plate that Peggy had ever seen. How could it be so slow without arcing any more than it had, she wondered. The batter in blue swung but missed.

"STEE-RIKE ONE!" the umpire behind the plate bellowed, and this time the blue crowd erupted in a loud, happy wail.

"Wasn't that a marvelous pitch?" Squeally asked. "Wonderfully slow."

"Yeah, marvelous," Peggy said. "If it was any slower it would have gone backwards."

"I know!" beamed Squeally.

What in the world was going on here? Peggy was puzzled. The green pitcher puts a slow one directly over the plate, the blue batter misses, and the blue rooters wail their approval.

"The *blue* fans cheer when a *blue* player at bat gets a strike called on him?" Peggy loudly asked Squeally, staring in disbelief.

"Sure. The green pitcher threw a perfect strike. I'll explain it.

"You see, it all started when a Mr. Ruth told The Chosen One, a boy named Marvin from Marvelsville, all about the rules some thirty-six million years ago. This is what happened. When Marvin emerged at Out and formed, he found himself just outside a place called Yankee Stadium. He heard an enormous roar, and in a minute or so, lots of people started streaming out of the place. Marvin asked a man what had happened, and he said, 'Ruth and Gehrig have done it again.'

"Marvin had asked, 'Done what?'

"The man said he had to get home and to ask them. So Marvin waited and when two men finally came out of the stadium Marvin heard an excited crowd around them calling their names, Ruth and Gehrig. After awhile, Marvin managed to get up to the two men and ask them what they had done. Mr. Ruth said, 'You're joking. You don't know? Come on, kid, I'll tell you.'

"So Mr. Ruth, Mr. Gehrig, and Marvin walked to a place called a bar, and although a lot of people were crowding around them, Mr. Ruth sat Marvin in a booth while he drank something called beer and explained the whole game to him. He told him how the field was arranged, the number of players, their positions, everything. Marvin had a mind like an encyclopedia and he remembered everything he was told."

Squeally continued, "Mr. Ruth said things like, 'Now, kid, the object in fairball--that's what we call the game--is for the pitcher to throw the ball as slow as he can, and right over the plate so the batter can hit it. That's fair, isn't it?'

"Marvin nodded, and Mr. Ruth laughed, clapped him on the shoulder, and gave him some more rules.

"Mr. Gehrig kept interrupting and saying, 'Don't do that. Come on, Babe, give it to him straight.'"

"I *am*, Lou. The God's honest truth."

As Squeally was telling the history of fairball, Peggy saw the next pitch loop slowly, ever so slowly, over the plate and the batter in blue smacked it right over the pitcher's head, over the second baseman's head, squarely into center field. She saw the umpire's signal and heard her bawl out "FOUL BALL! STEE-RIKE TWO!" and she watched amazed as the *blue* fans erupted again in a delighted wail. Their batter had swung, hit a ball right down the middle of the field, and it was a *foul* ball? *Strike two?* And the *blue* fans were delighted?

As Peggy was trying to sort this out, Squeally continued, "Mr. Ruth would laugh and have another beer and tell Marvin about some of the strategies of fairball, such as purposely dropping a high fly ball instead of catching it because of course the fielder should be fair to the batter who has hit a nice long ball.

"Mr. Ruth had a lot of beers and gave Marvin a lot of rules. Sometimes Mr. Ruth would stop and ask, 'Now, kid, you gettin' all this?' and he would clap Marvin on the shoulder, almost knocking off his very large, very dark sunglasses, and he would laugh some more, harder with each new beer.

"Marvin would adjust his glasses, say, 'Yes sir,' and he *was* getting it. All of it. He remembered everything.

"Finally, after more beers and when Mr. Ruth's face was quite red, Mr. Ruth said, 'Lou, my gals are waiting. See you tomorrow. Now kid, I've told you everything there is to know about fairball, so you go home and organize some games, okay?'"

"Marvin thanked Mr. Ruth, and when he went back to In he reported to The Council on The Gift what he had chosen to bring from Out--fairball. The Council nodded gravely and sometimes asked questions as Marvin patiently explained the game. Then they voted and unanimously approved of The Gift, and had the rules and strategies recorded. Fairball seemed to be a good game for children, they thought, though they were puzzled as to why grown men such as Mr. Ruth and Mr. Gehrig would engage in it. Soon youth leagues were forming throughout In, and fairball quickly became the national pastime."

Peggy's mouth was hanging open. She said, "You've got to be kidding."

But now she was distracted by two mothers standing near her, one in green, one in blue. The one in green was arguing that the other mother's kid in blue was a better ballplayer than hers. But she was being contra-dicted. "Nonsense," the mother in blue was shouting back, "your kid is a whole lot better than mine."

They seemed about to come to blows when Squeally said, "This next pitch looks like it will decide the championship. Come on, Squirts!" she yelled.

By now, Peggy thought she might have figured out why, when the pitcher seemed to be throwing a fastball, it was actually slow, very slow. The only explanation that made sense to her was that as the ball left the hand, the tips of the pitcher's fingers gave it a fast backspin which slowed down the flight dramatically. She thought it must have taken a lot of practice to achieve such a skill.

The Squirts' pitcher in green wound up carefully, deliberately, and finally, in releasing what seemed as if it should be a fastball, instead, as if in slow slow motion, he let loose what must have been a world record slow pitch, noticeably slower than his first two. It rose in a slow, slow loop and gradually, ever so gradually, dropped toward the plate. Peggy thought that the blue batter would have to be the world's biggest klutz not to knock this one out of the park. As the batter waited for the ball to cross the plate, he puffed out his chest, grandly raised his arm and pointed to the wall of centerfield.

There was a sound of the crowd sucking in air, waiting, waiting, as the ball slowly, ever so slowly, entered the center of the strike zone. The blue player, bat now on his shoulder at the ready, tensed, looked at the almost stationary ball, and

--didn't swing-----

"STEE-RIKE THREE, YOU'RE OUT!"

With that there were screams of joy--from the *blue* fans! Their player had just been struck out.

"We won, we WON!" the blue fans wailed in delight.

"Are you nuts," Peggy shouted at the closest blue fans to her. "He was struck out."

"I know, I know!" a blue fan shouted back. "Isn't that *WON-derful!*"

The green fans had now gotten their voice and were squalling out at the umpire, "You bum, that was a *ball*, not a strike!"

They were criticizing her for calling their pitcher's throw a strike????

"This is getting curiouser and curiouser," Peggy said. This indeed was the strangest dream she ever had, she decided.

Now several mothers in green ran onto the field and started berating the umpire for not calling a ball on their pitcher, and this prompted mothers in blue to surge forward and begin arguing with the greens. Amid the hubbub the umpire was almost knocked over.

"They're right. We shouldn't have won," a blue voice shouted.

"Yes, you should have," a green voice countered. "Your team was much better than our team!"

Now the greens and blues in the stands were shouting at one another and arguing that the other team was better than their own. Mrs. Squires screeched above the noise, "Come on everybody we're leaving!"

And leave they did. In a few seconds they were outside the ballpark, headed for Koloa to take them home.

The flatworm vendors outside were now busy calling to the crowd rushing past, "Hot flatworm pods, get your pods before they're all gone! Just a few more left."

Squeally said, "I'll get some for you and me," and Peggy wrinkled her face and said, "Don't bother." Squeally looked in surprise at her but just said, "Okay."

When they reached Koloa, Squeally told her, "Squatty's going to the Games Dinner tonight with his team. It's traditional. The two teams get together to congratulate one another." She was going to add that the teams would have a delicacy, blind flatworm steaks, to celebrate, but it was apparent that Peggy wasn't interested, so she just said, "He'll be home later."

Peggy thought that opposing teams getting together after a game to congratulate one another was weird, but she clambered aboard Koloa with the others and they made their rocking, swaying way out of the parking lot and onto the road back toward Low Meadows. Because old Koloa had only seven legs, other people, most of them on young blind wolf spiders, rushed past and got well ahead of them.

Mrs. Squires said, "Peggy I'm sorry you had to witness such un-sportsmanlike behavior they all should be ashamed of themselves the fans I mean the teams were perfectly wonderful and each deserved to win don't you think so S.Q.?"

S.Q. nodded sagely, and Peggy nodded in agreement too, not know-ing what else to do. But she turned toward Squeally beside her, having forgotten in all the commotion that she was not speaking to her.

"I don't get it," Peggy said. "The blue player could have put that one over the wall. He pointed where he was going to hit it, but he just let it go by, took strike three, and lost the championship."

"No he didn't," Squeally answered. "He won it for them."

"*Won* it?"

"Of course. He could have hit a home run, but that wouldn't have been fair to the pitcher who had pitched such a wonderfully slow pitch. So he let it go by. This is *fairball*. Don't you know how the game is played?"

"-----Uhhh, sure. I play it all the time."

"Of course!" Squeally said. "I knew you must play it! All the kids do. You've just been teasing me, making believe you didn't understand the game. You know the motto, 'It doesn't matter whether you win or lose, it's all in being fair.'"

"Sure," Peggy said. "I know that. Everybody who plays fairball knows that."

Eight

During the ride home to Squiresville, Peggy was seated between Squeally on one side and her father, S.Q., on the other. Up to this point, Peggy had gotten an initial warm smile of welcome from S.Q. back at the Games, but he had said nothing other than to yell along with the other fans in green to cheer on the blue team. Squeally had explained during breaks in the noise that he didn't say much, and he was the handy man around the house, doing lots of odd jobs. Now, as they were riding, she whispered carefully to Peggy that after her father finished a job, her mother often had to call in a professional to "touch things up a bit." In the tone Squeally used she revealed a deep love for her father, and she reached across Peggy to his shoulder and gave him a pat and a big smile.

Squeally's hand on S.Q.'s shoulder acted like a switch that turned on his speech, and he smiled and said, "Peggy, we're pleased to have you visit us," and began pointing out sights along the way. He was obviously a nature lover, explaining how in many thousands and even millions of years some of the cave formations they were passing had taken shape. Squeally said. "My older brother Squatty got a lot of his scientific curiosity from Dad." S.Q. smiled and replied, "Maybe. But he's a whole lot smarter than I. He's a real scientist--and I might add, psychologist and many other things."

"Yes, many other," Squeally said under her breath, nudging Peggy, "to include pain in the you know what."

"Now Squeally," her mother scolded, turning around from the seat in front of them, "I heard you you mustn't say that you know how much you love Squatty and how much he loves and teaches you I bet that Peggy doesn't say naughty things about her brother she-----

"Mother, she doesn't have a brother. She's an only child."

"Oh, Peggy, I'm sorry you don't have a brother it's nice to have brothers and sisters in a family but it's also very nice to be an only child isn't that right S.Q.?

S.Q. nodded.

Peggy thought it odd that Squeally knew she was an only child. Oh well, she reasoned, hallucinations don't need explanation. They are, after all, delusions.

On the outskirts of Squiresville, Mr. Squires said to Peggy, "We're approaching Low Meadows. I think you'll find it to be a very handsome neighborhood. It's the best looking one in Squiresville."

"Yes," Squeally joined in, lots of my friends live here."

S.Q. added, "And the parks have some beautiful collection ponds. We'll detour a bit and see one of them."

"What are they?" Peggy asked.

"You'll see. One of them is not far ahead."

Squeally made some clucks, and they went downhill toward the river. Peggy could see that Low Meadows, now behind them, was on a plateau above the river. S.Q. said he thought the pool ahead was the nicest one close to Low Meadows, and Peggy, through her moonglasses, had to agree that the pool she saw now beside them was beautiful. The water was perfectly still and clear, and along the edge and bottom of the pool lay thousands of creamy white pearls of different sizes, most of them like marbles.

Peggy was speechless.

They all climbed down from Koloa and went to the waterside.

Mrs. Squires said in a tone of awe, "We love to come here and look while we can the pearls this time are the most beautiful we've seen in probably twenty or thirty thousand years don't you think Squeally I'm so glad that Peggy is seeing them before they're gone they-----

"Gone?" Peggy interrupted. "How could they be gone? There must be thousands of them here."

"Yes, here now," S.Q. said. "But when high water comes, it rushes over the river bank into the many pools in this area and often sweeps everything out. One can never tell if the next high water will bring something to settle when the water recedes or not. Sometimes there is nothing. Nothing is left behind. But other times the water might bring pearls. They might be gray or brown pearls, misshapen, not like these perfectly rounded white ones. The unblemished white ones are not nearly as plentiful as others. And one time, a short time ago, maybe only a few thousand years, I forget, the water left some beautiful white helictites. After high water, the children of Low Meadows rush to the pools to see if anything has been left, and if so, they run back through the streets calling out what they have found--'Cave pearls in Flowstone Park'-- 'Helictites in Shelfstone Park' or whatever it is that has been displaced from somewhere upstream and left for all of us in Squiresville to admire."

Squeally added, excitedly, "Sometimes we and our neighbors up in Scenic Heights have a pool party. We bring baskets of food down toward the river and play games around a pool and have a great time."

S.Q. had said 'a few thousand years'? That was a *short* time ago? Then Peggy recalled that in In, people treated time much differently than people in Out.

She shook her head, puzzled, and asked, "Helictites? What are they?"

"C'mon, I'll show you, Squeally squealed. "I see a few on the other side of the pond."

The two girls rushed over, with Squeally's parents Squeezy and S.Q. right behind them.

"You can put your hand in the water and pick up a helictite, but be careful because many are fragile," Squeally cautioned.

"May I have one," Peggy asked, astonished at how beautiful the helictites and cave pearls appeared, lying under the surface of crystal-clear water.

S.Q. chimed in, "Yes, you can take anything you find in a collection pond because it's been dislodged or broken off from its original location. We love what we find in nature. We never even touch speleothems--that's a general name for cave formations. We can walk on flowstone and shelfstone if we're careful not to step on any portion which might break off. Such beautiful, fragile formations as green sulfur crystals or jade-colored stalactites must be left alone for everyone to enjoy in their original setting."

Peggy knew about stalagmites and stalactites but had never heard of other cave formations.

She dipped her hand in the cool water, carefully reached for a helictite and brought it out.

"It's beautiful," she said slowly, turning it over and looking at it from all angles. "It looks quite like Spanish moss, intertwined, except that Spanish moss is not white, and it's soft. This is white, and hard, not soft-- all the strings are fixed in place. They don't bend and twist to the touch."

"And you will never find another piece just like this one."

Like our snowflakes? Peggy wondered, but it was unlikely S.Q. would know, since snowflakes obviously would never be seen in In except possibly drifting into a cave mouth, then melting quickly in the warmer cave environment.

Peggy carefully put the piece of helictite back in its place and reached into the water, pushing her hand through a multitude of cave pearls and suddenly felt something much bigger. She clasped it, drew it out of the water, and all of them--the Squires family and Peggy--almost at the same moment said, "Ohhh-----

"I've never, not ever, seen one this big-----and perfect," S.Q. gushed. "I can't believe it!"

Squeezy and Squeally were just as astonished, and all three began talking at once, saying how big and beautiful this cave pearl was.

Peggy could not speak. She just held it, turning it around and around in her hand. She couldn't believe it. The pearl was almost as big as a baseball, and quite heavy. And amazingly beautiful.

"Peggy," Squeezy blurted out, "I've never seen such a big one why it must be a record don't you think S.Q. and beautiful it's as beautiful as--oh I can't think I------" she gasped.

"May I keep it, or should I put it back?"

"No, it is yours," S.Q. said. "Because anything left in a collecting pool will in most likelihood be pushed on downstream at the next high water we are allowed to keep a small amount for decoration, and to teach our children about the beauties of nature. We're just honored to have been here when you found it."

Chattering, the four of them climbed back up on Koloa who began laboring uphill on the path which led to the flat ground of Low Meadows. They were all so excited they talked almost at once, exclaiming what a rare find Peggy had made. She passed the pearl around so each of them could hold it, turn and admire it. Finally she stuck it in the pocket of her shorts where it made a big bulge, and she didn't care one whit if this was just a hallucination. Finding such a treasure was wonderful, hallucination or not, and she knew she would wake up from this crazy, fun journey with a big smile because she had done it.

During the ride, Peggy suddenly realized that even though the air was still cool and damp she no longer wished for a sweater. It was as if the warmth of this family somehow encompassed her and left her feeling warm. She wished she hadn't said mean things to Squeally back there in the Grotto of Tears.

The road through Low Meadows was wide, and Peggy tried to listen as one or the other of the Squires would point out something. Peggy vaguely realized that Low Meadows indeed was a beautiful section of town, with spacious, pretty houses and yards and large, healthy, blind wolf spiders which fairly glistened, unlike Koloa whose hard coat was quite rough looking, with scrapes and scratches in some places. Squeally had said that mostly workers lived there, not professional people, and Peggy couldn't understand, but she had too many things in her mind to straighten out now. Besides, as they exited Low Meadows and began a steep climb on a narrow road she was more concerned with the side of the road on her left. Just a few feet away, the ground disappeared into the dark. They were now passing through Middle Manors where houses were smaller, not impressive. In some of the backyards against the cave wall the hanging "bacon" formations got only an automatic, non-thinking, "Yes, they're beautiful," from her. She became terrified as the road got steeper and came closer to the abyss on her left.

Squeally was piping off in her strange, shrill voice and Peggy could not pay attention. Instead, through her moonglasses, she fixed on the perilous road and hardly heard Squeally announce,

"Here we are, home in Scenic Heights."

Heights for sure, Peggy could agree, but Scenic? These very small houses were rather haphazardly clustered together. She had closed her eyes and only felt Squeally helping her down from Koloa and up toward her house. "See," Squeally was saying proudly, and Peggy opened her eyes only enough to see a sign on the door, 'Proud Parents of the Chosen One.'

"Mother had it done in glow-worm paint so everyone would notice it," Squeally said. "It's for Squiggly, my younger brother. He was the Chosen One."

Peggy had no notion of what that meant, but at that moment the door opened on a boy and a dog. The dog was jumping excitedly and 'whoof, whoofing, over and over, pawing Peggy and looking into her face, trying to lick it.

"Whoof!" he repeated delightedly.

"Mugs?-----_Mugs_??" Peggy blurted out.

Nine

Joyous Reunion

I t couldn't be! It must be the hallucination. But it felt so good that Peggy reacted without thinking, squatted, and wrapped the dog in her arms. He looked a little goofy wearing moonglasses, but who cared? He whoofed and kissed and pranced and pawed her over and over. Just as dreams sometimes can be wonderful, this delusion was wonderful.

"Yes, it's Mugs, and I'm Squiggly," the boy with strange, almost translucent, skin said with a big smile. "He's glad to see you."

"I-----I-----I don't know what to say. I thought that my grandfather had buried him."

"Oh no, no. Mugs was The Gift!" Squiggly said with passion. "Mr. Henry let me have him so I could bring him back to In and The Committee could replicate him so all the children of In could have dogs. Your grandfather is a wonderful, kind man," said Squiggly.

My grandfather? How could Squiggly know-----? This weird trip was a doozy.

Further explanation was interrupted by Squiggly's mother bending over and wrapping her arms around both Peggy and Mugs. Peggy forgot about hallucinations and just sank into the warmth and goodness of the large woman and the reverie of being with Mugs again.

Squiggly's mother, Squeezy, kissed Peggy's forehead and said, "Mr. Henry is such a nice man we love him and are so thankful we just love him don't we S.Q. just such a wonderful man he let Squiggly have Mugs and it won't be long probably no more than twenty thousand years before the Science Committee gets its first births of puppies from their replication process won't that be wonderful Peggy when all the boys and girls in In have their own doggies of course they won't all look like Mugs they'll be different kinds of doggies but they will all be wonderful and-----

S.Q. interrupted his wife--which might have been a historical occasion--saying, "Yes, Squeezy, but you are much better at management than science, and-----

"Oh, S.Q. you are so right I'm going to leave the science to-----

Peggy lost track of who was saying what as the Squires all tried to explain at once. What seemed to have happened was that her grandfather had been in In and had given Mugs to Squiggly. That must have been hard, very painful, for him to have given up Mugs. But here was Mugs, his coat whiter and shinier, and his arthritis not seeming to bother him as he bounced around her like a much younger dog, looking funny in moonglasses. Life in In was obviously very good to him.

For the first time in a long time, Peggy felt close to her grandfather.

But this was an illusion. She would soon wake up.

She didn't wake up, and Squeezy was saying, "Since Squatty is having blind flatworm steaks at the Games Dinner a real treat they're getting harder and harder to get at the market we're going to have them too you do like flatworm steaks don't you Peggy my goodness what a silly question everyone loves flatworm steaks so I'm sure you will enjoy them."

Peggy figured that in a hallucination you might just as well play along with the plot line before it changed into something else, and Mrs. Squires' look indicated she expected an answer, so Peggy stammered, "Uh--yes--they are rather hard to get any more, and expensive, but we do have them now and then."

"Good," Squeezy said, "now S.Q. dear if you will prepare the steaks I'll do the moss salad and mix up some What'siss and girls you may go upstairs and freshen up for dinner and Squeally please tell Great Great Grandfather Squires that dinner will be ready soon and you will call him so let's go look in on Squishy for a minute he must still be asleep since I haven't heard anything from the baby's room Squiggly does such a nice baby-sitting job helping his aunt and-----

In a moment they were looking in on the sleeping Squishy, who looked angelic. Then they quietly left and Squeally led Peggy upstairs. Squeally knocked on the door of Great Great Grandfather Squires' room, and after no response, whispered to Peggy, "He's asleep, I think. He sleeps a lot. Old people sleep a lot." But her second knock brought the muffled reply, "Come in."

As they entered, the old man--ancient-looking, actually--pulled himself more upright in the rocking chair. All Peggy could see of his body was hands and head, the rest being covered by a very out-of-date suit with vest and shining black shoes. He looked like an illustration in a Charles Dickens book. In fact, everyone in In looked somewhat like that with their old-fashioned clothes. His white collar and cravat stuck out from a neck so scrawny his head seemed likely to break off at any moment. His withered but still almost transparent skin was so thin it was like misty, wrinkled plastic over bones.

"Welcome, Peggy," he grated.

How could he have known who she was, Peggy fretted, since the only Squires who knew her so far had been with her at the Regional Youth Games and during their trip home to Squiresville. Come to think of it, how had Squiggly known her when he had been at home with his aunt baby-sitting Squishy? But--oh yes, Squiggly had known about her grand-father and Mugs and-----

Oh, this was all so very confusing.

They entered his room and Great Great Grandfather reached out his gnarled, shrunken hand for Peggy to take.

She took it warily, as if touching cold bones. As he squinted directly at her, she saw his very light gray irises. Those eyes were magically intense, as if they had witnessed the beginning of time and everything thereafter.

"Peggy, it is good to see you," he laboriously uttered, pulling the words up from somewhere down deep inside. He said in Squeally's direction, "We will talk later."

Squeally replied with unmistakably profound respect, "Yes, Great Great Grandfather."

The meeting was over, signaled by a weak raise of the ancient man's finger.

In Squeally's room now, Squeally said, "The bathroom is across the hall. And you can put your cave pearl on your bed here." Squeally pointed, and Peggy put it in the middle of the bed.

"Sure is big--and beautiful," Squeally said.

"Sure is," Peggy agreed, proudly.

slowest fairball pitch in history had eventually made its way over the plate, the front door quickly opened and Squatty strode into the room, home from the Games dinner.

He burst into the conversation, "Small difference what year, dummy! On the way home I think I figured out the molecular differences that determine whether an organism develops into-----

"Who cares, smarty," Squeally said and gave him an elbow as he came past her chair.

"Now, children!" their mother scolded, "Such behavior in front of a guest we'll have no more of that will we S.Q. you must speak to them later-----

"Oh Mom, he always thinks he knows everything-----

"Better than knowing nothing," Squatty shot out, but was cut off by a particularly fierce look from his mother.

"Squatty dear," Mrs. Squires said, "This is Peggy she's visiting from Out isn't it wonderful to have her she-----

"Oh hello," Squatty said to Peggy casually, hardly glancing at her as if girls from Out were everyday visitors. And with that, he launched back into his molecular theory. Peggy noticed, now that she saw him close up, that his face was similar to that of Asians, and through her glasses his skin looked a little darker than Squeally's or Squiggly's. He was cut off by his mother saying that it had been a long day for Peggy, and Squeally should take her upstairs so they could go to bed.

"Thank you, Mother!" Squeally replied gratefully, and as she led Peggy past Squatty to the stairs, gave him the hip.

The last words Peggy heard from the top of the stairs before they went into Squeally's room were, "S.Q. you really need to-----

It indeed had been a long day. As Peggy lay in bed she held her cave pearl, looking at it, turning it, rubbing it against her cheek, making it warm. It was her special treasure. Then she lifted the moonglasses from her eyes and saw only darkness. Utter, complete darkness. She shuddered. How could anything be absolutely dark? And how could darkness produce such beauty as the pearl?

She tried to think, but overtaken by fatigue she drifted toward sleep, comforted somewhat that with her moonglasses now firmly back over her eyes, she would at least be able to see Squeally in the next bed. She hated that--feeling a need for someone else--at least someone other than her own mother. Her last half-conscious thought was that in the morning she would awaken from this confusing, crazy dream, and all would be normal again.

Eleven

HITBALL

B ut in the morning Peggy was still in the Squires house eating breakfast with Squeally. Squatty and Squiggly had gotten up early and
taken Koloa down to Low Meadows for an aerobics class. Mr. Squires
was attending to Squishy and changing his bedclothes, and Mrs. Squires
had already gone to her factory. She had left a note: 'Squeally why don't
you take Peggy to Wiggly World there is a glow-worm show that should
be interesting I would go with you but we're testing a new line of tissue
today so have fun Love, Mother PS There is fresh dulse bread on the
counter and cold fish in the icebox I think Peggy would like that for
breakfast you can buy something for lunch have fun.'

This was a strange breakfast, quite unlike bacon and eggs or oat-
meal or Cheerios, but Peggy was hungry and she actually liked the
dulse bread and fish. But an icebox? Why no refrigerator? Come to
think of it, she had seen no evidence of electricity in Squiresville. The
glow-worm paint of Squiggly's sign on the front door was the only evidence of light she had seen in In after leaving the cave entrance behind,
and it was gentle, low-intensity light at that.

Peggy said, "I can see how you easily enough get fish, but what is dulse bread, and where do you get it?"

"We buy both at the market in Low Meadows." Squeally explained. "Most of the fish and all of the dulse, which is a form of algae, come from our fisheries. We mostly eat it as a snack or buy it in flour form to bake into bread. Many of the In caves open underwater directly into seas, so In has a booming seafood business. Our coastal fishermen and women go underwater close to the cave exits where they easily get all we need of varieties of seafood--and quickly escape back into the cave in case of danger."

Squeally asked, "Would you like to go to Wiggly World? It has all kinds of rides and shows and fun things to do and see."

"Sure, why not? But first I'm going upstairs to get my pearl."

Peggy wasn't sure why she wanted to take it, especially as it was heavy and made a big bulge in her pocket that was a bit uncomfortable. But it also made her feel good, knowing it was right there with her.

They went out to the driveway where a small, blind wolf spider was waiting for them.

"The boys took Koloa so we're borrowing Miko from our next door neighbor Mrs. Scoot, Mother's good friend. She has a large transportation company, so we get rides any time we wish. We like Miko. He's young, and fast, and--sporty."

As Peggy climbed aboard and strapped herself into her seat she noted that Miko was a magnificent specimen, perfectly groomed and shiny and, unlike old Koloa, he had all eight legs. Two of them in the front were anxiously pawing the ground. Squeally scampered up, fastened her belt, and Miko's front legs pawed faster and faster as his back legs sank, like a 100 meter dash runner settling into the starting blocks. Squeally squeaked out a command and--whoosh!--they were off.

Miko had taken only one stride forward before he swung hard left. At his abrupt turn, Peggy, on the rightmost seat, got a terrifying glimpse of the dark void over the river far below and nearly shrieked, but Squeally poked her and called out, "Miko likes this trip down to Low Meadows, lots of great curves. You'll love it!"

This narrow road was right at the edge of the cliff, and the racing Miko was *blind*.

"Oy vey!" Peggy gasped, held tightly onto her moonglasses and squeezed her eyes shut.

"We love Koloa, but Miko will have us there in a quarter of the time. See, we're already through Middle Manors, and Low Meadows is just ahead."

In a matter of Out seconds, Miko had zipped past the sign, "Welcome to Low Meadows" and was braking so hard that all eight feet were screeching, drowning out Squeally's delighted shrieks.

"Peggy," she said breathlessly, "I think that was a record. Miko must have wanted my guest to have an especially thrilling ride. He's usually just a little slower."

With eyes now open and a look which she hoped conveyed delight rather than fear, Peggy replied, "Please thank Miko for me."

Squeally clucked, and Miko sank to the ground as Peggy patted his side while she climbed down. Peggy said, "Good boy, Miko, nice ride," as she thought quite otherwise. When Squeally clucked again, Miko raced back up the hill.

Waiting were a dozen or so boys and girls of varying skin pigmentation and facial features. About half of the girls wore very old style blue blouses with Watersville Warblers printed on the front, and a player number on the back. The rest of the waiting group was from Squiresville. All of the girls wore old-fashioned pantalettes and dresses similar to Squeally's. The boys wore loose trousers and caps.

"Well, hi, Wallis," Squeally called and waved at one of the girls in blue. "Did you win yesterday?"

"Naturally," the tall girl named Wallis replied. Squeally led Peggy over to meet her.

"Peggy, this is Wallis Waters. While we were at the fairball championship, the Warblers were playing their championship game of hitball at another venue close by. Wallis is the team captain. The team also has boys, of course, but she's the captain. Wallis, this is Peggy, my friend."

Instead of saying 'hello' Wallis replied, "May I ask where you got those clothes?" She was looking at Peggy.

"Well," replied Peggy, who thought the question impertinent, "probably at the mall."

"The mall. Never heard of it. But that's understandable. Mother and I don't shop for strange avant-garde fashions. We favor the classic look."

Peggy's hackles were now up and she said, "Yes. I can see you prefer clothes of Yesteryear--way, way Yesteryear."

Before anything else unfortunate could be said, Squeally quickly announced that the Squiresville boys and girls and Peggy were going to Wiggly World. "How about you Wallis?"

One of the other blue team members piped up, happily, "We are too. But where is Cedrik Centipede? He's late."

"Sure is," Squeally agreed, and explained to Peggy that Cedrik, a blind centipede, was their transportation to Wiggly World. He could take a large group on bench seats that stretched the entire length of his long back.

One of the girls in a blue blouse was carrying what Peggy took to be a ball they used for hitball, whatever that was.

"You play hitball don't you?" the girl called to Peggy good-naturedly, and before Peggy could reply, she was catching the ball the girl had tossed to her.

Wallis announced coolly, without asking anyone, "We will have a round of five points while we're waiting."

The boys and girls in blue and the Squiresville kids quickly took their places. The ad hoc Squiresville team formed in the middle of a circle the Watersville group made.

Wallis said, "Peggy, since you are Squeally's guest, you may make the first throw." Peggy did not much like the cold tone, and especially did not like Wallis's presumption of being the leader of this group. But the blue team had begun circling, all of them warily watching Peggy in the middle.

The somewhat velvety ball was about the right size. "Dodgeball," Peggy muttered to herself. So that's what hitball was, just a different name.

Peggy moved her arms back and forth, feinted twice, then threw hard at one of the girls in blue. The instant the ball left her hand, Peggy knew she had made a bad throw. It would be a miss, well behind the girl who was her target. But the girl quickly turned and jumped directly in the path of the ball, taking a hit squarely on her chest.

Her teammates in blue called out in delight what a good hit she had taken, and when Peggy just stood there, befuddled, they called, "Peggy, you're out. You have to get outside the circle so we can continue."

"What do you mean *I'm* out?" Peggy called. "*She's* out!"

Now all the girls on both teams were riled, several calling at once for Peggy to get out of the circle. With that, Wallis came striding directly at her, hands on hips.

"You're out. Get out of-----

"What do you mean I'm out. I hit her right in the middle of the-----

"Right! That's exactly what you did, so you're out!" she said, menacingly.

"This is nuts, you don't know the game of dodgeball."

"What's dodgeball? Some ridiculous game you and your friends in those funny clothes play? This is *hitball*. If you throw a terrible ball, the way you did, it's a miracle anyone could move fast enough to get hit, especially in the middle of her chest."

Squeally, embarrassed, thrust her way between the two girls, trying to explain there must be some misunderstanding and-----

At that moment a dark-colored centipede with only a few rows of seats strapped to his back hurried up to the group. He moved forward in a wave-like rising and falling motion similar to that of caterpillars.

"Cedrik Centipede, where have you been?" Squeally scolded, then instantly added, "Oh, you're not Cedrik, you're Cephus." She reached up and took down a note taped to his side. She read it to the group: "Sorry. Cedrik is sick today. Cephus will take you."

A groan came from the Squiresville kids who frequently used centipede transportation and knew most of their names. Squeally hoped the animal had not sensed it, and tried to quiet those who were saying things such as:

"Doofus Cephus."

"Must be real short-handed today if they sent him."

"We'll be lucky if we get there."

"I heard that last time he got lost."

Then a commanding voice cut through the grousing, "Everybody, get aboard or we won't get to see anything!"

The voice was that of Wallis.

Peggy was steaming. First the embarrassing business of not having the right clothes. Then the foolishness of hitball. Now Miss Know-It-All was giving the orders.

It was Peggy who had always taken charge.

Peggy!

Not someone who thought she was a big shot just because she was captain of a stupid hitball team.

Hmph! *Hitball!*

Twelve

The kids all scrambled up and took seats. Peggy got jostled out of position by the crowd and when she looked up, Miss Bossy was in the prime seat just behind Cephus's head. Peggy and Squeally had to take the only seats left, in the last row. Squeally said, "Normally, blind centipedes have dozens of legs, but Cephus has only--let me count them--fourteen pairs. They use him only when they have to, and just for short hauls."

Now Wallis was giving more orders: "All right, everyone, settle down, buckle your seat belts." Then she made a clucking sound and Cephus moved forward in a rolling motion like that of a horse on a merry-go-round which goes gently up, then down, and up and down. The girls around Peggy giggled at the pleasant motion, and it even made Peggy a bit less cross. Rubbing her pearl in her pocket also helped.

On the outskirts of Low Meadows, they came to a fork in the road. A sign at the left-hand fork had a sign pointing to Squabblesville: 2,623 SLs, Squallville 3,623 SLs, Squeamishville 4,944 SLs, Watersville 5,133 SLs, Goldville 6,783 SLs. The sign on the right-hand fork had only one destination, Wiggly World, 1,487 SLs.

"What in the world are SLs?" asked Peggy.

"Soda straws, Squeally replied. "Didn't you notice them hanging from the ceiling of The Grotto?"

Peggy had to admit she hadn't, having been absorbed in looking at other beautiful cave formations. "How long is a soda straw?"

"Well, it's the length of the broken soda straw which long ago the scientists placed in the Weights and Measures Room of Measurements Cave. An SL means Straw Length."

Cephus had slowed down, looked at the left fork, then the right, and stopped at the intersection.

"Oh, poor Cephus. He's confused," said Squeally to Peggy. "I think this might be his first trip, or more likely he's forgotten. "

Other kids around them were not as kind, and in snatches of their impatient talking all at once Peggy heard:

"This Doofus-----Doofus Cephus-----

"-----we'll never get there-----

"Did you ever?----- "

Cephus turned his head toward the rear, and Peggy could interpret the gesture only as confused and pleading for direction.

Above the kids' noise, Wallis loudly clucked, harshly ordering, "Right fork. Right!"

Cephus lowered his head as if ashamed and set off gamely down the right fork.

Squeally clucked and called out loudly, "That's okay, Cephus. It's okay." Wallis turned around, and with a reproachful look, called to Squeally, "*I'll* be the one to talk to him."

Squeally was embarrassed, and Peggy's face flushed with anger. She had to swallow hard to avoid intervening.

After awhile she found herself slowly calmed by the scenery--beautiful flowstone formations, atop some of which were rather haphazard but attractive pieces of stalactites and other cave formations which had broken loose from far overhead in some forgotten past and fallen in a pile. It was as if a superbly talented but eccentric sculptor had suddenly been startled and knocked over his work table, spilling wonderful works which had broken into fragments.

As they rode, tensions eased and the kids launched into song. The melodies were lively and pleasant, but there were so many unfamiliar words that Peggy strained to make sense of them, just as if she were hearing a foreign language which she understood only sparingly.

Then someone called out, "The Wiggly World song," and they began happily singing a song anyone could understand. It began:

We're on our way to Wiggly World
A wonderful world to see,
Rides and shows, as everyone knows,
A treat for you and me.

Each boy or girl, seated from front to back, would sing a verse, and then the next one would take a turn. As Peggy's turn got closer, she had no idea of what to sing. Now Squeally did her part as she elbowed Peggy to get ready to sing.

Gulping, Peggy let loose with what just popped into her mind:

Why in the World is Wiggly World
A wonderful world to see?
I don't know, come on let's go
You, and you, and me.

All of the kids turned toward her, clapping and laughing, and calling out their congratulations for a verse well done. That is, all but one.

Wallis kept looking straight ahead, saying nothing.

Thirteen

WHICH ROAD TO TAKE?

After more songs, suddenly up ahead was a man in uniform, holding up his hand in the 'Stop' signal.

Cephus must have sensed what was ahead of him, and his fourteen pairs of legs slowed.

"Who is that?" Peggy asked.

Squeally said, proudly, "He's one of our Squatter County sheriff's deputies."

Wallis clucked and Cephus stopped.

"You see," Squeally explained, "Studious Stick from Sticksville was the Chosen One some time ago and he came back from Out carrying The Gift and recommended it to The Committee, that uniform."

Peggy didn't understand much of that. Squeally continued. She thought the deputy's uniform was spectacular, and, realizing that Peggy through her moonglasses could see only shades of gray and had to more or less guess at other colors, she described it: dark blue trousers, scarlet tunic with white belt around the middle, shoulder straps, and a tall, black bearskin fur hat. The hat was so heavy it slid down over a deputy's nose and caused sneezing. The gift had been replicated to outfit the entire sheriff's department. Squeally didn't know where Studious Stick had found the uniform.

"Buckingham Palace," Peggy said, and this time it was Squeally who didn't understand.

The deputy's bearskin hat was down over his eyes, and he was sneezing as he called out, "Road closed."--Ah-Choo! "Blocked by rock slide. Take a side road."--Ah-Ah-Choo!--"Detour. On the right up ahead you will see a sign to Wiggly World."-----Ah-Ah-Ah- CHOO!"

At Wallis's clucks, Cephus set off down the side road--too slowly for Wallis and she was angry. "Stupid centipede. I won't get to see anything I wanted to see." She clucked Cephus into more speed, and now the girls were getting quite a ride, up and down fast, up and down faster.

Not far down the side road they came to the sign--or rather, *two* signs--two signs fairly close to one another, each alongside a separate narrow road. Peggy saw that the roads diverged as they moved off into what gradually became total darkness as viewed through her moonglasses.

Cephus abruptly stopped his legs, lurching the girls forward as their transport skidded to a halt halfway between the signs, one now to the left and one to the right of where the girls sat atop him.

The sign to the left read, "To Wiggly World, half as far."

The sign to the right read, "To Wiggly World, twice as long."

"This is great, just great!" stormed Wallis. "Idiot deputy. Moron, loony! Which road do we take?

What are we supposed to do now?"

It wasn't really a question, just a frustrated outburst. Peggy found herself smiling ironically at this first crack in Wallis's cold demeanor.

The kids were now nervously chattering

"What are we going to do, I think-----

"It must be the one on the right. It's the first one we came to-----

"No, I think it's the other one. It looks as if-----

"I just want to go home," one of the girls in front of Peggy said, and started to get teary.

But at that moment, out of the darkness between the two side roads came what Peggy could only describe as a mist. It wafted closer, and closer until it floated into and wrapped around them, so dense that Peggy could not see Squeally sitting next to her. But she felt her hand gripping hers.

"Oh Peggy," Squeally said. "What is happening?"

Two voices came out of the mist, one sweet and melodious, which said, "Take my road, children."

The other voice, harsh and crackly, said, "You little brats, you'd better take my road if you know what's good for you!"

"Ohhhh," the girl in front of Peggy sobbed as Squeally squeezed Peggy's hand harder and said,

"What do we do?"

Just then the mist dissolved and in front of them, one standing beside the left sign and one the right, were two women. At least one appeared to be a woman, angelic, a beautiful young woman in a long, flowing dress. Her almost translucent face was radiant. She was standing beside the left sign, saying gently, "Children, come, take my road to Wiggly World. It's only half as far."

"Heh heh," cackled the other, a hunched over old hag wearing a tattered black dress and black conical hat with a wide brim. According to Squeally, her face was a hideous green and purple.

"You believe that? If you do, it will be a short trip and you'll never return. My road goes to Wiggly World, and it's twice as long, but at least you'll get there, heh, heh, heh!"

With that, many of the kids, some boys included, were now fighting down tears. They were poking one another and asking what to do, which road to take. Some wanted the short way and thought the old hag was lying, but some wanted the long way because at least they would

195

get there. Most of the kids now seemed to be leaning toward taking the short way, that of the beautiful lady. But they were all confused.

"We'll take a vote," a shaky voice from the front said. It was Wallis, uncharacteristically unnerved.

"A vote!" Peggy feistily erupted. "You're the leader and you want to take a vote! Kids, there's only one road we must take."

At that, Squeally regained her confidence, knowing that Peggy would make the correct choice, the road on the left, the road offered by the beautiful lady.

"The road on the right!" Peggy said forcefully.

Everyone gasped.

"The right? It can't be." Wallis said, "We should vote."

Peggy called out, "It's a ruse. A trick. I've seen this a million times at Halloween. You get offered sweet candy by the pretty princess and sour candy by the witch. And you take the sweet candy and it sends you right through the roof it is so sour. Or the sweet princess invites you to enter her door and when you get in there all kinds of ghouls and ghosts jump out at you. Squeally, tell Cephus to take the road on the right."

Although the girls had no idea what Halloween was, or princesses, witches, ghouls, or ghosts, Peggy's confidence had inspired them, and Squeally clucked. As Cephus set off down the road to the right, leaving behind the beautiful lady's lament of "Oh dear, Oh dear," the group began to sing

> We're on our way to Wiggly World
> A wonderful world to see,
> Rides and shows, as everyone knows,
> A treat for you and me.

Many happy, impromptu verses followed.

Fourteen

DANGER!

The roads they had traveled from Low Meadows to this point had been in a cave so huge Peggy could not see the ceiling. But now, dead ahead, the road entered a fissure so narrow that Cephus slowed to ease his way past the jagged entrance, and had to wind his way around 90-degree bends with dank walls so close on both sides that occasionally the seats rubbed them, and the riders had to lean to the inside to avoid being scraped. The singing had stopped, and now they were frightened again. Peggy slowly lifted her glasses. When she had done this before, she had seen total darkness. But the dark she now experienced was worse, much worse. Maybe it was because the chasm they were in seemed to squeeze absolute darkness into a totally evil darkness.

With her glasses now back down over her eyes, and a gray world returned, Peggy called out, in a voice more confident than she actually felt, "Remember, the sign said 'To Wiggly World, twice as long' so although our ride may be slower, at least we'll get there."

But the way ahead remained tortuously narrow and jagged, and the going was slow. No one was speaking as they scraped along, hoping the way would open up so they could go faster and get out of this creepy place. Peggy looked behind and saw a mist approaching, closer and closer and then it enveloped them so they could see nothing, but in a moment it wafted on ahead. And best of all, they could see that the walls ahead now receded from the road a little, just enough so they could pick up speed again and get out of there. Soon they were in the clear, and Cephus had a bit more room to make his way, winding around the hairpin curves. "Whew, about time," one of the girls exclaimed.

They exited a curve and entered a short straight stretch. "Heh, heh," came a voice out of the cloud ahead. "Well, my little dears, you took my advice."

The mist melted away and there was the old hag, standing beside the road, in front of the next curve. Cephus came to a stop, trembling.

"Good for you children. You're almost at Wiggly World. But first, here is a preview. It's feeding time for Skelton, our gatekeeper. You're going to watch him eat. You'd like that wouldn't you?"

Not wanting to disagree with this old, ugly woman, some of them said, "Okay. Might as well. If it doesn' t take too long. "

"Oh, it won't take long. He's hungry. He's going to eat-----
"YOU!"

The kids were terrified, clasping one another. Wallis and the girl next to her were clutching one another. They were crying, as were others. Peggy struggled against her fear. She wasn't sure if she should tell them this was just part of the ruse, or if she should succumb to the horror that swept over them.

Peggy fought off the dread and was just about to tell everyone it was a deception when the hag cackled, made a clucking sound, and said, "Come on out, Skelton. Mealtime. Nice, pretty boys and girls. Show them how handsome you are. Heh, heh."

Out of the darkness a huge claw poked around the corner, like that of a crab, or a lobster--but more sinister looking. She heard clacks as it and then another claw struck the stone floor.

"A blind pseudoscorpion!" Squeally shrieked. "It will poison us and eat us."

Peggy had never felt anything like this terror, much worse than the instant scares of Halloween that quickly turned into a kind of chilled delight when she realized that the horrible things confronting her weren't real.

This huge beast was *real*, and it was clacking its way toward them, ejecting a stream of foul-smelling liquid from the tips of its claws. Its two clouded sightless eyes waggled ominously back and forth, and its hideous mouth was wide open. Peggy tried to say something but terror clutched her and she could not speak.

"My pretty Skelton, good boy," the hag cooed.

Nothing was pretty about him. This whitish, reddish-brown creature moving toward them was twice as tall as the hag and it had hard shells protecting much of its body.

Squeally was looking at the thing in horror as she shrieked, "It's going to shoot venom on us, grab us in its pincers and, and eat us!"

Cephus was struggling to turn around to run away, but bending his body as much as he could, his sides were scraping the walls and he continued to struggle. The kids were tossed side to side and up and down in their seats, screaming, as Cephus desperately thrashed, trying to free himself.

"Oh, my lovelies, my handsome boys, my pretty girls," the hag cackled, "Skelton is hungry. Thank you for taking my road."

Peggy cringed away from the creature as it came closer. Its mouth with sharp teeth was closing and opening, hungrily. With a few more lunges it would be on them, shooting its poison over them and grabbing them in its pincers and stuffing them into its mouth. But with a final huge heave, Cephus pulled himself around so that his rear end was now pointed at the beast, and Peggy and Squeally, in the rear seat, were almost within its grasp.

For some reason which she could not explain later, Peggy's hand slid into her pocket and grasped her cave pearl. The beast was now at eye level with her and some of its stinking venom spattered against Cephus. Now only a few feet away, a claw was reaching toward her head, opening and closing, shifting, searching for its prey. She drew out the cave pearl and hurled it as hard as she could, directly at the huge opaque eyes.

CRACK! The sound was like that of a hammer striking a hard surface. The head of the creature instantly retracted, then slowly lowered as if stunned, and its entire body flopped onto the road.

"Oh, my Skelton, my pretty boy. What have you done you little tramp?" the hag screeched. "My precious, beautiful boy. You hateful----oh, oh," the hag gasped and began to dissolve into a mist. As the vapor floated away into the darkness, Peggy could hear, "What have you done? What have you done?" over and over, getting fainter and fainter until she heard it no more.

Cephus, now nearly free, was faced in the direction from which they had come, and Peggy was almost thrown off as she unbuckled her seat belt and scurried down his side, jumping the last few feet onto the road.

"Peggy, what are you *doing*?" Squeally shrieked at her as Cephus broke free and raced ahead, away from danger.

"Stop him. Stop Cephus!" Peggy cried out.

She ran up to the pseudoscorpion, an enormous hulk which was moving slightly, one claw flopping up and down. Peggy's head darted from side to side, searching. Rasping sounds of labored breathing came from the creature, and it was trying to stand up. She had to work fast, searching, trying not to step in the gooey patches of venom.

"It better not be under him. Where are you? Where *are* you?" she cried out.

Finally, there it was! The monster's twitching leg bumped it and rolled it off the road. Peggy ran and scooped up her pearl, stuck it in her pocket, raced away from the stinking monster and chased Cephus down the road as Squeally managed to slow him, and finally bring him to a trembling stop.

Squeally reached down and grabbed Peggy's hand as she clambered up Cephus's side, scrambled into her seat and buckled her belt. With chest heaving, Peggy glanced back and saw a defeated, dazed Skelton wobbling away from them, fading away into the darkness.

Close call!

Peggy had gotten aboard just in time as Cephus now set his legs pumping, scraping his body along walls, dashing around curve after curve, carrying them back until they burst out of the crevice and into open country once again.

The kids who had been crying and screaming were now quietly sobbing, thankful to be safe. Then one of them called back, "Thank you, Peggy," joined shortly by others calling their thanks. Wallis turned and said, "Thank you." She seemed to have meant it.

"Wow," Squeally said, "I thought you had gone nuts back here."

"Maybe I did," was the panted reply.

Thrilled as she was that no one had been injured, and she was safe, Peggy slumped and paid no attention to the congratulations from the group. Underneath the elation was the realization she had led the group to take the wrong road, a huge mistake from being over-certain of herself that could have cost the lives of everyone.

Fifteen

Wiggly World at Last

After what seemed like a long time, they were nearing the deputy's post on the main road. He held up his hand to stop Cephus who wanted to get back to Low Meadows as fast as his many legs could take him. But the deputy remained in the middle of the road with hand raised, and Cephas stopped.

As the deputy lowered his hand and stepped briskly to the side of the road he intoned "Road open again--Ah-Choo!--Rock slide cleared away --Ah-Ah-Choo!--Resume travel on main road, turn-off to Wiggly World straight ahead." He pointed. "Ah, Ah, Ah CHOO!"

Cephus obviously wanted none of Wiggly World, and he turned his head left and started toward Low Meadows. The girls looked at Peggy and one of them said, "Peggy?" obviously meaning, what do we do now?

Peggy was drawn out of her funk by the question, and she said, "Stop Cephus, Squeally. We're going to Wiggly World."

Squeally smiled, clucked, and an unhappy Cephus obediently stopped.

"Oh, Peggy, are you sure?"

Peggy said, "I'll probably never get to Disney World, and all of us were headed to Wiggly World, so let's go there."

Squeally had no idea what Disney World meant, but she clucked and Cephus turned around. They were on their way to Wiggly World, leaving Ah-Choos behind them.

During all this commotion, Peggy had not heard Wallis say anything more. But no matter. Not long after, they went through the arch with the big glow-worm painted sign above them:

Welcome to Wiggly World

One of the girls started, and all of them joined in. Wallis was quietly singing with the others. They made up silly verses as they sang

Now we're here in Wiggly World,
A wonderful place to be,
Rides and shows, as everyone knows,
A treat for you and me.

How did it happen, back on the road,
Abeast against a girl?
She bonked him on the head, you see,
Heaving her great big pearl.

That's why we're here, she had no fear,
Skelton was his name.
She jumped down, retrieved her pearl,
The hag was put to shame.

So here we are in Wiggly World,
Happy as can be.

The girl with the pearl, how she could hurl!
Is our friend, our own Peg-gy.

The girls and boys giggled and laughed and poked one another as they made up new goofy verses.

Squeally said, "You see, I knew they would like you."

Peggy thought that her throw was more than a little lucky, but here they were in Wiggly World, and it was time to put what had happened behind her and try to have fun.

The kids hurried down a path and through stone turnstiles. No tickets required? "This is free?" Peggy asked.

Squeally seemed a bit surprised, "Free? Certainly. They're all volunteers. The people who manage, the helpers, everybody. And the animals too. During their training, if they show any sign they would rather not be doing this they are released back to where they came from. And even later they can quit at any time and be returned. Most of them stay, and some have been here for a long time. They seem to enjoy being part of the entertainment."

Just then two millipedes came humping up to them, dressed in red and black costumes--at least Squeally said they were red and black. The kids began calling out, "Hi, Mikkel, Hi Millie," as Mikkel reared up on a few dozen of his back legs and then took what seemed like a bow, and Millie in similar manner made a deep curtsy. "They're the stars of Wiggly World, Mikkel and Millie Millipede. There are so many stories about them. We've all heard the stories from early childhood. Everybody knows and loves Mikkel and Millie," Squeally said.

They all clapped in appreciation as the millipedes wound among them, rubbing their heads against them and getting petted in return.

Mikkel and Millie then circled around them, and in unison, as if someone had thrown a switch, sign boards lighted up. Words in glowworm paint provided a menu of recommended attractions:

The Cave of Healing

SHOWS

Winnie Wiggly, The Wondrous Wigglewoman, take path to your left
Warty Wiggly, The Wicked Wiggleman, take path to your right
Crayfish Concert, take path to your front
Glow-worm Gala, take path to your rear

RIDES

Centipede Circus, departs from Track 1 directly ahead
Millipede Madness, departs from Track 2 directly ahead

Many more shows and rides were listed, but Peggy thought she would start with the Crayfish Concert, and, having had more than enough thrilling rides in In, would skip them altogether. Squeally said she had made a good choice.

"You've been here before?" Peggy asked.

"Several times, but I love it each time. Sometimes my mom and dad come, or my brothers come with me, or sometimes just my school friends. There are often new attractions. The glow-worm show is new. The crayfish show is almost the same, but it thrills me every time I see it."

Sixteen

CRAYFISH SPECTACULAR

Several of the kids in the group joined Squeally and Peggy as they set out down the path to their front while the others went off toward different venues. Soon Peggy's group entered through a crevice and came out into a large cave.

Ahead was a broad, shallow pool, and ushers motioned them toward chunks of stalactite with flat tops which served as stools spread out along the edge of the water. When Peggy was seated she noted that the water surface was perfectly still, and through the crystal-clear water she saw that many large white rounded stones packed closely together formed the pool bottom.

When all were seated, two small children dressed in white carried a handwritten sign in front of the stools which read, 'Crayfish Concert.'

Squeally said, very quietly, that the sign had been glow-worm finger-painted by the children. Peggy thought, "Give me a break." This was nothing like the on-line videos of Disney she had watched, with bright, flashy displays announcing the attractions. This show was going to be a dud.

Across the water and beyond the far bank was an array of what appeared to be vertical, closely aligned pipes of a huge church organ."Oh, wonderful," she thought. "Just what I need, an organ recital."

"Those are a hundred broken soda straws of different diameters and lengths," Squeally offered.

Before Peggy could respond, in the profound stillness of the cave the white bottom of the pool began slowly to move. What was going on?

In a moment, the surface of the water at the far bank was broken quietly by gleaming white, blind crayfish, which Peggy had thought to be the white stones in the bottom of the pool. They slowly began to emerge from the water, a hundred of them, close together, heading away from the audience toward the array of vertical soda straws.

"Ohhh-----the audience gasped. The sight of the densely packed crayfish, a mass of gently rolling, gleaming white backs, was astonishing. "Beautiful," Peggy breathed.

The moving crayfish made a soft rustling sound like a soothing breeze wafting through autumn leaves. They kept coming and coming out of the water until a final line of them emerged and waved their broad tails up and down in unison as a kind of salute. A lone crayfish was now leading. It raised both claws and clacked them. At the signal, the mass of crayfish began to fan out slowly, continuing to move away from the audience. As they approached the three lines of soda straws, each crayfish moved to a straw. The crayfish who had clacked climbed onto a low platform, raised a claw, and clacked twice. In perfect precision, in the lines of crayfish each raised a claw at the side of its soda straw, waiting. Peggy and other kids around her inhaled in excited anticipation.

The conductor crayfish clacked, and several claws struck straws one time only. The tone was beautiful, perfectly harmonious. Then the conductor clacked again and a player crayfish struck the shortest, thinnest straw. A very high, beautiful clarion note sounded. One by

one the conductor clacked, and a player would strike another straw, a bit longer and broader in diameter, producing a slightly lower tone until, having worked down the musical scale through several octaves, the last note was reached, a deep, resonating bass. Then the conductor raised both claws and clacked a downbeat. With that, some of the hundred players struck a note, followed rapidly by others striking their notes in rhythm as the conductor directed. The sounds were somewhat like those of xylophones. The effect was a short, brilliantly harmonious piece that reminded Peggy of hummingbirds hovering for an instant at flowers, followed by honey bees buzzing from one flower to another. It was a bright, sunny tune that seemed not at all out of place in this dark cave. The cave roof produced an acoustical effect that to Peggy seemed like surround sound, enveloping her, holding her spellbound. The cheerful melody made Peggy feel as if she herself were a hummingbird or a bee flitting here and there, sampling the heavenly nectar which she would take home to share with friends. At the end of the composition, Squeally and Peggy and all the kids clapped loudly, Ooh-ing and Ahh-ing their approval.

Peggy, being a piano player, knew a good deal about music, and this orchestra was superb. The crayfish concert featured a variety of selections. Each was different from the preceding one--some similar to waltzes, some to marches, others to romantic music, and one to a symphony--similar, yes, but more unusual and more beautiful than any music Peggy had ever heard. She thought that a heavenly choir could not have given such a captivating, intriguing performance. She did not want it to end. The thought of so many blind crayfish being trained to strike their individual straws at just the right moment to create such music was beyond her comprehension. She almost asked Squeally to explain it, but any explanation would fall so far short of the reality of what she saw and heard that she just wanted to cherish this moment, and so she simply said to Squeally, "This is beautiful."

The last number was heroic, the kind that made one feel proud to be even a small part of some great event. Deep, throbbing sounds like drum rolls introduced fanfares of high notes, followed by flourishes up and down the scale. It was breathtaking, and too soon it was over.

For some seconds there was silence.

Then, at the conductor's clack, the one hundred crayfish reared upright, turned and bowed to the audience. The conductor raised his arms in thanks to his players, then did an about face and he too bowed to his audience. Squeally, Peggy, and everyone else jumped up and applauded loudly, shouting Bravo! Hurrah! Well done! The applause went on for perhaps a minute or two. Then the conductor came down from the platform, and the front rank formed behind him. They began moving slowly back toward the pool as the other ranks fell in to their rear, the mass making the same gentle swishing sound as before. The audience remained standing and clapping and calling out their appreciation. As each crayfish rank reached the edge of the pool they simultaneously raised their right claw in acknowledgement of an appreciative audience and quietly went back into the water. Soon all were submerged, and Peggy saw once again what appeared to be closely packed white stones lining the bottom of the pool.

"Wow" Peggy gushed to Squeally, that was beautiful, so magnificent-----

"I know," said Squeally. "I've seen it a few times, and each time the music is wonderful."

Some of the kids in their group excitedly agreed. They especially liked the heroic last number, saying it made them feel proud, just as if the crayfish orchestra was their very own hometown performing group. One of the kids from Watersville joked that they should try to hire the conductor for their school band and get rid of Old Lady Waggles, the band director who had been there so long their grandparents had been in her band.

Seventeen

GLOW-WORM GALA

Before they knew it they were on the path leading to the glow-worm show. Squeally said, "This is quite a hike. We have to go almost to one of the exits from In. The glow-worms feed on flying insects, and we don't have any of those in the totally dark countryside we're now in, the troglobite region of absolute darkness. That's the only problem. The glow-worms instead are in a troglophile area where it's still quite dark, but not totally. We'll just have to put up with it. I like total darkness, don't you?"

Squeally abruptly stopped talking, and said, "Sorry. I know you like light although I have to admit I don't know why."

"No problem," replied Peggy. "Dark is okay. I've liked just about everything here--except -----

"Except Skelton," one of the boys laughed, mimicking the old hag, "Oh, my Skelton, my pretty boy. My precious, beautiful boy." Everybody laughed. The fun they were having in Wiggly World made Skelton and the hag old news, and somebody broke into song,

Now we're here in Wiggly World,
A wonderful place to be,
Rides and shows, as everyone knows,
A treat for you and me.

All joined in, adding funny verses as they skipped along.

In a while the path curved, and Peggy saw very faint light on the cave wall ahead, so faint she was unsure if that was what she was seeing. Also, she felt a slight breeze and realized it was the first one in what so far had been the completely still atmosphere of In.

"Are we still in Wiggly World?" she asked Squeally.

"Yes, this part of it is quite close to Out. That's why there's a breeze."

As they rounded the next corner, they came to two small children in the path, each dressed in a glow-worm costume.

"Hi, I'm Glover Glow-worm," said the boy. "And I'm Gloria Glow-worm," the smaller of the two piped up. In unison they chimed, "We're here to welcome you to Glow-worm Gala, a wonderful experience you will always cherish."

The costumes were those of glow-worm larvae, similar to what butterflies look like in their caterpillar stage. The costume legs were black with light spots, and this theme went all the way up the bodies to the necks. Covering the children's heads except for their faces were hoods in the same pattern of black with spots, and on the top of each hood were two short antennas.

"Oh, you are so cute," Squeally said.

"Thank you," said Gloria, and with that, the two children in unison spun around so that their backsides were facing the group of boys and girls, and instantly their rear ends lit up, Gloria's with what appeared to be a bluish-white light, and Glover's with a greenish-blue light. At that, Peggy's group gasped and applauded.

The two little glow-worms turned back around to face them, and Glover explained, "In reality glow-worm lights are to attract prey, but we won't hurt anyone." "No," Gloria added, "We like you. Just follow our lights to Glow-worm Gala!"

And with that, Squeally and Peggy and the rest of their group followed, singing goofy lyrics to the Wiggly World song, laughing and poking one another in fun. A boy from Watersville and a girl from Squiresville were shyly holding hands--actually, just holding fingers at this point--and another boy and girl were playfully nudging one another.

Soon the group went through a fissure and beyond it was a wide, almost still, stream. The darkness was not total, so Peggy slid her glasses up onto the top of her head and discovered she could see almost as well without them.

"Can you see okay?" she asked Squeally.

"Sure. it's fairly dark here. And the glow-worm lights are not so bright as to bother me. It's only that horrible sunlight and moonlight of Out that is so frightening."

That statement brought Peggy back to the realization that this was all a hallucination, and she would come out of it and wonder what had caused it. This was much more complex and confusing than any dream she could remember.

Suddenly there was a burst of several bluish-white and greenish-blue lights at the edge of the stream. Dancers in glow-worm costumes who were larger than Glover and Gloria, probably teen-agers, moved in a line, then a colorful circle. As their dim lights flashed out onto the stream, Peggy could see several small boats lined up at a dock. The dancers stopped dancing and circling, moved to face Peggy's group and broke into song

Glow little glow-worm, glow and glimmer
Swim through the sea of night, little swimmer
Lead us lest too far we wander
Love's sweet voice is callin' yonder
Shine little glow-worm, glimmer, glimmer

Hey, there don't get dimmer, dimmer
Light the path below, above
And lead us on to love.

Squeally said, "Wonderful!" to which Peggy replied, "Yes, very sweet but the words are jumbled. When I was a Brownie we sang it lots of times as we watched fireflies, and the words were different. I have the Mills Brothers CD."

Squeally had no idea what that meant. A hand-holding couple in front of them nudged one another and giggled at "Lead us on to love" as the glow-worms sang on, ending with,

This night could use a little brightnin'
Light up you little ol' bug of lightnin'
When you gotta glow, you gotta glow
Glow little glow-worm, glow.

Everybody clapped, and then the head glow-worm said, "Now you may enter the boats for your gala journey, four to a boat." The other glow-worm performers moved ahead to act as guide and helmsman, one per boat.

Peggy, Squeally, and the two kids holding hands were greeted by a costumed glow-worm at the rudder for their boat, the first in the line of boats. "Welcome aboard. The stream is very slow and shallow, so there's no danger." She asked each one's name and said, "I'm Glenda Glow-worm. You're in for a treat. As we drift along you can ask me any questions." The stream was indeed slow, and no paddling was needed, just Glenda's gentle hand at the rudder to steer around the several curves where overhead stalactites, draperies, and soda straws hung down, and on the surface, stalagmites poked upward. With her glasses on top of her head, Peggy could only vaguely appreciate the scenery. That is until they turned a bend and overhead was an awe-some display.

"Ooohh-----" the travelers breathed out. It was as if they suddenly had sat down in a vast open meadow with a clear sky filled with what looked like a galaxy far overhead, so densely packed with light that much of it looked like a Milky Way, a bluish-white glowing expanse of heavenly objects so close to one another that the eye could not distinguish individual stars until at the edges a few appeared, and then more and more farther out. At what seemed to be a far-distant horizon another mass of greenish-blue light, somewhat brighter, reflected from the calm surface of the stream.

"Fantastic," Peggy said, and struggled for other terms that would do the scene justice. Squeally was pointing out patterns that particularly pleased her. The two kids behind them were so quiet Peggy turned to see if perhaps they were transfixed by the splendor. Instead, the girl had her head on his shoulder and was looking up into his face. Peggy whispered, jokingly, to Squeally, "I guess they must have been here before and seen all this." Replied Squeally, "Yeah, right."

As they floated under the magnificent canopy, Peggy asked, "Why are the colors different?"

Glenda responded, "We're not entirely sure. One of the theories is that because there are different kinds of glow-worms, one type prefers one location in the cave, and the other likes another. Another guess is that the cave wall has certain minerals in it that reflect a light of different hue."

"Those glow-worms are so high overhead, I wish I could see some close up," Peggy said to Squeally.

"Don't worry," was the reply, "we'll see some later." In the meantime, they drifted and watched as the scene overhead slowly changed. As they went around a bend, far ahead was another kind of scene, this time not on the cave ceiling but just above the water level. Instead of a mass of light that looked like a galaxy, there appeared to be bluish-white, fuzzy spheres rising from the ground, as if a strong wind were blowing them sidewise as they rose. Interspersed were horizontal bands of gray-purple ledges. The combination of colors and lines was beautiful.

Squeally watched for a time, then impishly glanced over her shoulder, turned to the couple behind them and said, "Do you see that?"

"What?" said the boy, pulling away from the girl's lips he had been about to kiss.

"Oh, never mind," Squeally said, turning back to the front, elbowing Peggy and grinning.

"Thanks a heap!" said the boy.

The next light show was different. High on the ceiling the lights appeared to be patches of clouds, and the girls tried to find objects in them. "There's a dog, like Mugs," Squeally exclaimed. "Do you see it?"

Peggy followed the pointing of Squeally's finger, and said, "It's more like a zebra."

"A what?"

"That's like a gray horse only with black stripes-----oops, horse, I know, I'll explain later. But see, I found a P. See?" She pointed. "For Peggy!"

"Yes. Now let's see if we can find an S for me." Momentarily Squeally said, "There it is. See it?"

What Peggy saw when she followed the point looked more like just a blob, but said, "Sure, there it is!"

"Okay, Peggy, just around the next bend you're going to be able to see glow-worms close up."

The ceiling of the cave slanted down, closer now to the water surface. What they saw overhead looked like thousands of glow-worms hanging down, very near one another. They seemed to be glowing strings of bluish-white beads.

"How beautiful," Peggy said. "I'd love to have one around my wrist as a bracelet, or wear one as a necklace."

Up to this point Glenda had been mostly quiet, letting her charges absorb the beauty as they encountered it, personal treasures to be individually cherished. But now she spoke up. "Peggy, glow-worms are surely beautiful, but you would find them sticky and messy if you tried to wear them. You'll see very shortly what I mean."

"Yeah," agreed Squeally. You'll see!"

They rounded another bend, and ahead of them was a long flow-stone shelf jutting out from the wall of the cave a little above head level of people seated in boats. The sight was spectacular--thousands of glow-worms attached to the underside of the shelf, all of them having dropped "fishing lines" which were the glowing "strings of beads" which Peggy had wanted to wear around her wrist and neck. The current was so slow here that it took some time for Glenda to maneuver their boat up so close that the glow-worms were only a few feet from Peggy's face.

"This is gorgeous," she said.

"Yes," Squeally agreed, "but watch." Just then one of the strings of beads in front of Peggy's eyes shook violently, and Peggy saw that a flying bug of some kind had gotten stuck in the glue-like string, and its wings were fluttering frantically to get loose.

Glenda spoke. "Flying insects are attracted by the glow-worm lights, and instead of finding food they become food." Peggy stared as the glow-worm slowly reeled up its catch to be eaten. Then she noticed that several other "fishing lines" were shaking. The long line of glow-worms was in motion which, from a distance was no doubt beautiful, but close up was not so nice. Glenda must have seen Peggy's expression because now their boat was slowly moving back out into the water, and the farther away they got, the prettier the scene became--glittering, shimmering lights.

Glenda explained that it was part of the cycle of life in a cave, necessary for existence.

As they came around the next curve, Peggy was glad to see that the cave ceiling was once again quite high overhead, and the masses of glow-worms were looking like a faraway Milky Way, glittering in a clear night. From somewhere to the rear in the line of boats came a song

> Glow little glow-worm, glow and glimmer
> Swim through the sea of night, little swimmer
> Lead us lest too far we wander
> Love's sweet voice is callin' yonder
> Shine little glow-worm, glimmer, glimmer
> Hey, there don't get dimmer, dimmer
> Light the path below, above
> And lead us on to love.

Enjoying once again the scene of the distant glow-worms overhead, Peggy turned and saw that the boy behind her was finally getting his kiss.

Eighteen

EXPLAINING DISNEY WORLD

On the trip back to Squiresville aboard Cephus Centipede the kids were singing the Wiggly World song again, and Peggy sang along with them. Peggy noticed Wallis singing, and Wallis smiled at Peggy, and Peggy smiled back.

After a lot of singing, a long rocky ride aboard Cephus, and some hand-holding and nudges and jokes, it was Squeally who said, "Peggy, you spoke of Disney World."

One of the boys said, "Yeah, what's this about Disney World? In is vast--most of In has never even been explored according to reports, but you'd think we would have at least heard of Disney World--if there is such a thing."

"Oh, there is," Peggy assured the group.

"Is it as nice and as much fun as Wiggly World?" asked one of the girls.

"Well-----it's different, but fun."

"Does it have a Crayfish Concert or a Glow-worm Gala?"

"No," Peggy smiled, "not really."

"Well, what does it have?"

"Lots of things. For instance, the Haunted Mansion. This is a spooky, scary ride in a gloomy Doom Buggy, and on the way you see scary things like ghosts and ghouls and-----

"Whoa. What in the world are ghosts and ghouls?"

"Well-----ghosts, they're--they're souls of dead people who come to scare you in the dark--they-----

"You mean they're dead and they walk around?

"Well-----sort of, they-----

"Come on, Peggy," a boy said sarcastically, "this is some kind of fantasy."

"Yes! Just like the one I'm having now!" Peggy huffed.

The kids laughed without understanding a bit of what she meant.

"C'mon, what else does this Disney World have besides ghosts?"

"Well, there's Splash Mountain. It's-----

"What's a mountain?"

"A mountain?-----It's-----it's kind of like a huge stalagmite, and you ride down a water chute and go real fast."

Squeally added, "I bet it's something like riding a blind cave fish downriver, getting splashed and all wet."

"You're right, Squeally," confirmed Peggy.

"What's the most exciting thing about Disney World?" Wallis asked.

"Well, I guess that might be Space Mountain, it's -----

"Here we go up another giant stalagmite," a boy interrupted as Cephus made a hump, and several kids laughed until Wallis said, "Hush, Squash Face!" which got another round of laughs.

"Go ahead, Peggy, tell us about Space Mountain, and don't anyone interrupt. Save your questions until she's done."

"Thanks, Wallis," Peggy said. "Space Mountain is like a ride through space. First you see out into space where you see stars, comets, and a space station. It's a little like looking up during Glow-worm Gala where you see glow-worm lights looking like the heavens-----Uh, the heavens are like the ceiling of a very tall cave. Then you get into something like a spaceship--whoops-- a spaceship is like a-----a long, thin clamshell--and you get buckled in so you don't fall out because the ride is going to be very fast and it takes sharp curves and you get terrified but thrilled at the same time. Then the spaceship you are in gets pulled up high, then levels off, and lights flash slowly at first-----

"Lights! one of the kids said. Are they brighter than glow-worm lights?"

"Well, yes."

"That's abominable, atrocious!"

Nonplussed, Peggy continued, "Then as you go down through a tunnel the lights flash faster and faster, and then you see lots of stars, and you race through lots of turns and sharp climbs and steep drops and all this time you and everybody else is screaming at the tops of your lungs until finally you go through a swirling red tunnel and come to a stop. Even though you've been terrified, you want to do it again-----or at least you say you do."

"Wow!" some of the kids said. One of them offered, "It sounds great. I don't really know what you mean by space, but that ride puts the fastest cave fish trip downriver to shame, even when you launch off Big Falls and splash down into the river below. But thanks, Peggy. You must like that Space Mountain ride a lot."

"I haven't gone on it," she replied ruefully.

"What? Then how do you know what it's like?"

"Well-----I may have gotten some of it wrong, but kids have told me about it, and I've looked it up on Internet."

Before she even got the word out, she knew what was coming.

Sure enough, "Internet?" a couple kids asked.

"It's too complicated. Maybe I'll tell you in my next hallucination."

"Your next what?"

"Squeally," a girl leaned over and whispered, "does she always talk like this?"

"Only sometimes. If she has enough time she can usually make you understand."

That line of curiosity was cut off when a girl asked which Peggy preferred, Disney World or

Wiggly World.

"Well, they are so different--one has bright lights and loud music and fast rides and lots of things to eat, and the other has-----well, they are different."

Some more singing and more rolling up and down on the back of Cephus brought them to the fork in the road with the sign, Watersville 5,133 SL, and at Wallis's clucks, Cephus stopped. A millipede with many rows of seats on his back was waiting.

"Hi Milfred," Wallis called out cheerfully.

She turned and said to Squeally and Peggy, "Well, this is where we get off." With that, the boys and girls from Watersville climbed down. Peggy climbed down with them.

"Peggy," Squeally said. "We don't get off here. We go on to Squiresville."

"I know."

Peggy walked over toward Wallis, who in turn was walking toward her. They met and wrapped their arms around one another.

"Wow, you can sure throw a wicked cave pearl," Wallis said.

"And you throw an awesome hitball," Peggy replied as both smiled and hugged.

"Goodbye, Peggy. Have a good ride home."

"Sure, and goodbye. I hope we can see one another again--soon."

A final hug and the two girls parted.

Nineteen

PEGGY LEARNS MORE ABOUT IN

B ack home in Scenic Heights, Squeally and Peggy had much to relate about the adventures of the day. At dinner Peggy was so busy
explaining what happened that she could not even remember what she
had been told they were eating, which, come to think of it, was probably
just as well. At one point Squeally proclaimed excitedly that yes, Peggy
had indeed beaned the monster. At that, what might be taken as a smile
came from Great Great Grandfather. Peggy watched the corners of his
lips rise slightly, hoping that his face didn't crack and splinter.

As Mrs. Squires cleaned up the kitchen and put Squishy to bed, and
Mr. Squires set about one of his repair tasks, the ancient man and the
others were seated in the living room, listening as Peggy asked questions.
She did not understand many things about In, and in fact wondered if
she understood anything at all.

"For one thing," Peggy asked, "how do you get to be a million and
more years old?"

"Simple," said Squatty, the scientist in the family.

"Oh, yeah, simple to him," Squeally needled. "He thinks he knows
everything."

"Well, if you would go to science meetings or maybe even just try listening to your teachers in class now and then instead of giggling and poking the boys you might learn something too. You and Crazy Cronus." He was a kid in Squatty's class whose only apparent interest in life was to dress up in kid-size Squat Squad fatigues and dream of the day he could join the force.

Squiggly, in a rare defense of their older brother said, "He does know a lot, doesn't he, Great Great Grandfather?"

The ancient man nodded almost imperceptibly, but enough that Peggy thought he might crack his neck and have his head roll off.

Squatty, ignoring Squeally, launched into a lecture about the Ages, on how life on Earth began--about three and a half billion years earlier. "In fact, in In, inside the earth, the earliest life appeared as single cells of matter, earlier than in Out," Squatty said. "Why was that?" Squatty asked, then answered his own question. "Well, in the beginning, the surface of Earth was being bombarded by meteors and other bits of matter, and volcanoes were spewing out lava and toxic fumes, making life on the surface impossible. However-----(and here came the dramatic utterance) --" it was *safe* inside Earth -----"

"Conjecture." interrupted the ancient man. "Possible, maybe even probable, but not certain." His words came in crisp clicks as if he had a block of marble in front of him and he was the sculptor, chipping away pieces in his slow but focused attempt to unveil a Truth within.

"Yes, I was just going to say that, Great Great Grandfather."

"Oh sure!" retorted Squeally.

Squatty ignored her and continued his lecture, looking at Peggy, "Homo Sapiens--your 'Wise Man'--huh, 'Wise Man' indeed!" Squatty snorted. "He came only about two hundred thousand years or so ago. Did you know that, Peggy?"

"Well--uhh--of course. Sort of."

"And by that time, Great Great Grandfather had already been living almost forty million years. Just goes to show how much better In is than Out."

"Stick to the science," chastised the old man.

"Yeah, stick to the science," echoed Squeally, earning a frown from her great great grandfather and a dirty look from Squatty.

"But how can you people be so old, millions of years?" Peggy asked.

"Because In is a much better place than Out."

"Stick to the science!" the old man said.

"Uh, yes Sir. The production of life requires energy, and in In, sources of energy are deficient, and it must be used carefully, and life forms take a long time to develop, but once they do, they use energy very efficiently-----"

Peggy interrupted, "And that's why you people live longer?"

"Well, sort of."

Great Great Grandfather said, "Sort of ? That is not a scientific explanation."

"Well, I'm still investigating, and-----" Squatty trailed off.

Peggy asked, "And why is it that in one family, skin colors and facial features are so very different? You mother is very dark-skinned, your father Latino, Squeally and Squiggly extremely light-skinned, and you are quite Asian-looking."

Squatty, not understanding most of what she said, especially 'Latino' and 'Asian', replied confidently so as not to betray his lack of insight into these complex matters, "Simple," then lapsed into a convoluted explanation about factors of reproduction, time, and distance that left more questions than it answered. He was saying, "You see, in In we have billions of caves reaching out in all directions, most of them unexplored."

"Not simple," the old man corrected. And it is probably trillions of caves, not billions."

"Yes, trillions," Squatty said. "And they reach out so extensively, and into so many areas of In with so many different environments that with intermarriage people are born with different skin colors and features. The theory is that these get passed along so that when women give birth they never know what kind of baby they will have. And this trait goes down to future generations.

Squatty now lapsed into being a humanist, which indeed he was, in a way. "And what difference does it make? A baby is a baby, and after several million years babies grow up to be men and women, and what difference does it make? None, so far as I can see."

Peggy may not have understand much of what had been said, but she kind of agreed. "And why do all of you wear such old-fashioned clothes? Hasn't one of the Chosen Ones brought back from Out some more modern ideas?"

From Great Great Grandfather came the utterance, "Like war? Not actually modern, but much more deadly."

Squatty tried to explain, but that left Peggy shaking her head.

"Whew," said Peggy. "I'm immensely confused about lots of things, but especially one thing bothers me--the size of caves here in In. When I was in Out, I only saw a small hole with a little water coming out of it, but when I was sucked into In with Squeally, suddenly I was in a huge cave next to a river and-----

"It's all relative," interrupted Squeally.

"She's right, for once," added Squatty in a sarcastic tone which prompted a slowly-developing, ever-so-slow but lasting scowl from his great great grandfather.

Squatty explained, "Our Science Committee has a much different interpretation of 'cave' from what you people from Out have. To us, a cave is actually much smaller than a cave in your terms. Big ones grow from little ones, sometimes because of water flow, sometimes from earth tremors, things like that. Then there are huge ones, many times bigger."

Peggy thought of the hole in the side of the hill which she had entered, only to find it a large cavern when she was inside. "Then I'm-----I'm tiny right now-----ohhh."

"Don't worry. I said that everything is relative. You look okay to me."

"Yes, but-----oh-----my head is swirling-----ohhhh."

Peggy knew that this whole thing was an illusion, and in a few seconds she would wake up and -----

Twenty

GOING HOME

When she did awake she was in bed in Squeally's room, and she was wearing a funny old-fashioned nightgown. Her head was foggy and she could only vaguely remember the night before: Mrs. Squires' long hug, then climbing the stairs, getting into bed, putting her pearl beside her, and saying good night to Squeally. So much had happened, and she had been tired. Very tired.

She dressed, put her pearl in her pocket and, somewhat refreshed, she went down, found them all at breakfast and joined them. There was a lot of chatter, questions and replies, but she could remember very little of it, or what she ate. When all were finished it was time to say goodbye.

She stood and Mugs was against her legs, rubbing up tightly to them. Suddenly Peggy was buried in Mrs. Squires' hug.

"Oh Peggy you darling darling girl oh S.Q she is such a sweetheart isn't she I just wish-----" She slowly released Peggy then pulled her back for another hug, let her go again and dabbed her eyes with her handkerchief. S.Q. put his arms around Peggy, kissed her cheek and passed her to Great Great Grandfather. His lips on her cheek felt cold and cracked, and Peggy saw a tear in the corner of his eye. She patted his shoulder, tenderly, both in affection and so as not to shatter him. Then it was Squatty who reached out his hand and told her to come back. He had more to tell her.

Squiggly said, "Peggy, it has been wonderful of you to visit us. Please tell your grandfather I miss him and want him to come back soon. And tell him I'm taking good care of Mugs." He choked and had to turn his head away.

When Mugs heard his name he reached his front paws up to Peggy's waist and looked up lovingly at her. She bent and kissed his cute little squinched-in face, and again, one more time. It was a puzzle. Indeed her grandfather had been here before her.

Wow!

Finally she and Squeally went to the door. She gave a sorrowful little wave back at everyone as she and Squeally went outside, and she heard Mugs' forlorn whine as the door closed.

In a kind of trance she climbed aboard Koloa, the faithful old blind wolf spider, and Squeally clambered up beside her. At the clucks, Koloa moved and in not many swaying steps downhill left Scenic Heights and the Squires home behind.

Peggy was not much aware of what they passed on the slow, rocking ride down. Squeally pointed out some pretty draperies and stalactites in the rear yards of Middle Manors, and Peggy could only nod. Then they were in Low Meadows, and Squeally was still pointing out the sights, trying to get a response, but Peggy didn't feel like talking. Koloa ambled along the plateau and then began the steep descent to the river. Soon Squeally clucked, and Koloa slowed.

"Peggy, you'd like to see the pool again where you got the pearl, wouldn't you?"

Peggy said nothing, then quietly, "No, I don't think so. No thanks." She reached into her pocket and rubbed her pearl. The first time at the pool had been perfect. So perfect she did not want to spoil it with a second visit which could never be as good as the first.

"Okay." Squeally clucked and began to hum self-consciously.

Angie, the blind salamander was waiting at the dock. They got down from Koloa, and Peggy patted his side and said quietly, "Thank you, Koloa. You are such a good old boy." Squeally clucked, and Koloa turned, and Peggy thought his face was sad. She raised her hand in a little wave, and she hoped that even though he couldn't see it, he would sense it. Then he started slowly back up the hill, head down as if sad.

Angie lowered so they could climb aboard. At Squeally's cluck, she started swimming across the still lake. Squeally was humming some strange tune and pointing out things to notice as they moved. Peggy looked and replied now and then, "mm hmm" but nothing much registered.

After quite a long time, Squeally asked, "Do you want to visit The Grotto?"

Peggy said nothing, then finally replied, "Yes."

Squeally clucked Angie through the entrance. The view for Peggy this time was different. Through her moonglasses she could see that the magical stalagmites and stalactites were still there, but they seemed more somber, as if they were saying a mournful goodbye. The stillness in the cavern was the same, and the little waves from Angie tinkled against the stalagmites, and Peggy again could feel the melancholy-----this time, though, a different kind of melancholy.

They came to the same place where they had stopped before, and Peggy asked, "Could we get out?"

"Certainly." Squeally clucked.

From the flat expanse of flowstone Peggy surveyed what seemed like an enchanted room of the stone castle she had seen earlier. She looked again at the waved draperies and the white and silver stone flowers that grew out of cracks in the rocks.

On her first trip into The Grotto, she had wanted to absorb all the beauty by herself.

Alone.

She had wanted to cry.

Alone.

She had renamed this place The Grotto of Tears.

But this time she wanted company, and she slipped her hand into Squeally's. They sat down on the same flowstone shelf where Squeally had said, "You don't have any friends, do you."

This time was different. Much different. Peggy said, "You are my friend, aren't you?"

"Of course. You know I am. I'm your forever friend."

Peggy squeezed Squeally's hand and sat quietly, letting it all sink in, this magical place, this great friend.

They just sat for several minutes. Then, "You're wonderful," Peggy said, and felt a flow of goodness, of total happiness inside her.

They sat for a long time, hand in hand, Peggy feeling the magic of the cave, and of her friend.

After awhile, Peggy sprang up and said, "Let's go. I want to remember this always, just like this."

Atop Angie again, they moved toward the grotto exit in silence, and Peggy turned, got one last look, and they were out once more into the lake where she burst into song

We went off to Wiggly World
A wonderful world to see,
Rides and shows, as everyone knows,
A treat for you and me

Squeally added a funny verse, and they both sang several more goofy ones until Peggy sang out

Glow little glow-worm, glow and glimmer
Swim through the sea of night, little swimmer

They finished that verse and followed with several silly made-up ones, and ended at the top of their lungs with

Glow little glow-worm, glow
Glow little glow-worm, glo ohh ohh ohh!

Big Falls was just ahead, and Angie gave them a ride over, and beyond it, fully as thrilling as the first one when they had come upriver. Beyond the falls, Rhapsody, the blind cave cricket, was waiting. They climbed up and she did her thing, carrying them in terrifying leaps and landing finally in the twilight zone near the exit of the cavern. They were within walking distance of Out.

No more happy singing now. Squeally said, haltingly, "You won't need your moonglasses anymore." Peggy took them off, handed them to Squeally, blinked her eyes, and found she could vaguely see the closest objects in this twilight. The girls thanked Rhapsody and bade her goodbye. She took off in a giant leap back toward the dark zone.

The two girls walked slowly along the river, talking softly about some of the things they had done, trying not to think of what was ahead. Around the next bend, Peggy could see much better, and the moonglasses on Squeally's face had darkened to the point of being almost sunglasses again. Soon, too soon, they were almost at the cave exit. The river made such a loud rushing noise the girls had to raise their voices in order to be heard.

They stopped, and Squeally said, quietly, "Peggy, I guess this is it." Squeally was having a hard time but managed to say, "Go straight ahead and be sure to be outside the cave. When you are outside, say 'Form.'"

"Yes. I will." Peggy put her arms around her friend, and they hugged and tears came. "Goodbye."

As Peggy walked toward the cave opening, Squeally called, "Please come back."

Peggy blubbered out, "I'll try."

Several steps, bright sunlight, and now the cave was at her rear. Peggy said, "Form."

She felt funny. She was dizzy. Her thoughts were all mixed up. She looked down to see a trickle of water by her foot, the big rock nearby, and, misted by her tears, she saw her grandfather's house through the trees.

༄༅༷༅༄

"Peggy," her mother was calling, "would you come in and help me with the dishes?"

For a moment she could say nothing, then raised her arm and wiped the back of her hand across her eyes.

"Yes Mom," she called back.

She entered the house with her hand in her pocket hiding the pearl, and she skirted around the back of her mother who was bending over the sink.

"Did you have a nice walk?"

"Not bad," she answered, hurried up to the bedroom, put the pearl in her dresser drawer under some clothes, and came back down to wipe the pots and pans. First, though, she gave her mother a big hug and said, "I love you."

"And I love you too, honey." Her mother turned her head, soapy hands still in the sink, and gave Peggy a kiss. "Grandpa and Grandma are driving back. Be nice to Grandpa. He gets very tired when he goes to counseling."

Peggy smiled and said, "I will."

Twenty-One

ANOTHER JOYOUS REUNION

Near suppertime, when she heard the car come up the driveway Peggy hurried out to greet them. Her grandfather looked tired, somewhat stooped, but he waved and smiled.

"Grandpa!" Peggy gushed, rushed over and put her arms around him.

"Well!" Henry replied. "What a nice homecoming," and he softly took her head in both hands and kissed her and hugged her.

Melanie, her mother, and Laurel, her grandmother, exchanged looks of surprise.

"Come on in and I'll get some cold soft drinks. You both look as if you could use them," Melanie said and hugged her parents.

Despite being tired, her grandfather seemed stronger and more-- 'normal'--was the only word Peggy could think of. During supper he said some nice things about Doctor Shepherd but didn't go into detail on his counseling. Afterward, while the ladies were doing dishes, her grandfather suggested they take a little walk. Peggy first went upstairs, got the pearl, put it in her pocket with her hand over it so her mother and grandmother wouldn't ask about the bulge. She and her grandfather went out the back door onto the deck. Dusk was coming on.

"Where would you like to go?" he asked.

Peggy pointed at the hill which began to rise only a few yards away.

They walked without talking, Peggy slowing her steps as her grandfather began breathing heavily, making his way uphill into the woods.

"Gosh, I'm out of shape," he said. "Got to do something about that."

"We can go slower."

"Thanks, I'll make it."

They came to the big rock. Peggy had been bursting with the need to tell him, and as soon as they sat down on the rock she pulled out the pearl, and put it in his hand.

It took a moment for him to realize what he was looking at, and another to grasp the significance.

There was only one place she could have gotten it.

"Peggy!" he burst out.

She had been thinking for hours how she could tell him, and what she could say.

"Grandpa." She snuggled against him. She had rehearsed her first words over and over and now she forgot. "I-----

When she could not speak he said, in amazement, "You were there."

After a moment of baffled silence, he said again, "You were *there*." He put his arm around her, pulled her to him, and kissed the top of her head. "Actually there."

"Yes."

For what seemed a long time, neither one could talk, and then Henry asked, "Did you see him?"

"Mugs? Yes, and Squiggly."

"Oh!" Henry was trying to contain himself. "And-----and they're okay?"

"Yes, they're wonderful. Mugs looks and acts so much younger. He bounces around and jumps and smothered me with kisses."

"Oh, thank God. And my little friend Squiggly?"

"He's fine, too."

"Listen to us," Henry said. "We're talking as if all this happened. People would think we we're loony. And, you know-----

"What?"

"I-----I was almost losing faith. I almost told Dr. Shepherd that I was having hallucinations. I wondered if all that was possible. But then I thought, I didn' t have Mugs anymore. Then I wondered-----could he have just wandered off into the woods and died. But he wouldn't have wandered off from me. He was always with me, and I didn't say anything about it to Dr. Shepherd, and we had a good session. He felt I had improved. He-----

"Grandpa, you *have* improved, you-----

"I sure hope so, and here is the pearl. Huge. I didn't see any this big, by far." He turned it around and around in his hands. "Tell me about your trip. Did Squiggly come and get you?"

"No, Squeally. I thought I might be going nuts, and you'd have to take me to Dr. Shepherd's with you, and-----

Henry laughed. "He would have had his hands full, wouldn't he-- two loonies who unformed, and went up a river in a cave almost in our back yard, and-----

Peggy giggled, "But here's the pearl to prove it. Oh, Grandpa, we know but we can't tell anyone, maybe not even Mom and Grandma or they'll pack us off somewhere."

"Especially not your mom and your grandma," Henry laughed.

"Yeah, they'll know then that I for sure caught PTSD from you."

They laughed and squeezed one another.

"Tell me what you did," Henry said.

This set off a string of stories among them, about exciting trips up-river, and beautiful cave formations, and bonking a pseudoscorpion on the head, and-----

"You mean you hit him with this pearl?"

"Yeah, right square on his noggin."

Henry laughed and came back with, "We also had a scare with a whole herd of pseudoscorpions, and Mugs saved Squiggly and me and-----

This went on for awhile, Peggy telling him what a great friend Squeally was, and Henry saying that Squiggly was special. After awhile they just sat, quietly, thinking, as night came on. Every now and then, one or the other would say some more about their adventures in In. But most of it could never be told, not even to one another. There are some things a person wants only to cherish and not even try to tell.

Finally, "It's quite dark. We need some moonglasses," Henry said. "Time to go home."

He hugged her, bent and kissed her cheek.

"Grandpa, what can I do with the pearl? We don't want Mom and Grandma to see it. How could I possibly explain it?"

Her grandfather put his hand on his chin, thought, and said, "Why don't we put it here by the hole and cover it with some leaves and ground mulch? We can look at it whenever we want."

And that's what they did.

She threw her arms around his neck and squeezed and kissed him.

"I love you, Grandpa."

"And I love you, Peggy."

They climbed down off the rock, and the little stream made gurgling sounds as it trickled out of the hole. Behind them was In. They were in Out. The house now had lights on, and they walked toward it.

Part 3

HENRY, PEGGY, SQUIGGLY, AND

SQEALLY: A DOG SHOW?

One

FRIENDS FROM IN

The summer had been enjoyable for Peggy. She was having fun with girls she increasingly could call her friends. One of them told her she wasn't so bossy anymore. Others just liked being with her without thinking why, a change from the past in which she always had to direct everything.

So, it had indeed been an enjoyable summer, that is, until the day her mother Melanie said, "Peggy, I'm sorry to tell you, but I thought you needed to know. Your grandfather has been drinking again."

"Oh no, Mom, no! What happened?"

"Grandma isn't sure, but she thinks she may know what started it. They were watching TV, and a news clip came on that showed soldiers fighting and some were badly wounded, and your grandfather just burst into tears, went out and got into the car and drove to a bar and began drinking."

"Oh, no, no." Peggy's voice trailed off.

For a few weeks, Peggy was subdued and not having as much fun with her friends, but then came better news. Her grandfather Henry had gone back to see Dr. Shepherd at VA and seemed to have stopped drinking.

But this was an all-too-familiar PTSD pattern for him, and Peggy did not have much hope. Her grandmother, though, had not given up on him, as she had done before, and her news was increasingly optimistic. One day she invited them to come for the weekend.

School had been in session for three weeks, and the leaves were changing, the air crisp. The drive to the country was beautiful, and Peggy's anxiety ebbed. When she stepped out of the car at her grandparents' house in the clearing in the woods, she breathed in that wonderful fall aroma of sunshine, woods, and new-fallen leaves, and she was happy. Even anxious to see him.

Her grandfather came around the corner of the house on his lawnmower. He waved, quickly stopped the machine, and hurried to greet them. In a moment he was hugging and kissing her, and she was saying to herself that she wanted him to be well.

The afternoon was wonderful. Her grandfather had a familiar treat--a ride in his boat that he rowed around the small lake across the road from their house. It was like old times beginning when she was only a baby and did not remember, but she recalled well those lake outings when she was probably four or five years old, and the several since then. Today was much the same, her grandmother and mother sitting on the rear seat, she on the front seat looking down into the dark brown northlands water, and her grandfather in the middle, rowing. They first heard faint honking, and he stopped rowing. He was listening and looking over their house and the wooded hill beyond. The noise got increasingly louder as the flight of Canada Geese came into sight above the trees behind their house, the raucous honking mingled now with a whooshing sound as they braked directly over their house, nearing the lake, looking for a landing. But when they discovered the unwelcome boat they made a last-second swerve. As the flight continued off into the distance, the honks seemed to be chastisements, of disappointment at not being able to land.

Grandmother Laurel smiled, saying, "Remember how Mugs would sink in his legs, twist his head and scowl up at the geese?"

"He sure didn't know what to make of them," agreed Henry.

"Sometimes he'd bark back at them, but usually just scowl," Peggy added. "He was so funny."

It was always the same, wonderful early fall days--the same, yes, except in the past few years when her grandfather was drinking so heavily, and their visits to his house got fewer and fewer. A new feeling of dread swept over Peggy. Would he ruin everything today?

"Grandma," Peggy asked, to relieve her tension, "do you remember when I was little and you took me down to the lake just before sunup? The geese on the water were honking like mad, getting ready to leave. And when we scared them by getting too close they all at once exploded up off the water, and I never heard such a racket, the pounding of their wings to take off, and their honking."

"I do indeed remember, honey. There must have been several hundred of them."

"I know. I had lain awake for some time that night, hearing them come in. They just kept coming and coming, flight after flight. I never heard so many overhead. And Mugs had enough of that. I heard him barking at them downstairs."

"Yes, he was funny for sure."

Her grandfather laughed. "He could stand it for just so long, and then he couldn't put up any more with their nuisance. He was something else."

"He was special," Peggy's mother said, sadly, thinking of Henry having to bury him up behind the house in the woods they so much loved. No one wanted to dwell on that, so they went on enjoying their boat ride.

While her mother and grandmother were busy getting supper, Peggy and her grandfather took a walk. They chatted, looked over the fence for Breeze, Mr. Myser's old horse, didn't see him, picked some wild blackberries along the road and ate them, and lazily watched the neighboring farmer's cows. At some point Peggy asked, "How are you feeling, Grandpa?"

"I'm feeling well, especially when you're here."

"And when I'm not here?"

He said nothing at first, then, "I'm doing better than I did a few weeks ago. I'm doing very well. Don't worry, I'm doing well." He knew that she knew, but that was enough said for now.

They walked back toward the house, chatting about her school, her friends, the beautiful colors of the leaves, and then they fell quiet. Henry had been thinking of how to tell her that he was sure, this time, he would be all right. It was hard, but he would be all right. Just yesterday the two farm boys had raced past him at the mailbox, yelling, "Hey Nutsy Fagin, have you gone bonkers yet today?" Henry had just smiled and waved to them, getting a finger in return.

After walking some more, Peggy asked, "Grandpa, have you gone to look at the pearl?"

Her question startled him. "No. It's yours, and if you want to-----"

"But it's kind of yours, too, Grandpa. We share it."

244

And share it they did. How could either of them tell anyone else about it--that she had found the very large, perfectly beautiful cave pearl in the fantastic world of In? How could she tell anyone about Squeally, her friend who had invited her to In? Squeally with the alabaster-like skin and pale grayish eyes?

And how could Henry tell anyone, especially Laurel or Melanie or even Dr. Shepherd, about Squeally's brother, Squiggly, his little friend who lived in In? Who would believe him? Who could ever believe there was such a place as In, and that you could get there by going up the hill into the woods behind the house and finding the small hole where a trickle of water flowed out and ran down the hill? How could you tell anyone that small hole was the entrance to In? How could you say that Squeally and Squiggly called the other world Out--the land where Peggy and Henry lived? Who would suppose that you could go to In just by saying secret words and believing you could do it?

No one would believe it.

But Peggy had brought the pearl out from In early in the summer and Henry had helped her hide it in the woods near the large rock, covering it with dead leaves and ground mulch next to the small hole that led to In.

"Grandpa, let's go see it."

As they walked up the driveway her mother Melanie called from the front deck, "Hey you two explorers, supper will be ready in a little while."

"Okay, Mom. We're just going up into the woods," Peggy answered.

"Well, don't stay long. It's getting dark. I'll call you for supper."

Henry and Peggy went around to the back of the house and started into the woods, trudging uphill. They had the rock in sight. Henry said, puffing, "Whew, I'm out of shape. Have to get in shape."

"That's what you always say, Grandpa. I'll believe it when I see it."

"Oh yeah, little whippersnapper?" he panted. "When I get in shape we'll have a race, and I'll beat you uphill to the rock."

"That'll be the day!"

"What day is that?" a squeaky voice asked.

Startled, Peggy could not miss that high-pitched tone. There could be no other.

"Squeally!" she exploded in astonishment, so loud she hoped her mother was back in the house, which she was.

There stood Squeally in her funny clothes, old-fashioned dress over pantalettes. Behind her was her younger brother, Squiggly, in a similarly old-fashioned frock over trousers. Both wore broad-brimmed hats from which locks of light hair, almost white, stuck out. Their strange-looking clothes covered their light skin, so light it seemed translucent. And protecting their highly unusual eyes were very large, very dark sunglasses.

The greetings gushed out all at once.

"Squeally!" "Peggy!" "Mr. Henry!" "Squiggly!"

It was a mishmash--Squeally's high squeaky voice, Squiggly saying 'simple,' questions, answers, hugs and kisses all around, chatter so mixed it was hard to distinguish who was saying what to whom-----

"I've missed you so much!

"Me too!"

"It's been so long!"

"Forever, how've you been?"

"Great, just great."

Mugs?" Henry asked.

"Wonderful, playing all the time, happy," was Squiggly's reply, which anyone in the real world would not understand because rational people certainly don't believe there can be a world called In and another called Out, and most definitely don't believe that an old, arthritic dog buried in the woods behind a house can be playing all the time. How could anyone understand that?

When the tumult finally settled, Peggy had her hands outstretched, holding Squeally's hands, looking at her, smiling, and Henry had his arm around Squiggly, beaming down on him.

Squiggly turned his face up and said, "Mr. Henry, we want you and Peggy to come back to In. We've got something to show you. It's-----"

"It's about Mugs," Squeally cut in.

"You'll like it," Squiggly assured them. "You'll really like it. There's going to be-----"

"A Dog Show," Squeally butted in. And Squiresville has been named the host village."

"The First Annual Dog Show," said Squiggly proudly.

"What?" responded Henry. "A dog show with one dog?"

"Oh, please come and see. You will be so proud of Mugs."

"Well, that would be nice," said Henry, "but we'll be called for supper in a few minutes, and-----"

"No problem," Squeally piped up. "Don't you remember, time in In is different from your time in Out. Peggy, tell your grandfather you were worried about coming with me to In for three days and your mother would be frantic, but-----"

"Yes, grandpa. You must have had the same experience. You were in In for a couple days, and when you got back to Out you'd only been gone a few seconds."

Henry's head was swimming. "Yes, but--a dog show? I don't know about that."

"Oh, Mr. Henry, you'll have to see it," pleaded Squeally. You will be proud of Mugs."

"Grandpa, let's go, please?" said Peggy, thinking of the fun times.

With Squiggly, Squeally, and Peggy all pleading with him, an incredulous, reluctant Henry thought about it.

What could be more rational than for a person from Out to go to In for a dog show? But a dog show by one dog?

What the heck. The kids on the road knew he was nuts. Nothing to lose.

"Okay. We'll go."

"Yea! Yes!" the kids gleefully called out, causing Henry put his finger to his lips--"Shhh! We have to be quiet."

So they quietly stood by the hole next to the big rock, and Squiggly spoke in a low, confidential voice, "Remember, we'll hold hands, and both of you make a wish to go with us, and-----

"And we have to say 'unform' and-----" Peggy said, well remembering the routine from her previous visit to In. She was cut off by a super-excited Squiggly who continued, "and then you have to add the secret words and believe."

He whispered the words into Henry's ear, just to make sure he hadn't forgotten from his earlier trip, and Squeally did the same to Peggy.

"Ready, Peggy? asked Henry. "Sure!" was her answer.

They did as instructed and the four of them instantly turned into tiny wisps and, as before, were sucked into the small hole where the trickle of water emerged from the hillside.

Two

Journey Up River

"Whew!" said Peggy, trying to clear her head.

"That's for sure," agreed Henry.

They were dizzy and disoriented. Instead of standing next to a trickle of water coming out of a small hole in the woods behind the house, they were standing on the bank of a river in a large cave that turned into a tunnel ahead of them. Even though Henry and Peggy had done this before, it was an experience not easy to get used to, as any reasonable person would have to agree.

"There! We're here," gushed an excited Squiggly.

Henry said, "Boy, that unforming thing is a zinger. I get confused."

"Me too," agreed Peggy.

"Just look behind you," said Squiggly, pointing back over his shoulder but not looking into the bright light of the cave entrance. "That's Out. I still don't quite understand why you like to live in a place with all that terrible sunlight."

"Well, I like it," Peggy retorted. "Besides, out there I'm regular size, and I found out last time I was here in In that I'm tiny."

"True," Squiggly confirmed, "but everything is relative. It all depends on your environment. We're in In now. You look fine to me. Don't I look all right to you?"

Henry said, "You look great, Squiggly. We're glad to be here with you."

Squeally squeaked, "And we're delighted you're here. But let's get going. We have lots and lots to show you."

Henry thought, but did not say out loud, Yeah, a dog show with one dog. At least it would be Mugs. He was super-excited at the thought of being with Mugs again. Before, he had thought this was all a PTSD hallucination. But he knew now that he wasn't imagining it. Only some Nutsy Fagin from Out could doubt it was real.

As they walked upstream on the narrow path along the river the cave became increasingly dark, cooler and very humid. Squeally and Peggy were skipping along ahead of Henry and Squiggly. The girls were giggling, recounting some of the things that had happened on Peggy's earlier trip: "Oh, my Skelton, my dear, dear boy," mimicked Squeally, recalling how Peggy had beaned the monster pseudoscorpion with her big cave pearl, and how the hunched over old hag wearing a scary black outfit had faded off into the mist, cackling, "My sweet dear boy, my dear boy, ohhh." The girls poked one another and laughed.

They turned a bend and Henry and Peggy had to slow down because it was getting even darker ahead. Squiggly and Squeally took off their sunglasses and handed them over.

"There. Now you have moonglasses."

If anybody had asked, "Why are they called moonglasses?" Squiggly would have answered, "Simple! You can see through them somewhat like you'd see on a moonlit night. At least that's what my older brother says. I hate the moon. Well, maybe not hate. It's not as bad as that horrid sun, but it's bad enough."

Henry and Peggy found the name of their glasses as funny this time as they did when they put them on for their first trips in In. During the war, Henry had used starlight scopes which enabled objects to be seen at night, but everything appeared as varying shades of green, from light to medium to dark. The moonglasses did much the same, only the objects appeared in shades of gray. Not great for seeing in the dark, but better than nothing. The path along the river and the walls of the cave and even some of the ceiling were now visible through their moonglasses.

Squiggly said, "Peggy, I told your grandfather on his first trip that moonglass lenses are made from a special crystal that is found in only a few places in In, and so they are scarce and precious. You'll have to ask Squatty about how they work. They're not perfect, but better for you than nothing."

"Be careful what you ask Squatty unless you want a lecture," Squeally warned about their older brother.

"I know" replied Peggy. "The last time I was here he got wound up and although I think I understood some of it-----

"He's a pain," Squeally said.

"No he's not!" objected Squiggly, then qualified his statement, "Well, yes, sometimes, but he really is smart. He's going to be the head of the Science Committee some day."

As they walked farther into the dark, Squeally said, "That's better. I can see much better now."

Peggy shook her head. She would never understand. She could have said she didn't much like the dark but it might have offended Squeally. Thinking about that, Peggy realized how much she had changed. Before, as she had traveled farther into In, she could have cared less about how Squeally felt, but by the end of her trip they had become lifetime friends. And now, that thought amused her. Lifetime? Squeally was about four million years old in In years. But what did that matter? As Squiggly said, everything in In is relative--size, distance, time, everything.

For what seemed like a long time they walked upriver along the path. They reached a spot where Henry said, "We need to be on guard and ready to jump into the water."

"Why?" asked Peggy.

"It's right about here that when Squiggly, Mugs, and I were coming back to Out we got attacked by a bunch of pseudoscorpions, and I would have been poisoned and eaten by one of them if it hadn't been for Mugs. He jumped at the huge thing and startled it, long enough for us to get into the river and swim out of their way. He was a hero that day, and so was Squiggly."

"Not really. It was all due to Mugs," Squiggly objected, "and besides, we don't need to worry now. After I told them about it, the Squatter County Sheriff's Department sent out their Squat Squad to drive the pseudoscorpions back into their nature preserve where they can't hurt anyone, and they have outposted this area with deputies to ensure its safety. I'm surprised we haven't come upon them by now."

The words were barely out of Squiggly's mouth when out of the dark just ahead of them came a sharp command:

"Halt! Who goes there?"

Henry, reacting instantly as a result of his Army days, spouted out, "Friend."

"Advance, Friend, and be recognized."

They advanced and again, "Halt!"

In front of them was a deputy sheriff in uniform. Henry and Peggy could not tell what color uniform she wore because they saw it only in shades of gray, but they remembered what they had been told on their previous trips to In.

Wielding a long police baton across her chest stood the deputy in dark blue trousers, scarlet tunic with white belt around the middle, shoulder straps, and what Henry and Peggy recognized as a big black bearskin fur hat. Squiggly and Squeally had no idea of the hat's material since they had never seen a bear, whatever that was, but they thought nevertheless that the uniform was magnificent. The hat reached up high on the deputy's head but was settled so low on her brow that her eyes were not visible. The deputies basically liked their uniform because it was so spectacular, but the hat was a problem. It was heavy and it slid down over their eyes so they couldn't see, and the fur made them sneeze. The captain of the Squat Squad was not happy with the hat because what good is a deputy who can't see and who sneezes all the time? He wanted to replace it with a fairball cap but for now was overruled by the Superintendent of Law Enforcement. This rotund gentleman loved pomp and circumstance, so to him the uniform was spectacular. He sat in his office and ruled on police matters. These took so much of his time he never visited the field to see what was actually going on.

"Identify yourself!"

Henry, being a former soldier, took over. "We are travelers."

"Ahhh--Chooo! How many?"

"This many." Henry held up four fingers.

Craning her head back, trying to see under the rim of her hat, the

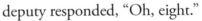

deputy responded, "Oh, eight."

Henry grinned.

"Destination!" she demanded.

"Squiresville," piped up Squiggly proudly. "We're going to see the First Annual Dog Show."

The deputy barked out the challenge: "Glow."

"Uhhh-----" Squiggly could not remember the password.

Squeally shook her head at him and said, "Little glow-worm."

The Cave of Healing

"Pass! Ah--Ahhh---Ahhhh----CHOO!"

As the four travelers hurried on past the deputy and farther into the dark, the two girls struck up the glow-worm song they had heard at Glow-worm Gala when they finally got to Wiggly World. That was after Peggy bopped the monster pseudoscorpion right between its blind eyes with her big cave pearl. The words weren't the same as the ones in the song Peggy had learned at Brownie camp, but they had fun with the tune:

> Glow little glow-worm, glow and glimmer
> Swim through the sea of night, little swimmer

Peggy added a line

> This path is getting dimmer and dimmer

But Squeally squeaked in with

> No it's not, I'm seeing better

Squiggly jumped in with

> You're just girls, and boys are brighter

And Peggy responded

> Watch what you say 'cause I'm a fighter

And Henry, who had put on a little weight, added

> These pants on me are tighter and tighter

They chortled at each new verse they created and sang loudly to be heard over the rushing noise of the river, ending with a raucous

Glow little glow-worm, glow
Glow little glow-worm, glo ohh ohh ohh!

Laughter, jostling, and hugs all around.

By the end of several goofy verses they had walked far upriver. Ahead, a very large fish maybe 20 feet long was waiting against the side of a dock, its tail and fins moving slightly to keep it in position facing into the current. Through moonglasses, the fish seemed to be alabaster white, like Squiggly and Squeally. Its eyes were not eyes at all, just chalky-white mounds, and strapped on its back was a platform with seats. Life vests and helmets hung on a rail.

"Ah, Silver, my good boy," called Squiggly affectionately, and he made strange clucking sounds in a code which children of In learn at a young age. The clucks cause vibrations the cave creatures can sense even when they have no ears. Silver swished his tail as if in delight.

"Silver's a blind waterfall-climbing cave fish," Squiggly reminded Peggy. "We'll show these girls what a fast trip is like, won't we Mr. Henry."

Remembering their swift, harrowing trip aboard Silver on his last visit, Henry affirmed, "We sure will!"

"No you won't Grandpa!" Peggy shot back. "Squeally, you can get Angie here can't you, and we'll show them."

"Sure! Won't take but a moment."

Squeally let forth a loud clucking sound similar to Squiggly's, and momentarily through Peggy's moonglasses she saw a familiar creature slowly surface at the dock, just behind Silver. Water rolled off its silvery-pink, almost translucent back on which was strapped some seats with life vests and helmets. It was not quite as large as Silver, but much more strange-looking. It had a blunt nose, no eyes, and blood-red projections where its ears might have been, which were, as Squeally had explained in their earlier trip, gills.

Peggy said proudly to her grandfather, who had not seen such a creature on his previous trip with Squiggly, "This is Angie. She's a blind salamander, a troglobite amphibian. She's wonderful. She can go in both water and on the cave walls and ceilings. Squeally and I will ride her, and we'll beat you to the Squiresville dock."

Peggy and Squeally exchanged gleeful high fives.

"We'll see about that, won't we Squiggly. Silver will leap Big Falls in a single bound, like Superman."

Henry burst into song

O ye'll take the high road, and we'll take the low road,
And we'll be in Squiresville afore ye.

He thrust his arms over his head like a runner winning the marathon.

Squiggly, not stopping to wonder what in the world he meant by Superman and the other strange words, danced around with his arms up, celebrating what was sure to be their classic victory.

Everybody climbed aboard, slipped into the life preservers, and clapped on helmets. Squiggly and Henry on Silver buckled seatbelts whereas Squeally and Peggy on Angie slipped into harnesses since Angie could climb walls and scoot across ceilings, and harnesses were needed when the girls were upside down.

Squeally clucked Angie into position beside Silver.

Squiggly said, "Ready?"

He leaned forward and made a strange clucking sound which caused vibrations the cave fish and salamander could sense. Silver responded with a nervous twitch of the tail. Angie raised one foot out of the water.

"Get set!"

Silver tensed and Angie put her foot back into the water, anxiously awaiting the signal.

Squiggly loudly clucked "GO!"

Three

THE RACE

Silver lurched forward, and Squiggly waved his hat and shouted, "Heigh Ho, Silver!" just as he had heard Mr. Henry do in their earlier journey up river. He still did not understand what it meant, especially when Mr. Henry yelled, "Get 'em up, Scout," but that didn't matter. They were off in a spurt, well ahead of Angie whose legs and long tail were not as well suited to swimming as were the fins and tail of Silver.

Peggy uttered a disappointed "Ohh-----" as she saw how far behind they already were.

"Don't worry," squeaked Squeally. "We'll catch up when we come to the series of small falls ahead."

Squiggly looked behind him and said, "See, Mr. Henry, I told you we could do it." But they were so far ahead that Henry through his moonglasses could barely make out the girls aboard Angie to their rear. The first of the step-like falls was just ahead. Silver's powerful fins and tail thrust him vigorously forward, but going up over falls was not as easy or quick as swimming in the river below the falls. Squiggly looked back again and said, "Oh, oh. They're getting closer. Come on, Silver!" He clucked excitedly and Silver responded with more effort.

"Ha!' squeaked Squeally, "we're gaining on them. Let's go, Angie," she said, then clucked. Angie sped up her swimming, paddling furiously with her feet and swishing her tail back and forth which gave her forward movement a kind of squirming effect.

By this time, Silver was approaching the second falls created by the tiers of flowstone.

Peggy said, "Come on, Angie!" and although Angie of course could not hear her, or understand even if she did, she nevertheless got to the bottom of the first small falls in good time. The girls could see the boys ahead, now on top of the second falls. Squiggly and Henry were waving back at them, shouting and laughing.

Peggy said, "Not good." Squeally replied, calmly, "Just wait."

At Squeally's clucking, Angie came up out of the water onto the bank of the river, and in a few more steps was at the wall of the cave. Straight up she shot, and Peggy was thrown back into her seat. Then Angie leveled off so that her body was parallel with the river, and Peggy was thrust hard left so she was looking down at the water, thankful for the harness that held her in her seat. Squeally had been thrust against her, and she elbowed Peggy and said, gleefully, "See, now we'll show them. They're only approaching the third falls. Angie is much better on cave walls and ceilings than she is in the river."

Angie sped along while the girls laughed. As they whisked past the boys below, they waved at them but got no wave back.

"Oh, oh," said Henry. He was not thinking so much now about the race as he was about the safety of the girls shooting past on the wall of the cave.

"They'll be fine," Squiggly assured him. "But they think they're so smart. Wait and see!"

Just as Silver crested the third small falls, Angie zoomed down from the cave wall and skidded to a stop on the bank ahead of him. "Hi, boys," the girls called out, giggling. Silver, as if ashamed, thrust mightily forward, and Squiggly shouted back at them, "You'll see!"

Big Falls was dead ahead, and the roar of the falling water was deafening. Angie settled down into the river as Squeally loudly explained, "She has both lungs and gills, and she likes to wet her gills frequently." Peggy could see Angie's dark, fan-like gills working hard, getting oxygen into her body. Then, at Squeally's clucking, out of the river and upward on the wall they exploded again and raced ahead.

Below them, Silver churned through the whitewater at the base of the high falls, gained speed and then leapt up, his body partially in the surging current that rushed over the crest of the falls, and partially out of it. He teetered on the crest, in danger of being swept back down.

Angie was moving fast upward and was now on the ceiling, arcing over the roaring falls below. Peggy had thrilled to this part of the trip on her earlier voyage upriver with Squeally and Angie, but this time, upside down, she looked below and saw Silver in trouble. Squeally yelled out at Squiggly and Henry, "Watch us!" but was certainly not heard due to the noise of the falls.

"Oh, no!" Peggy cried out in horror at the danger of Silver with her grandfather aboard being swept back over the falls into the swirling pool below. Squiggly was young and a good swimmer, but although her grandfather was wearing a life jacket and helmet, he was old.

Silver, though, with a herculean burst of fins and swishing of tail bested the current and thrust ahead, safely into the water above the falls.

"Wasn't that great!" beamed Squeally as Angie raced downward on the other side of the falls and slipped back into the river to wet her gills again. "Yeah, great," said Peggy with no enthusiasm.

She perked up however as she saw the calm lake ahead and knew there was now no danger to her grandfather.

Peggy and Henry must have had the idea at about the same time. Peggy said to Squeally, "Could we just make it a tie instead of beating them?" Henry, shaken from seeing Peggy upside down aboard Angie over the roaring falls, looked at Squiggly and asked, "What do you think about just calling it a tie? Can we get to the dock at Squiresville at the same time the girls do?"

So for the rest of the race the boys called out to the girls up on the wall of the cave such good-natured taunts as, "You're gonners," and the girls called back down, "We'll see about that!" Silver and Angie both sped along, but their pilots managed to bring them in to the dock at Squiresville in a dead heat--a tie.

"We won!' yelled Squiggly. "No you didn't, we did!' spoofed Squeally. "Angie was a teeny bit ahead." And everybody laughed, knowing the race was fixed. They hugged one another as Silver and Angie were dismissed with thanks and clucks, and the two cave creatures sank into the water and swam out of sight.

A new large sign in glow-worm paint greeted them at dockside:

WELCOME TO SQUIRESVILLE

Site of

FIRST ANNUAL DOG SHOW

Squiggly said, "There! Mr. Henry, see what you did!" He was so excited he tugged at Henry's arm and pulled him toward the sign.

"You did this! You gave me The Gift-----Mugs!"

What in the world could Squiggly be talking about?

The Cave of Healing

Wondering, Henry nevertheless felt pleased, enormously pleased. And at the same time old, incredibly old. It seemed as if a hundred years had passed--and that was in Out time, the time back home at his house in the woods. Old. A hundred years since he had gone to In with Squiggly. A hundred years since the boy he had come to love had asked him for The Gift. A hundred years since he had given him Mugs. Just thinking of it now overcame him with grief at giving up his old friend, the only one who gave without expecting anything in return. Mugs was pure love. Laurel loved Henry. Melanie and Peggy of course did too. But he had made their lives so difficult, and he knew it.

Trying not to allow sadness to overwhelm him, Henry slowly felt happy overtake sad--happy for Squiggly who got a dog to love and who would love him, a young-acting dog who, because of Squatty's potion was not arthritic, not in pain, but full of joy and play.

Squiggly. Mugs. A boy and his dog. What could be better than that?

"Mr. Henry, don't cry. Why are you crying?"

"I'm not really crying, Squiggly. I'm happy. I am *so* happy!"

In a moment Henry had three pairs of arms around him, hugging him, and he bent and kissed the brow of each child.

Then a strange-looking creature lumbered out of the dark. "Hi, Koloa!" the children called out. Henry joined them in their eager greetings. They all felt the same about him. "Good boy. Good old faithful Koloa."

The animal limped up to the dock and sank down, waiting for his riders to climb aboard. This blind wolf spider appeared to have had some bad times. His dull hard coat was scratched and dented in places, and one of his eight legs was missing. Squiggly petted his head, clucked, and said, "I'll get you some nice fresh amphipods when we get home." Koloa seemed to nod, and anyone who could detect smiles on a wolf spider's face might have seen a broad one on Koloa's.

The four happy travelers climbed aboard, and although going at Koloa's slow pace they were unlikely to need seatbelts, nevertheless, the benches strapped to his back had them. Mr. and Mrs. Squires had decided long ago not to embarrass this loyal creature who gave the family so much pleasure in his slow, swaying rides. Other younger blind wolf spiders who provided transportation were much faster, and it was prudent for their passengers to wear seatbelts, so Squeezy and S.Q. Squires had Koala equipped with them too. Koloa had seemed thankful.

So snap went the unnecessary seatbelts, and Koala ambled off in his uneven, rocking motion. Soon the path up to Squiresville became steep, and Koala's breathing got more labored. Squiggly clucked Koala into a pull-off so he could catch his breath.

"Peggy," said Squeally, "the pool where you found the cave pearl is just ahead. Do you want to stop and look?"

Peggy paused before answering.

"----- No-----no. Let's just go on by."

"Oh, okay."

On her first trip to the pool Peggy had found the cave pearl.

It was so large, so creamy white, so nicely rounded, so-----beautiful-----*her* pearl.

How could she ever expect to find another? And if she did find one-----larger, whiter she would-----

"No," she repeated. Her pearl was-----*perfect*. There could never be another to replace it. "Let's go on by."

And so they did. After two or three more brief rest halts for Koloa, they came to the plateau on which sat Low Meadows, the part of Squiresville where the largest, best-built and most attractive cut-stone houses were located. This was home to the working class--the janitors, road sweepers, seamstresses, and others who had needed large houses when they were young because most of them had large families.

The Cave of Healing

The professional people such as Mrs. Squires lived high above in Scenic Heights. Anyone who had never visited Squiresville and met the Squires family might think it curious that their home, like those of the doctors, professors, business owners and such in Scenic Heights, had little to commend it--small, perched as it was right up against the ceiling of the cave on the edge of a precarious cliff. When in his earlier trip Henry had first reached it by riding Koloa up that narrow, steep, dangerous road, he had shuddered when he looked down toward the lake below and found that his moonglasses did not allow him to see that far. All he saw was a dark abyss. But the Squires family lived there in perfect contentment. After all, since they saw wonderfully well in total darkness, there were few places in In which could boast such a view.

Four

The First Annual Dog Show

Low Meadows was quiet today. "Just about everybody in Squiresville is at the dog show," Squiggly pointed out. His excitement was at the bursting point as they went through the edge of Low Meadows and out into the open space bordering the town. Signs pointed to such places as Squabblesville, Watersville, Goldville. A much larger glow-worm painted sign pointed down a path:

To FIRST ANNUAL DOG SHOW

Sponsor: Highville Kennel Club

The path led off to the right. Squiggly excitedly clucked and Koloa ambled down it.

Henry instantly recognized where they were going. It was the open area where Koloa had taken him during his return from Squabblesville. There in Squabblesville he had had his counseling session with Doctor de Squawk, Squabbler-In-Chief, who had helped him so much. Dr. de Squawk had confirmed what Doctor

The Cave of Healing

Shepherd from VA had told Henry "You are not responsible for everything, but you *are* responsible for Laurel, and you *are* responsible for Melanie, and you *are* responsible for Peggy--responsible to love and be loved by them. It was not your fault, not entirely, but the fact is you have made their lives a mess-----*You are responsible for them and for yourself.*"

Now Koloa was heading toward the spot where, on his last trip, Henry was greeted by a deliriously happy Mugs wearing moonglasses. He had been playing with the children, a Mugs devoid of pain and looking years younger.

Henry saw a strange creature ahead of him. Suddenly Peggy saw it too. "Cephus!" she cried out. "Squeally, it's our Cephus!"

"I know," smiled Squeally.

Cephus was the unfortunate blind centipede whom some of the boys and girls riding him had called 'Doofus.' 'Doofus Cephas.' Despite his shortcomings, though, he had proved to be somewhat of a hero in carrying Peggy, Squeally, and the other riders back to safety, away from Skelton, the monster pseudoscorpion which Peggy had nailed right between the eyes with her cave pearl. Cephus had two passengers aboard. The small one jumped down.

All of a sudden Henry heard a frantic, joyful barking. "Mugs!' he cried out.

A beaming Squiggly called, "I knew you would be surprised, Mr. Henry."

The four riders scrambled down from Koloa and a delighted Mugs, with his moonglasses fastened over his eyes, was instantly in among them, yipping, moaning in joy, jumping up with his paws against their chests. They bent so he could lick their faces in rapturous greeting.

"Mugs!" gushed Henry, with tears in his eyes, taking slobbery kisses and giving hugs and kisses in return.

In a moment, Squatty came up to them. "I thought you'd never get here. Mugs and I have been waiting for ages."

Henry grinned. Ages. This short, plump older brother of Squeally and Squiggly, he remembered, was over five million years old, in In time. What would ages be?

Squatty seemed to have Asian-like facial features and skin coloration, although through Henry's moonglasses how could one be sure? Squatty squinted at Peggy and Henry through his clear crystal-lens glasses and said, "Good to see you, but let's get going to the dog show." This boy who was part scientist, part philosopher--and all lecturer--as usual had so many things going that he needed to get to the next event quickly so he could discover what science and great ideas he could wring out of it. After he analyzed important information he always felt compelled to pass it on to others.

So they set off, with Henry helping Mugs aboard Koloa. Squiggly sat on the other side of Mugs. As they traveled, Henry, teary, patted the dog's head, and Squiggly every now and then kissed Mugs. Seated between the two people he loved the most, Mugs responded in joy, giving them his crooked teeth, lopsided grin of sheer delight.

Following Koloa was Cephus with Squatty and the girls aboard. The blind centipede moved along in his wave-like rising and falling motion like that of a caterpillar. As Squatty pondered a thorny problem in physics, Peggy and Squeally sang, enjoying being carried by Cephus again. They made up The Dog Show Song:

We're off to see The Dog Show
The wonderful show of dogs,
They bark, they yip, they jump and nip
Scoot under your feet and make you trip
Those wonderful, wonderful dogs.

Henry looked at Squiggly and smiled as he listened to the girls singing their made-up verses. Cute songs but ironic. How do you have a dog show with only one dog?

"Where are they having the show?" he asked Squiggly.

"Well, they're building an arena in Highville for the shows that will begin next year. Mrs. Haughty from Highville has been influential in developing the Highville Kennel Club and so The Committee voted to put it there."

"Politics, huh?" replied Henry.

Squiggly, not understanding some of the strange things his friend said, just continued, "But this year the show will be outdoors in Fairball Stadium, which is where we're headed. That's where Squeally took Peggy to see The Regional Championship."

"I see," said Henry. But, for the moment, he didn't see at all, not just because if he lifted his moonglasses he would be in darkness so total he literally couldn't see his hand in front of his face. He knew, though, that what Squiggly said would become clear soon enough. It always did. However, a kennel club show featuring only one dog? Henry this time was befuddled. And a show outdoors? Inside a cave? But in In terms, that made sense. Someday he hoped to be able to think in In terms, like learning a foreign language and finally being able to think in that language. No translation necessary. "Whew!" he said to clear his mind.

Just then Squiggly said, "Do you hear it?"

"Hear what?" The screeching sound in his ears as the result of explosions and gunfire had gotten even worse since the war.

Squiggly clucked and Koloa picked up the pace as much as he could. "We're getting close," said the excited boy. "Do you hear it now?"

And this time, astonished, Henry *did* hear it. Dogs barking.

Dogs.

And instantly he remembered. How could he have forgotten? When Squiggly had asked for Mugs as The Gift, Henry, struggling to get over the shock, had agreed and said, "Mugs is a wonderful Gift. The Committee can replicate him." That's what Squiggly had wanted--dogs so that every child in In could have a precious gift like Mugs. Henry remembered that Squiggly had also said, "Once The Gift is brought back to In it is replicated into as many as are needed." However, that was for the Sheriff's department uniforms, the ones with the bearskin hats. But even then The Committee hadn't merely duplicated the one uniform which had been brought back as The Gift. If so, they would all have been the same size, and a big tall male deputy wearing a small uniform would look as ridiculous as a small female deputy wearing a huge one.

But an animal? A single male dog? How do you get a bunch of barking dogs out of that?

Henry's thinking was all mixed up. He was in a daze as they came to the parking lot of the stadium. The dog show was such an attraction they would have to park far out and hike quite a distance to get in.

But no! Several sheriff's deputies in uniform, each proudly riding a blind wolf spider, greeted the travelers and wheeled into formation, two by two in line ahead of Koloa and Cephus. They led the way down the path to the main entrance gate where they fanned out, halted, and dismounted. The deputies immediately posted to the side of Koloa and Cephus and helped the riders down.

Henry, still in a state of amazement, was saluted by a tall deputy. "Sergeant at Arms Squires at your service, *SIR*! Ahh--CHOO!"

Squiggly beamed and said, "He's my uncle, my father's brother!"

"Follow me, please."

The sergeant imperially led the way toward the main gate, with Henry, Mugs, and Squiggly directly behind him, trailed by another deputy leading Squatty, Squeally, and Peggy. As he marched, the sergeant tipped his head back severely in order to see under the rim of his tall bearskin hat. It is not good form for a senior deputy to bump into a gate while leading honored guests.

Over the gate was a huge banner. Henry stopped and craned his head up to admire it. Through moonglasses, unfortunately everything appeared in shades of gray. Squiggly, however, interpreted the colors for him. Against a gold background, the large letters in glowworm paint were done in a luxurious sapphire blue:

FIRST ANNUAL DOG SHOW

In the middle of the banner was an outline of a dog, the emblem of the show's sponsor, the Highville Kennel Club. The emblem bore some resemblance to Mugs, but Mugs probably would not have approved of it. Although Mugs in fact was a pedigreed dog, his demeanor endeared him to everyone. It would never have occurred to them to ask, or care, about his lineage. The emblem presented an idealized Mugs with head held regally high. Perhaps an outline depiction was chosen because it would not show the crooked teeth or goofy smile which would have disqualified him from competition.

Under the emblem were the words

The Committee

As Henry was to learn later, those words needed no explanation. In In were many committees--Science Committee, Health Committee, Environmental Committee--you name it. But The Committee was special. When Squiggly had brought Mugs to In as the Gift, at first the feeling was universal that dogs should be for everyone, children through adults, to love and to receive their unquestioning, total love in return. But somewhere along the line, perhaps in the early stages of discussing the breeding of dogs, a more restrictive idea crept in until the result was The Committee, from which came Standards.

Henry said, "See that, Mugs," as he pointed to the banner. Mugs looked up and gave Henry a goofy, crooked-teeth smile.

Thankfully, Sergeant at Arms Squires didn't bump into the gate, and the passage was made safely.

Ahead was the huge arena, its limestone floor covered by an immense green carpet. At the sight of Henry and Mugs, the crowd broke into a roar, and dozens of dogs of all kinds and sizes barked in greeting. Mugs at first was as astonished as Henry. Then he seemed to tune into the occasion and proudly pranced beside Henry and Squiggly right up to a podium, following the sergeant who bowed to a tall lady, elegantly dressed in the old-fashioned clothes of In. The sergeant briskly about-faced, sneezed, and, head tipped sharply to the rear, marched smartly back to the gate, leaving the travelers standing in front of the lady.

She held up her hand to quiet the crowd, but it took some time before the roaring, clapping, and barking settled into a respectful silence. She was so elegant looking that Henry was not sure if he was supposed to put his lips to her hand, bow, or what. Squiggly whispered, "This is Mrs. Haughty. Mrs. Haughty from Highville. That's not her real name, but it's what some people use--not to her face. Her real name is Mrs. Hedy Heights." Squiggly, being a well-mannered boy, smiled mischievously only a little.

From a distance she had appeared to be an elderly lady. Her hair, beautifully coifed, was silver-white. Up close, though, she seemed about the same age as Peggy's mother, Melanie--measured not in In, but Out years, of course.

"My deah, Mis--ter Hen--ry," she spoke loudly, distinctly, enunciating carefully in an aristocratic, upper crust manner. "On behaall--ff of Highville Kennel Clu--uubb, and all dog lov--ahhs of In, I welcome you to the Firrr--st Ann--uuahll Dog Show!"

More clapping and barking, more words to honor Henry, the donor of Mugs who had made all this possible. Words too to welcome Squiggly who had brought The Gift to In, and to Peggy, the girl from Out. And wel--come Mugs, pro--genitor of our pre--cious, pre--cious *purebred* dogs." Mugs, having gotten over his astonishment at such a welcome, grinned his lop-sided, toothy grin throughout the speech and looked up often at Henry and Squiggly. More speech, then final clapping and barking at the end.

An announcer with the Kennel Club emblem on his lapel took over and called out, And now, it is time for our first event, Meet the Breeds. The *purebred* breeds, of which we have seven breed groups comprising one hundred eighty-two breeds-----the *purebred* breeds are on *this* side of the arena (and he gave a grand sweep of his arm) whereas -----"

"Whereas?" Henry mused--a seemingly innocent word so often implying something less desirable.

"-----the *mixed breed* group is on this side." (No count of breeds, no grand gesture.)

Five

Strange Words and Concepts

Squatty led the way to the reserved Honor box on the purebred side of the arena. Next to it was the central, Premier box for The Committee. Looking across to the mixed breeds side, Henry could see no boxes, just bleacher seats.

He had little time, though, to contemplate this. Mrs. Squires, whose name was Squeezy because she greeted everyone with a huge hug, waved to him from the Honor box. When Henry entered she engulfed him in her large arms and gushed out her greeting, "Oh, Mr. Henry we are so delighted to see you we've been waiting so long and now you're here oh S.Q. isn't this wonderful here he is again-----"

'S.Q.' sounded like 'askew,' which characterized how this home do-it-yourself man approached his repair work, as well as the result of it. On Henry's earlier trip, Squiggly had said he felt sorry for his mother who had to figure out ways of calling in a professional to repair the damage without embarrassing his father. Squeezy's torrent of words continued nonstop until, in an instance of unusual boldness S.Q. said, "Squeezy, you're smothering him. Let him come up for air."

Henry was saved.

Squeezy held him out at arm's length and studied him as if he were a precious rediscovery of a long-lost relative. Henry was greatly fond of this large, dark-skinned woman who, despite her gushes of enthusiasm that made her seem a bit addlepated was in fact the highly intelligent and adept owner of a large paper products business in Squiresville. She proudly employed workers--those of Low Meadows who had the largest houses; and mid-level employees, up the steep road to Middle Manors where the smaller, less attractive houses were owned by the forepersons, accountants, and such; finally the executives of Scenic Heights who lived in the smallest, most drab houses like her own, perched high over the lake. These were heads of her departments, operations staff, and so forth. Her favorite employees were the ones from Low Meadows. She was always making it easy for them to purchase goods such as new shoes for thrift shop prices. Her employees loved her, and she loved them, but when the occasion arose she could be a disciplinarian in a manner that did not result in resentment.

In the embrace of Squeezy, Henry had not noticed the ancient gentleman.

"Great Great Grandfather Squires!" Henry said with pleasure.

"Hello again, young man," croaked the patriarch of the family, extending his bony hand to Henry who took it carefully so as not to collapse it into a pile of dust.

Good.

Now Henry might get answers to what was confounding him: How does a single male dog propagate so many breeds? Especially in such a short time? Henry had been gone from In only about four months.

When he posed that question, Squatty spouted out, "Simple!"

"Not simple," corrected the ancient man whose base of wisdom seemed to extend to the beginning of time. At least to the beginning of life on earth, more than three billion years.

Unfazed, Squatty began his lecture, "Cloning and Hermaphroditism. The Two Basic Concepts."

Squeezy and S.Q. excused themselves, saying they wanted to go look at the dogs. Henry suspected they had listened to too many of Squatty's lectures. Peggy rolled her eyes, and even Henry was puzzled. Cloning he thought he somewhat understood, but hermaphroditism?

"Cloning," Squatty said in his professorial tone, "is the process of making genetically identical copies of an original being, in this case a dog--Mugs. But cloning does not necessarily produce identical copies. Genes and environmental factors come into the equation."

So far so good, Peggy thought. She had done a fourth grade research paper on cloning, recalling Dolly the female sheep.

But now Squatty waded in deeper, describing the copying of genes in reproductive cloning. "Simple," he repeated.

"Not simple," corrected the ancient man as Peggy's eyes rolled once more. Squatty was in territory unexplored in her research paper. Even Henry was frowning, trying to keep up.

"So," said Squatty, "in cloning we got a copy of Mugs with which we could now proceed-----"

"We?' interrupted Squeally. "Don't you mean they? The Science Committee?"

"Wait a minute, Squatty." objected Henry. "Don't you need a female egg cell to make this process work?"

"Here is where we come to hermaphroditism. Simple," responded Squatty.

"Definitely not simple," rasped the old man.

Squatty went on as if the wise ancient man was a student who was interrupting his lecture. "You have to understand that in nature, some plants and animals can themselves produce offspring even though an opposite sex is not present."

"Wow!" said Peggy, slapping her forehead. She had learned some basics of reproduction in a school class during which she and some of her classmates tittered, but this was new information.

"True hermaphroditism occurs in rare cases in which an individual is born who has both some male and female tissues. We-----

Squeally said, "He means scientists of our Science Committee."

"As I started to say before I was so rudely interrupted, the scientists were able to exploit this situation because they discovered that Mugs and his clone had such tissues."

"You mean that Mugs is both male and female?" an astonished Henry asked.

"No, he is fully male. It's just that he did have enough female tissues for our scientists to work with. And they did it. Simple."

"Much more complex," corrected his great great grandfather. "Profoundly complex."

Squatty continued, as if the correction was unheard, "And mastering this process shows how much better In is than Out."

Holding up his finger, "Stick to the science!" the ancient man sharply rebuked the boy.

Peggy had given up, leaning back in her chair, looking up toward the ceiling of the cave, rolling her eyes.

Henry, though, persisted. "But it takes a long, long time to produce breeds of dogs. I've only been gone from In for about four months."

This time it was Squiggly who spoke, "But Mr. Henry, that is your Out time. Think what those four months are in In time."

The ancient man smiled in approval, if a tiny upward movement of the corners of his lips could be called a smile. Peggy was afraid that any more than that would crack his face into pieces.

Henry then saw it, sort of. Four months translated to In time might be thousands of years, tens of thousands, long enough for breeding and cross breeding to produce the dogs in the arena. His head hurt from trying to figure it all out. It was easier to think that it was a hallucination such as he had been convinced he was having on his earlier trip. But no, Peggy's pearl, which he had seen in Out, which he had held in his hands on the wooded hill behind his house, was the best evidence it was not just an illusion. All of this cloning and hermaphroditism business might become clear if he gave it enough time.

Henry shook his head quizzically. "Let's go look at dogs," he said.

Six

STANDARDS--PUREBRED AND MUTT

At that moment a boy of about Squiggly's age came up to the booth. "Hi, Squiggly," he said.

An excited Squiggly said, "Mr. Henry, Peggy, this is my friend Heston. Where's Haley?" he asked of Heston's sister.

"She had a test and couldn't miss it. She'll come tomorrow."

"Heston's mother is Mrs.-----Hedy Heights." Squiggly had barely caught himself before he goofed and called her Mrs. Haughty. "Heston is older but we have great times together. He has a purebred Trailhound named Trevor."

"Hello, Mr. Henry, Peggy," the boy said. We are so glad you could visit us, and delighted you gave Mugs as The Gift, Mr. Henry."

"Well, I'm pleased to meet you. I've never heard of a Trailhound."

"Oh, Mr. Henry," said Heston, "they are a magnificent breed. Trevor is actually Trevor de la Grand Duchy du Balmont."

"Impressive," said Henry.

"A mouthful," said Peggy.

"That's why we just call him Trevor," said Squiggly happily, quite oblivious to the irony.

Henry thought Trevor looked like a bloodhound, a magnificent one indeed, one who had that mournful look about his eyes, but Henry was to learn he was anything but sorrowful. He was full of life and joy.

Heston continued passionately, "Trevor perfectly meets The Breed Standard, the accepted guide developed by the Highville Kennel Club."

Squiggly contributed, proudly, "Of which his mother is chairperson. And chair of The Committee."

"I see," said Henry, with fingers on his chin. "And what, exactly, is the Standard?"

"Well," Heston replied, "generally speaking, there are such qualities as appearance, of course, and how the dog moves, and then there is temperament--how well he acts and reacts. Mother says that temperament is paramount, and judges place a high premium on it."

"Oh, *really*--temperament?" said Peggy, and might have said more but her grandfather nudged her.

Heston continued, "Yes, temperament is important in both dogs and bitches."

With that, Peggy choked down a yuk and instantly feigned innocent ignorance. "Oh, and what are they?"

Squiggly jumped in with, "That's what female dogs are called in the dog show business."

Peggy was struggling to maintain her composure. "Let me get this straight. Males are dogs, and female dogs aren't dogs?"

Heston said, "Yes, they're dogs in the general sense."

Henry, knowing a bit about dog shows, nudged her again and intervened, as much to keep himself from cracking up as to quiet Peggy. "Let's go look at some dogs," he said.

"Sure," said Squiggly. "Let's go see Trevor, and then we can see Scamp too. He's Squishy's dog. Squishy's too small to have one yet, but he loved the dog and gurgled and cooed and waved his arms and punched at him every time Scamp was with him. They love one another. I'm training Scamp until Squishy gets big enough."

"Scamp, huh," said Peggy. "As in Scamp de Royale Majesty?" Henry frowned at her.

"No, just plain Scamp," said Squiggly. "He's not purebred. He's a mutt."

Squiggly explained, "Scamp was plain-looking. He was the last of his litter to get adopted. I don't know how the people who chose the other puppies missed the sparkle in his eyes. My mom and dad could see he was full of mischief-- just like baby Squishy--always poking, pulling hair, and giggling at his misdeeds. So naturally they chose Scamp for Squishy.

Squiggly thought Peggy's name for Scamp was classy, and that's what he would put on his nameplate for the Show.

Great Great Grandfather Squires declined the invitation to join them, so the others set out for the purebred side of the arena. In doing so they passed close to where Mrs. Heights was still standing near the podium, conferring with the head judge, a splendid looking specimen in old-fashioned formal attire. Heston waved and called out warmly, "Hello Mother." He got a distracted slight turn of the head and raise of her forefinger in acknowledgement.

"She's busy," Heston explained.

Squatty whispered to Peggy, "She's always busy."

Behind them, on the mixed breed side, dogs were barking and howling. On the purebred side, though, the barking was minimal, just an occasional yip. Owners, dog trainers, and handlers work assiduously at keeping their pedigreed dogs from barking, which is their natural inclination. Since judges rate the show dogs on how close they come to the Breed Standard--so carefully developed, formalized, and tweaked across years and years of breeding--a playful bark at the wrong time could change a potential winner into a loser. Never mind, for example, that hounds tracking quarry presumably are most useful when they howl loudly, Standards are Standards.

They went past several cages containing beautifully groomed, well-behaved dogs. "Sure are wonderful-looking," said Henry and meant it. "Gorgeous," agreed Peggy. As they arrived at the Hound group, Heston studied the engraved nameplates on the cages to get an idea of Trevor's competition. One or two, he thought, had even more impressive pedigrees than that of his dog. It caused him some worry.

"Oh, Trevor is the best," Squiggly assured his older friend. "I'll bet he wins Best In Show."

"What about Scamp?" Squeally said forcefully.

"Huh! No chance," answered Squatty. "It's a miracle that mutts are even allowed to compete."

"Yeah," Squeally acknowledged. "Peggy, we had to petition hard, a lot of people. We had to make our case before The Committee, even carry signs outside their meetings. It just wasn't fair that Scamp and other dogs like him couldn't compete."

Squatty whispered to Peggy so Heston, who was a good kid, couldn't hear, "Mrs. Haughty was against it, and whatever she wanted she got. Except this time. Our side won in The Committee by only one vote."

Heston said, "I love Trevor. He comes so close to The Standard. He's a great dog."

Squatty pulled a folded manual out of his pocket. "Here it is, The Standard, Hound group. Hmm. Height. The mean height is--let's see, in Out terms--adult dogs, 25 inches, adult bitches, 23 inches."

When he said that word, Peggy held it in again. With difficulty.

"Weight," Squatty read, "seventy-nine pounds and sixty-nine pounds respectively. Expression is regal, dignified. Head, narrow, tapering." Squatty hmmed as he read to himself other requirements: outline of the skull, foreface--hmm--ears long, hmm, etc., etc. "Very precise," he concluded.

"Yes," said Heston, "and Trevor comes terribly close in every requirement. In fact he's perfect, I think, and I love him. He has a spectacular coat, don't you agree?"

How could anyone not agree? Trevor had short hair of a pleasant tan and black combination, and his loose skin lay in symmetric folds. Indeed he was a noble-looking animal.

Heston put Trevor on a leash and took him out of the cage. "He needs a little more practice in stacking."

"Stacking?" Peggy looked at Squeally who shrugged her shoulders.

"Simple," said Squiggly. "We handlers do it all the time. The dog needs to be presented in the best possible stance so the judge can appreciate his best traits and run his hands over him and study him to see how close he comes to The Standard."

As Trevor stood, Heston looked carefully at him and said, "Not bad for free stacked, but this will be better." He knelt and positioned Trevor's legs in an artificial, more acceptable stacking position.

Trevor stood there, perfectly calm, a most impressive dog.

"Great!" said Squiggly.

"Hmm," Peggy quietly said to Squeally who shrugged again.

Everybody petted Trevor affectionately, and he looked proud and handsome. Mugs liked him, too, and rubbed up against the bigger dog. Trevor replied by giving Mugs' shaggy coat a slobbery licking. Mugs grinned contentedly and returned the favor.

With Trevor back in his cage they walked over to the mixed breeds side of the arena, the mutts. It was just short of pandemonium. Barking, yipping, whining, spinning around in the cage, bad smells, frazzled boys and girls, some teenagers and adults who seemed to be what--owners--trainers--handlers ? Who could tell? What they seemed to have in common was a kind of nervousness at trying to prepare their mutts for competition. That, and a lot of camaraderie, encouraging one another, consoling one another. Strange goings-on for competitors. Maybe it had to do with having to band together in order to get The Committee even to allow them into the show.

Peggy, seeing this, thought back to the fairball game she had attended with Squeally where the object was to help your competitor win. She told her grandfather about it and said, smiling, "What a nutsy place, this In."

Henry replied, "I guess you might say that, but nice."

Scamp in his cage went bonkers when he saw Squiggly and Mugs, barking, jumping, twirling around. Squiggly had forgotten to put in an order for an engraved nameplate and, remembering at the last minute, he stuck up something that resembled a Post-it. It was hand-written: 'Scamp de Royale Majesty,' Peggy's facetious suggestion.

"Hey, little guy, glad to see us?" Squiggly greeted him. "Let's practice our stacking."

Apparently Scamp thought that was a marvelous idea, and when Squiggly got him on his leash and out of his cage he jumped and barked and tried to kiss everyone. Peggy thought he would need more than a little practice in stacking to have any chance. He not only was short and rotund but his coat was a crazy mixture of brown, orange, and a couple other colors which defied description. Squeally described it to Peggy who, through her moonglasses, saw only shades of gray.

Squiggly said, "Okay, Scamp, stand still. Let's do our stacking."

Scamp did everything except stand still and stack, and Squiggly had quite a wrestle with him even to get all four of his feet on the carpeted floor of the arena. He was getting slobbery kisses all over his face.

"Here, I'll help you," said Heston, and this turned into a three-way wrestling match which Scamp won. He barked and jumped in celebrating his victory.

"I hope he's better tonight in the group judging," said a downcast Squiggly.

And miracle of miracles, that night Scamp had such a good time prancing and cavorting his way around the circle that he stole the heart of the crowd. They laughed and applauded at his every trick, especially when he ran around handler Squiggly's legs, tripping him with the leash, and then robustly licking his face while he was down.

Now anyone who knows even a smidgen about dog shows should know that crowd response is not supposed to be the deciding factor in choosing a winner. And even a fool could be presumed to realize that even without a Standard for Mixed Breed--how can mixed breeds have a Standard?--a judge ought to know something about what he or she is judging. So whatever circumstances combined that night to lead to such a decision no one can say, but in the Mixed Breed group:

Scamp was the winner!

And Trevor de la Grand Duchy du Balmont?

The competition in the purebred Hound group was dignified and close, ever so close. As Trevor circled the arena on his leash he looked proud, and Heston his handler was even prouder. The crowd responded warmly and applauded loudly. And when Trevor stacked for the judge, Heston did not have to move even one of the dog's legs for better position. Then as the judge explored every part of Trevor's body with her hand--every part--she found that in all respects this dog well met The Breed Standard.

Trevor won Best in Breed!

That evening Mrs. Heights stood in front of the podium to present large, exquisite ribbons to each breed winner. Six winners in turn received their ribbon as she gave short congratulatory remarks, one by one. The announcer then said, "And last, from the pedigreed group, Hound, the winner is Trevor de la Grand Duchy du Balmont, owner Mrs. Hedy Heights, trainer and handler, Heston Heights."

The arena erupted in applause so intense it quashed any suspicion that the judging might have been influenced by her position as chair of the Kennel Club. Trevor had won fair and square.

Mrs. Heights looked down on Heston and Trevor, and said, regally, "It nat--urally gives me ex--traor--dinary pleasure, to present this ribbon in the Hound group to Tre--vor de la Grand Duch--y du Bal--mont." Mrs. Heights smiled at Heston and handed him a large ribbon in the Club colors of gold and sapphire blue. Trevor, gentleman that he was, held his head high. Heston did too, and nearly overcome with joy said, "Well done Trevor!"

At that instant, Scamp pulled the leash loose from Squiggly and showed his pleasure at Trevor's win by jumping on Heston and snatching the ribbon from his hand. He stood on his hind legs and showed off Trevor's prize, then trotted around the arena with it, head held high, strips of ribbon and leash trailing behind him. The audience howled and clapped madly in delight.

"Please," the announcer said, trying to quiet them. Please-----please." Finally Squiggly was able to catch Scamp and get him back to the podium where he relinquished the award and gave Trevor some slobbery, congratulatory licks. The announcer was able to say, "In the-----uhh-----" He was having a hard time bringing himself to say the words "----- *mixed breed* group"-----Whew! The struggle to say it had winded him. "----- the winner is-----*Scamp*, owner Squishy Squires, trainer and handler, Squiggly Squires."

The announcer had a stricken look on his face, having barely made it through that ordeal. As the crowd roared its approval, Scamp lay down and rolled around. He didn't come up until Mrs. Heights said, with a pained look, "I take great pleasure -----" She appeared to be having no pleasure at all as she tried to recapture her regal manner "----- in presenting this ribbon in the--uhh--*mixed breed*--group to-----long pause while she tried to say it-----*Scamp*."

More audience wild approval, lots of Squiggly smiles, plenty of Scamp shenanigans, and finally it was over. Now, the remaining challenge was Best In Show. The next evening would be historic, the selection of the first winner in what was sure to be a long succession of annual dog shows. Each of the seven winners of Best in Breed, to include Trevor, would compete for that honor, as well as Scamp, who surely would once again test the survivability skills of the announcer and Mrs. Heights.

Seven

LABYRINTH OF HORRORS

Lots of adventure stories about the next day's activities begin: "The day dawned bright and clear -----"

But in the Squires home in Scenic Heights, while Henry was waking up and fumbling for his moonglasses, there was no dawn, and most definitely nothing was bright and clear. He was confronted by total, absolute darkness. For a moment he felt that awe, that fear, that had gripped him on his first trip to In. "It's just the dark," he said to himself, and tried, not entirely successfully, to shake off a foreboding feeling even as he put on the glasses.

Late breakfast was scrambled spider eggs, dulse bread, and What'siss, the drink which got its name when Squiggly was a little boy only about a million years old and was just beginning to talk. A cup of the brown liquid was put in front of Squiggly and he had asked, "What'siss?"

Everyone was going to see the Best in Show selection except Great Grand Grandfather Squires who needed his rest, and the baby, Squishy, who would be cared for by his aunt. Squiggly wanted to get to the arena quickly to tend to Scamp, so he took Miko, a young blind wolf spider who was spectacularly fast. Miko was one of the many in their next door neighbor's large transportation business.

Henry, Mugs, and Squatty rode Koloa on the front seats, and Peggy and Squeally sat behind. The girls took up their dog show song, and Henry began to smile. That feeling of something not quite right was beginning to leave him.

> We're off to see The Dog Show
> The wonderful show of dogs,
> Scamp, he won by having fun
> And Trevor was wonderful too
> Trevor was beautiful
> And properly dutiful
> While Scamp ran around
> And brought the house down
> We're off to see The Dog Show
> Those wonderful, wonderful dogs.

Koloa's slow, rocking ride allowed for many more impromptu verses, and they finally arrived at the arena. Although he was still a bit out of sorts, the singing had lifted Henry's mood.

"Hi, Mr. Henry, Peggy," cried out a happy Squiggly. He had Scamp on his leash and almost had to shout to be heard above the dog's ecstatic barks of greeting. Mugs responded to Scamp with a fond yip and crooked-tooth smile.

"Hello, Mr. Henry, Peggy," called a smiling Heston. Trevor on his leash was trying diplomatically to sidestep Scamp's antics, but you could tell by Trevor's intermittent licks and head nudges of Scamp that he liked this little mischief maker.

"By the way," said Squiggly. "Where's Haley? I thought she was going to come with you today."

"She was, but her tutor told her he could go over her test with her, so she'll be along later."

"In time for Best in Show?"

"Oh, sure. She'll be here."

With both dogs on leashes the group set out on a slow tour around the arena to chat with competitors, some of whom Heston said were his friends. Squeally whispered to Peggy, "Or at least his acquaintances. It's difficult to make friends if your mother is Mrs. Haughty."

Trevor moved at a steady pace beside Heston, and Scamp was going loco beside, behind, and around Squiggly. Squatty, Henry, Mugs, Peggy and Squeally just tried to keep out of Scamp's way. The group found themselves near Mrs. Hedy Heights.

She was busy conferring with two show judges, one of whom, Payton Prestwood of Pridesville, had yesterday performed his duty by selecting Best of Breed in the Sporting category. The other, Ormund Oldsmith of Smithville would be choosing Best in Show, thereby concluding The First Annual Dog Show. "Oh deah, you will hahve such a difficult tahsk to per--form won't you," Mrs. Heights said to Mr. Oldsmith.

The judge allowed as to how having to choose Best in Show among the seven winners of Best of Breed would be problematic indeed. He said they were such perfect specimens.

Peggy whispered to Squeally, "I thought they were dogs."

Heston stopped near his mother. When Scamp saw Mrs. Heights he flattened himself on the floor and sized her up, wondering, no doubt, if he should bark in thanks at her for presenting his winner's ribbon or growl at her for no particular reason. Whichever, at least for the moment he was quiet.

Mr. Oldsmith and Mrs. Heights talked until finally she noticed Heston and said, "Yes?"

"Mother, would Mr. Preston take a look at Scamp and give Squiggly some advice for this evening's Best in Show?"

"*Scamp?*" said Mrs. Heights. "For *Best in Show?* That would be droll indeed. Mis--tahh Prest--wood, would you be so kind as to look at-----*Scamp?*"

Henry felt like smacking her, but Squiggly, not understanding her contemptuous tone, was thrilled. "Really? That would be fantastic!"

Mr. Prestwood, whether to please the chair of the Kennel Club or more likely to have a little jovial sport, said, "I would be delighted, Mrs. Heights." He looked down at Scamp who was tipping his head side to side as if trying to decide whether to jump in joy or bite him, and said, "Hmm. If he weren't just a crossbreed, what group does he come closest to? Hmm, I would have to say--hmmm. The coloring is all wrong for--hmmm--but there's nothing to be done about that now, I suppose. And his dimensions are dreadful for a--hmmm. He is terribly--and frightfully----- If there were such a thing as Crossbreed Standard, I fear he would not even come close even if I could place him-----."

"Yes," I see what you mean," said Mrs. Heights, primly. Had Henry not been a guest in In, and had not one of Heston's classmates come rushing up, Henry might have decked the judge. And maybe scowled at Mrs. Heights.

But Heston's classmate, out of breath, was gasping, "Mrs. Heights, Haley's wolf spider got spooked and ran off with her-----down the road to the Labyrinth of Horrors!"

"What! Are you sure? Oh, no! No!" She clasped her head in her hands. "No!" she shrieked.

"I tried to stop him but he was too spooked."

"What is that place? Henry shouted.

Squatty cried out, "A wild nature area of poisonous animals."

Henry grasped the boy's shoulder. "Can you show me the way?" he shouted. "Here!" he said, and thrust Mugs' leash into Mrs. Heights' hand. "Take care of him. Kids, let's go!"

"We need to take Trevor too. Maybe he can track her!" Heston called out desperately.

"And Scamp, too!" shouted Squiggly, running with Scamp barking hysterically alongside him.

Peggy and Squeally were also racing toward the main entrance.

Heston's classmate was pointing at a blind wolf spider which was breathing hard from the long run to the arena to give the alarm. The boy quickly told Heston and Squatty where Haley had disappeared down the road to the Labyrinth of Horrors. Henry, Heston, and Squatty clambered aboard the blind wolf spider, hauling Trevor up with them. Squatty's clucking sent the spider shooting ahead. Trevor let out a manly bay just as if he was warming up to get Haley's scent in his nose.

Squeally, Peggy, Squiggly, and Scamp scrambled up on Miko and raced to catch up with the spider ahead. Squiggly had to hold onto Scamp who was frantically barking.

"Squatty, what is this Labyrinth?" Henry shouted?

"It's an immense area of tunnels and caves, hundreds, probably thousands of them, with poisonous animals. When kids get to Squiggly's age, the Sheriff's department holds orientation days for school classes. They take field trips guided by deputies, and the Labyrinth of Horrors is the worst of all. There were other danger areas they took us to such as the one you passed on your way upriver. The deputies outpost all of them and put up warning signs, but sometimes there have been accidents, and someone strays into an area and is never heard from again."

At this reminder, Heston began gasping over and over, "Oh, Mr. Henry, we've got to find her!"

By this time Miko was alongside them, and Scamp was barking wildly and Trevor howling with all his might. Henry had to help Heston hold onto Trevor and he shouted into Heston's ear, "We will find her. We'll find her." But Heston could not stop weeping. "She's my little sister," he sobbed.

293

They raced along for some time and Henry shouted at Squatty, "How much farther?"

Squatty shouted, "Not much."

Henry shouted again. "What kind of animals? How many?"

Squatty shouted back, "Several kinds, probably hundreds. Pseudoscorpions, centipedes, spiders, and more. All poisonous."

"What do you mean spiders? We're riding a blind wolf spider. And we ride Koloa all the time."

Peggy called over to Squatty, "Yeah, and centipedes? What about Cephus?"

"That's something else. They're domesticated, have been for ages. No poison in them. No time now. I'll explain later," he shouted.

Despite the gravity of the situation, Squeally called to her grandfather, "He sure will. You're in for a lecture."

Squatty shouted to Henry, "The Labyrinth extends into the troglophile zone. That makes it doubly dangerous. There are poisonous creatures there who don't even come into our troglobite zone."

Squiggly added in a shout, "And it's harder for us to see there. That awful light! Not as bad as in the trogloxene zone near exits to Out, but bad enough."

That made Heston sob. Henry could not put his arm around him and still hold onto

Trevor, but he called, "It's going to be okay, son." He wasn't so sure himself, but Heston stopped crying and was staring ahead.

"Look, there's a deputy!" Heston shouted.

Through his moonglasses, Henry could barely make him out in the distance. Then they were coming up hard on him and got a shouted "Halt, who goes there!"

Mr. Henry yelled a bad word which one might translate as, "Like *fun* halt!

Did you see her?" Henry bellowed.

The deputy had a hard time seeing anything at all under the rim of his bearskin hat; nevertheless he had seen the terrified spider with the girl on top. He shouted that in fact he almost got run over as he tried to stop them. He had sense enough now to jump out of the way of the two blind wolf spiders and point down the road. He called after them, "Take the turnoff at the sign!"

"Heston," Henry shouted, "do you have anything of Haley's so Trevor can get a scent?"

"Oh----no! I-----wait! She hugged me before I left this morning. Do you think that will do? Maybe Trevor has already picked up on it. He has been howling enough."

Trevor indeed had gotten her scent from Heston's clothes. Henry thought that trailhound Trevor was some kind of bloodhound. He sensed that the dog wanted desperately to be down on the ground, racing along, nose down, tracking her.

They came to a huge sign in glow-worm paint pointing down a side road that led into a tunnel.

EXTREME DANGER

KEEP OUT!

LABYRINTH OF HORRORS

Poisonous Wildlife

Entrance Without Deputy Sheriff Escort Forbidden

Trespassers Will Be Heavily Fined, or Imprisoned, or Both

If You Survive!

"Ohh!" Heston was sobbing again.

"Halt!" came the shouted command. Another deputy was holding up his hand.

"Halt like ----!" Henry shouted, inserting another bad word. "We're going after the girl! Did she come through here?"

"Yes, but halt! You can't enter!" shouted the deputy. Peggy and the youngsters of In heard some more bad words too often used in Out but seldom in In. By now the deputy was blowing his whistle, hard, and with a red face was yelling, "The mounted patrol will be here! You'll be arrested!"

More bad words from Henry as they dashed past.

Behind them they heard AHH ---- CHOO! Ahh --- choo! Ah choo until the sneezing faded away and they could hear it no more. Trevor was baying crazily, and Scamp was barking at full volume.

At high speed they came to another sign

YOU ARE IN GREAT DANGER

TURN BACK

YOU WILL BE KILLED AND EATEN

BY POISONOUS ANIMALS

Turn Back and Face the Court

Only Fines and Prison are Behind You

Horrible Death Is Ahead of You

Trevor's nose confirmed Haley had been taken through this tunnel, so she must be ahead. They raced on until they came to a crossroad.

"Oh, oh!" said Squatty. "This is where it *really* begins."

Two signs were at the crossroad. The one with the arrow pointing at the tunnel to the left read

CAN'T YOU READ?

YOU ARE IN EXTREME DANGER

TURN BACK IMMEDIATELY

Deadly Pseudoscorpions Ahead

Last warning

TURN BACK!

The sign with arrow pointing to the tunnel on the right said

PLEASE!

CONSIDER YOUR FAMILY

How Will They Feel?

They Love You

Venomous Centipedes and Spiders Ahead

You Will Be Poisoned and Eaten

TURN BACK!

All well said. But what do you do about a girl on a runaway mount?

Eight

GREAT DANGER

Which arrow should they follow? Something needed to be done, instantly.

Henry shouted, "Get Trevor down!" and he himself jumped to the limestone floor of the cave.

Dumb, done in the heat of the chase. His arthritic knees buckled and hurt terribly from the shock of the hard landing. Heston helped Trevor down, but it was a tough job with the squirming, baying dog who was struggling to get loose.

Henry called to Heston, "Give me the leash!" He could not chance having it pulled out of Heston's hand. What could anyone do if Trevor got loose, raced off after Haley's scent, and followed it for several turns deep into the labyrinth, out of eyesight? How could anyone then know which tunnel Trevor had taken? One would look the same as another, and the far-off baying could be coming from any of them. He must hold onto Trevor at all costs!

Heston carefully gave Henry the leash and the dog tugged hard, sniffing, baying, working the scent while tugging Henry along behind him.

Henry shouted to Squiggly who had climbed down with Scamp in his arms. The boy had all he could do to hold onto his struggling, frantically barking Scamp. "Squiggly," Henry called, "give the leash to Squatty, and don't let go until he gets it. Squatty, wrap it around your wrist. Don't let go!"

Squatty was not much taller than Squiggly, but he was heavier and stronger. Scamp was going nuts, wanting to get loose and race off with Trevor on the chase, free of leashes. Trevor, though, had his nose to his business, and his business was to track Haley. He strained to go down the tunnel to the right. A wide, shallow creek ran through the tunnel, and Trevor was following the scent on one side of it.

Trevor let out with a deep bass HOWOOO, HAWOOOO. To Peggy it sounded like a profoundly personal howl, and it was. Trevor loved Haley, and she needed him to find her. Scamp's frantic ahroo, ahrooah was much higher in tone, and Peggy interpreted it as appreciation for the good job Trevor was doing.

Trevor the pedigreed hound tugged Henry down the tunnel to the right, howling, with Scamp the mutt trying to pull Squatty faster. Henry's knees were hurting him, and he was desperately trying to ignore the pain. With her grandfather and the boys on the ground, Peggy climbed onto the wolf spider in front and, not knowing how to cluck, motioned for Squeally to go around her and take the lead atop Miko.

"Good boy, Trevor, good boy," Henry shouted. Heston was now also holding onto the leash, helping Henry.

After tracking some distance, Trevor all of a sudden seemed confused. His howling dropped to loud huffs as he sniffed right and left, trying to pick up the scent. Shaking his head, nose still to the ground he pulled Henry and Heston forward a considerable distance. Twice he turned around and went back a short way, nervously sniffing, trying to figure it out, and then resumed his forward thrust, but with not so much conviction. Scamp was also confused, and he stopped barking, just watching Trevor at work. Henry was limping badly, and all of them on the ground were breathing heavily from the hard work.

"How you doing, Heston?" Henry huffed.

"Okay," the panting boy answered and called out plaintively, "Trevor, you've got to find her. Find her, boy!"

But there was no scent.

Squatty called, "Mr. Henry, shouldn't we go back to the sign? Maybe we should have gone down the road to the left."

Just then Henry had the thought that perhaps Haley's spider had left the bank and run in the creek. If so, that might account for why Trevor was confused. No, the hound wanted to go straight ahead. Henry called, "We'll keep going forward."

In a short time Trevor erupted in a loud baying, then sniffed right and left. He thrust his head back and bayed some more, tugging hard, HOWOOO, HAWOOOO!

"He's got it again!" shouted Henry. He saw water spattered on the limestone where Haley's spider had come back out of the creek. Scamp was delighted-----ahroo, ahrooooah!

The tunnel opened ahead into a large cave with rocks dotting the floor where they had spalled from the walls and ceiling. The humid air of the tunnel had turned rancid in the cave. Everybody was drenched with sweat. What was that awful, pungent smell?

Immediately Squatty shouted, "Centipedes!"

Something large, as tall as Henry, darted out at them.

Ever the scientist even in a crisis, Squatty yelled, "Watch out for the head. The forcipule fangs will inject poison!"

Scamp jumped at the horrible head as it came striking down, the fangs barely missing him. Having been startled by such an unusually aggressive prey, the centipede whipped sideways and struck again.

But Squatty had yanked Scamp away and they were both in the stream. Scamp barked fiercely at the thing and strained against his leash to get at it. Squatty took no chances that it would swim after them and he splashed their way toward the other side in the knee-deep stream, with Scamp tugging to the rear, splashing and savagely barking his defiance at the monster.

Henry had dragged Trevor into the water, along with Heston hanging onto the leash. "Oh!" screamed Heston, "it has killed Haley!"

But Trevor, tugging Henry and Heston, struggled up on the far shore and instantly howled. He had the scent again. It led back in the direction from which they had come.

"No," Henry shouted, "they got away."

At the centipede's attack, Squeally frantically had clucked Miko into the stream, and Peggy's spider had followed. All were now on the opposite bank hurrying back away from the danger, and Trevor was howling along the trail.

They made their way as quickly as they could back to the sign that had warned about centipedes and spiders. Trevor, nose to the ground became supercharged. Henry was in so much pain and so exhausted he just let the dog lead them. He was dizzy and nauseated by the time they came to the next sign. It read

YOU ARE GONERS NOW

UNLESS YOU TURN BACK IMMEDIATELY

Many Crossroads Ahead

You Will be Lost

All of Them Lead to

DOOM

Henry was hurting, disoriented, and staggering. Someone was calling "Grandpa" from--where?

"Grandpa!" Peggy shouted. "Get back up there on Miko! Here, we'll help you." Peggy and Squeally jumped down, took him under the arms and by some strength that comes only as a miracle in dire emergencies, the two girls hoisted him up into a seat and snapped the seatbelt on him. Henry was so close to passing out his head lolled on his chest. Peggy told Squiggly to get up there beside him and hold onto him.

Peggy shouted, "Heston, Squatty, hang onto those leashes! Haley's life depends on it! Now let's get going again!"

The frenzied baying and barking and lunging that accompanied Peggy's orders signaled that Trevor and Scamp wholeheartedly agreed. They had gone only a short distance when Trevor's baying suddenly reached a new, frantic pitch.

"Heston, Squatty, hang onto those dogs! We're close!"

Instantly out of the dark ahead a wolf spider loomed and shot past them, racing to their rear with no one in the seat on top.

"Oh no! That's Caleb, Haley's wolf spider!" Heston screamed. "Oh, no!"

With Haley obvious having been thrown off her spider, Peggy shrieked again, "Hang onto those dogs!"

Too late! Trevor's desperate lunge pulled Heston down and in tumbling he lost hold of the leash. Worse, Squatty, in trying to help him up, lost his grip on Scamp's leash. Trevor, freed, raced ahead, baying hysterically, with Scamp just behind barking wildly, the leashes bouncing after them.

Peggy, Heston, and Squatty ran after the dogs calling frantically for them to stop. At that moment they saw a huge spider ahead, and on the cave floor beside it, a dark shape.

"It's Haley!" screamed Heston.

Trevor leapt, and with his weight and speed, knocked the much larger creature over.

Squatty ridiculously shouted, "Watch out for the chelicerae!"

"Help!" screamed Haley. She, Trevor, Scamp and the poisonous wolf spider in an instant were a squirming mass of arms, legs, screams and vicious barks. The spider was the first one out of it, racing away as fast as his eight legs would go. Right behind him were Trevor and Scamp.

"Squeally, Squiggly, stop them!" screeched Peggy. "Catch the dogs!"

Henry shook his head to clear his mind. The dogs were racing into what might be dozens, hundreds of poisonous spiders.

Heston and Peggy had Haley on her feet. She was sobbing uncontrollably, grasping Heston, blubbering, "I'm okay. I'm okay."

Squeally aboard Miko was in hot pursuit of the dogs, with Henry and Squiggly on their spider close behind. "We'll never get them to stop," screeched Squiggly. "The spiders will-----" He couldn't say it. How could he tell his baby brother when he got bigger that he couldn't save Scamp?

But Trevor slowed. He wobbled, then sank to the ground. Scamp raced ahead, barking and jumping fiercely at the spider's rump.

Suddenly he realized he was alone in the chase.

Where was Trevor?

Scamp abruptly stopped barking, turned, and came back to his friend. Seeing him helpless, twitching on the ground, he whined pitifully and licked Trevor's face over and over.

With Haley crying but safe in Peggy's arms, Heston ran forward, cuddled his dog and wailed, "What's wrong with him? Trevor, what's wrong?"

Squiggly came up and said, "He got bitten. The spider must have gotten him. He's been poisoned."

"Oh no!" screamed Heston. "No, no!"

In pain, Henry somehow got himself down from his spider. As an Army medic he had known about snake bites, and, lacking any other means, he would try to squeeze as much of the venom out of the wound as possible.

But in an instant, behind them, out of the dark came five or six spiders racing directly at them.

The kids held their heads in their hands and screamed.

Nine

Henry, though, who had been in the middle of danger so often he had paid the price of PTSD, shouted with what little strength was left in him, "Here comes the cav!"

Not exactly the cavalry. It was the Squat Squad, the mounted patrol of the Squatter County Sheriff's Department who were charged with keeping dangerous predators within their wild nature preserves. The deputy out at the road had quickly told them what happened and they had immediately ridden to the rescue, guided by the sound of the dogs until the howling and barking had abruptly stopped, and by then they had the group in sight.

They pulled up and vaulted off their mounts.

"Everybody okay?" called the squad medic carrying a first aid kit.

Henry said, "Everybody except our hound dog. And Haley has bruises and needs checking out."

These deputies were an elite bunch. Their captain had finally gotten to choose the Squad's uniforms. Consequently, unlike the rest of the deputies who stood guard or directed traffic, they wore sensible uniforms with fairball caps--no bearskins--and field uniforms rather than colorful dress uniforms. They could see, and didn't sneeze. (Someone, Plato perhaps, said it's always better if law enforcement officers can see and don't sneeze all the time.)

The captain and his men and women troopers were a thorn in the side of the Superintendent of Law Enforcement. He could fume in his elegant office all he wanted, but, never going to the field to check on performance, it finally came to this: How could he dispute the testimony of the citizens who had been saved from disaster by the actions of the captain's Squad? He caved in and the Squad got its practicable uniforms.

The medic hurried up to Haley, quickly looked her over and said, "Bruises and scrapes. I'll be back." But Trevor was another matter. One of his long floppy ears had been sliced and was bleeding. Worse, his front shoulder showed a puncture wound and swelling where the spider's fangs had struck.

"Here," the medic said, snatching gauze and a compress from his bag and handing them to Henry.

A combat medic doesn't need to be told what to do, and Henry pressed the compress against the split in the ear and with the other hand swabbed blood.

The medic quickly gave Trevor a shot from something resembling a syringe. Henry didn't have to be told it was a pain killer. Next came a shot of anti venom serum.

With a knife the medic deftly scraped away hair around the wound on the shoulder, then squeezed both sides of the swelling. A gray, foul-smelling liquid mixed with a little blood oozed out. The medic placed a venom extractor over the fang punctures and pushed the plunger. The tube filled with a mixture of venom and blood. He ejected the mixture, put the instrument back over the wound and pushed again, repeating this action a few more times.

"Nice work," said Henry.

"You're not doing so badly yourself," replied the medic.

"Will he be all right?" Heston asked frantically.

The medic just raised a hand in a signal to be patient.

Heston and Haley still had their arms around one another but they were no longer crying, and instead intently watching the medic and Henry at work. With an instrument that resembled a stethoscope the medic was listening to Trevor's heart and lungs. Then alternating between swabs and a needle with something like catgut thread, the medic worked at suturing the dog's ear. Scamp, who had been quiet but nervously wiggling while watching the procedure, was now licking his friend's face. Trevor tried to respond but only weakly lifted his head and twitched.

Not able to contain himself any longer, Heston asked, "Please. Will he be all right?"

The medic put antiseptic liquid on the ear and the puncture wound and looked into Henry's eyes. What did that look mean? Long pause. Then the medic said, "He won't feel so hot for awhile, and he will have a long scar on his ear, but he will be okay." Henry nodded.

"Oh, thank you!" gushed Heston, and he and Haley, clasping one another, joyously swung back and forth.

Three spiders raced up to the group. On top were two sergeants and the captain. No saluting, just hand clasps and pats on the shoulders of their men at the scene. The captain's unit was proudly called just The Squad, but in fact it was company size, comprising platoons and squads. They had a lot of badlands territory to cover. Henry remembered his platoon sergeant, platoon leader, and company commander. He had no experience with men above company level and was suspicious of higher level command, but his company leaders were great. Most of the poor leaders and men had been winnowed out by the time he joined the unit. Combat compressed the rest into truly a band of brothers, and they shared a bond which few people other than those who serve together in stressful, dangerous circumstances will ever know. The captain's Squad, consisting of both men and women, no doubt were a band of brothers

The medic quickly swabbed Haley's scrapes and squirted a liquid on them. "We'll take the dog. We'll be faster," the medic said.

Heston and Haley begged to be taken back with Trevor, and the medic nodded. They quickly climbed up on the blind wolf spider beside him and their dog. Heston petted Trevor and said, "You're going to be all right. I promise. You're a winner. Remember?"

With that, the Squad unit which had first arrived on the scene sped off. Scamp watched and whined pitifully after Trevor as they disappeared into the dark.

The captain and his sergeants stayed behind and helped Henry and Squatty board Miko, then helped Squiggly and Scamp up onto the other spider.

Peggy climbed into a seat beside her grandfather and held onto him. "How are you doing, Grandpa?" she asked.

"Better," he said. He knew that was the case because the pain was back, something he often had not much noticed in the midst of the great danger.

"Captain," Peggy called. "My grandfather hurt his knees. Do you have anything for pain?"

The captain nodded, and one of the sergeants came over, reached up and put a few pills in Henry's hand.

Henry said, "I'm supposed to take two of these and call you in the morning?"

The sergeant, not understanding Out clichés said, "Sir, take only one a day."

Squatty added, "You'll be in never-never land if you take two."

The girls had gone through a lot, and as they rode, Peggy began to sing to herself, quietly, sadly, slowly, almost in a monotone, with some pauses between words

We went to see-----a dog show-----

A wonderful show-----of dogs-----

Scamp, he won by having fun-----

And Trevor-----was a winner too-----

Her voice trailed off and there were tears in her eyes. "Grandpa, Trevor is going to be all right, isn't he?"

"Yes, honey. He will be all right."

With that assurance, Peggy brightened somewhat and Squeally on the wolf spider to the rear joined her in tentatively, haltingly, hopefully singing

We went to see a dog show
A wonderful show-----of dogs,
Trevor was beautiful (pause)
-----And properly dutiful
While Scamp ran around
And brought-----the house down
We're off----- to see a dog show
They're wonderful, wonderful dogs.

The pill had a marvelous effect on Henry. By the time they reached the road leading back to the arena he was singing along with the girls, but with a gusto which cheered them. Henry felt no pain. As he sang off key 'We're off to see a Dog Show' for the umpteenth time, with what was left of rational thought he pondered this question:

What indeed would become of the dog show? One of the star attractions was out of action, and without his friend in the contest, Scamp would be in no mood to appear even if there would be a Best in Show event.

When they arrived at the arena they could hear a few dogs bark intermittently. When Henry got down in the parking lot he limped unsteadily toward the main gate. Peggy was holding his arm and he was singing 'We're off to see a Dog Show.' Then he would grin goofily down at Peggy and whistle a few bars. "Wonderful night, isn't it Peg?"

When they went through the gate and came out on the floor of the arena the place exploded in applause. Henry, wobbling, looked behind to see what they were going nuts about.

"Grandpa, it's for you," said Peggy, smiling up at him. "Do you think you can walk better?"

"Sure!"

Henry held up his head, pulled his shoulders back and said, "How's this?"

"Wonderful!" But she wasn't so sure.

It actually was not bad at all. He was walking fairly steadily, and the applause showed no sign of stopping.

Mrs. Hedy Heights rushed up to Henry. Behind her were Haley and Heston, still holding onto one another.

"Mr. Henry, thank you! Thank you!" she called out above the noise. "How can I ever thank you enough!"

There was no "My deah, Mis--tah Hen--ry," just a crying woman squeezing him in her arms and thanking him over and over. "Thank you!"

Haley and Heston threw their arms around Henry, and they joined in, "Thank you, thank you!"

Mrs. Heights now had her arms around Haley and Heston, saying to Henry, "You've given me my children back. No, not back, you've given me my children!" She was crying and kissing them. "*My children!*"

No Mrs. Haughty now, just Mrs. Heights, mother of Heston and Haley.

The applause died down and then became a hush, broken by only an occasional bark of a dog somewhere. Mrs. Heights led them to Scamp's cage on the mutt side of the arena. He was happy and yipping, but he did not whirl and bark out of control. He acted like a dog who had learned something.

Next to Scamp's cage, in fact flush against it, was another cage, and the nameplate read, 'Trevor de la Grand Duchy du Balmont.' A dog with such a pedigree on *this* side of the arena, the *mutt* side? Inside stood a wobbly, but recovering Trevor. Mrs. Heights put her hand over the nameplate covering all but 'Trevor,' and said, "Mr. Henry, Trevor thanks you too." Trevor managed what seemed like a smile and leaned against the bars of his cage. Scamp stuck his nose between the bars and happily licked his friend.

Henry, in his pleasant fog, hadn't noticed another cage. Now he saw it, and inside was Mugs. On his face was a big lopsided grin showing lots of crooked teeth.

"Mugs was worried," Mrs. Heights said, but I gave him some special treats, pieces of dried flatworm steak."

"That's good," said Henry, who seemed to be returning somewhat to normal. "Well, I suppose you have things to do. What about the show?"

"What about it?" said Mrs. Heights "I asked Mugs and Scamp and Trevor, and they all wagged their tails. That means 'On with the Show!'"

And indeed, Mugs and Scamp wagged again in agreement. Trevor weakly twitched his tail.

Mrs. Heights asked about Haley's rescue, and Henry was telling her how well the dogs had performed. As they were talking, judge Payton Prestwood, who had yesterday selected Best of Breed in the Hunter category, came up to Scamp's cage and said, "Hmm, little boy--er--Squiggy was it?--Squidgy?-----"

Squiggly, always a sweet boy, politely said, "Squiggly, Mister Prestwood."

"Whatever."

The judge yesterday had told Squiggly that his dog's coloring was all wrong. And his dimensions too. He had said that if there were such a thing as a Standard for mutts, "I fear he would not even come close. "

Now, looking for more sport, he was saying to Squiggly, "If you're going to have Grunt in the Best in Show tonight, maybe you would appreciate some more advice."

"Certainly."

But then Squeally bluntly corrected, "It's *Scamp*, Mister Prestwood. *Scamp!*"

"Whatever."

At that moment, Mrs. Heights saw the judge, turned to him and said, "Mister Prestwood! I heard you offer to give Squiggly more advice.

Don't you think what you did and, to my shame, I allowed yesterday is enough? More than enough?"

"Er--Mrs. Heights, I think-----

"Mr. Prestwood, no one cares what you think. I've heard from you all I ever want to hear."

Henry, giddy, wanted to give her a big kiss. If what Mrs. Heights said wasn't a permanent dismissal of Mr. Prestwood from judging he would-----In his mixed up condition he couldn't think of what he would do, so as the man slunk off to contemplate his fate, Henry just called merrily after him, "Good night Mr. Prestwood. And good night Mrs. Calabash, wherever you are."

Mrs. Heights smiled although she had no idea what he meant, and attributed it to his pain medication. She put her arm around Squiggly and said, "You don't need advice. Scamp is a perfect show dog just as he is. And he is a hero."

Ten

THE SHOW MUST GO ON

The evening event built to a crescendo. "Whew!" Peggy said. "Grandpa, I've never seen so many people in one place." The parking lot was not only full, it overflowed well beyond the arena. People were arriving from all over In. Or at least from the several surrounding counties since most of In had not even been explored and other communities were far distant. In her previous trip, Peggy was informed that In consisted of billions, maybe trillions of caves and tunnels which were huge in In terms but could be less than an inch or so of Out dimensions.

Mrs. Heights could have been seated in the premier Committee box as chairwoman of the Highville Kennel Club, sponsor of the show. Instead, she asked Henry if she and Haley might join him and the Squires family in their adjacent Honor box. "Pleased to have you," was Henry's reply. His speech was somewhat better now, but he still felt tipsy from the pill. He seated Mrs. Heights next to him, with Peggy on his other side. Mugs lay on the floor next to them, snoozing contentedly. Having survived all the excitement and with Best in Show yet to come, who could fault him for taking a nap?

Henry and Peggy were survivors too. Not just of the Labyrinth of Horrors, but of the delighted hugs and gushes of admiration from Mrs. Squires. She, S.Q., Squatty, and Squeally were seated in the row behind. Great Great Grandfather Squires had arrived and Henry seated him in the front row, and Haley beside him.

Henry began chortling. He said, "Squatty is quite the scientist. A hero scientist. He kept us informed of the dangers. The centipede was attacking. 'Watch out for the head,' he shouted. 'The forcipule fangs will inject poison!' *Forcipule* fangs! Just what we needed to know at that instant."

Henry turned and gave Squatty a playful poke. "But in all seriousness he was great. Indeed a hero." That prompted a hug of Squatty by Squeezy, his mother. She hugged and rocked him back and forth. Squatty was buried so deep in the embrace that Henry feared for his life, but then Squatty struggled up for air.

"Where's Heston?" asked Peggy. Haley told her he wanted to be with Trevor but would join them later. "Same with Squiggly," Peggy replied. "He's with Scamp."

Excitement built. The announcer gave some preliminary information about dog breeding, pedigree requirements, and the show. He received unexpected and unwarranted applause. What he said wasn't all that spellbinding, but this crowd was worked up. They were participants in a historic event, the First Annual Dog Show, with the final event just ahead. When he said, 'Next, Best in Show' they erupted. Peggy feared that the vibrations from thunderous applause and shouts might collapse the ancient man into dust, but he sat there intact with the tiniest smile marking his approval. "Thank goodness he didn't clap," Peggy said slyly to her grandfather. "His hands would have pulverized."

The announcer provided far more information than interested Peggy. She twiddled her thumbs, looked around, tried to estimate crowd size by counting rows then multiplying by what she thought were the numbers of people in the rows, and finally gave up. The task was far too burdensome. The crowd, though, had not lost interest.

The competitor dogs were now brought out and the handlers led their charges to knee-high cubes, each of which heralded a group name on all sides in oversized letters. As the dogs appeared, mingled with the general applause were surges of noise as group or breed supporters spotted their winner and watched him or her being led into position beside a cube, each of which was done in the colors of the Highville Kennel Club: gold with sapphire blue lettering. The seven perfectly spaced and aligned cubes for the seven purebred groups faced one side of the arena, the most desirable side which provided the best view of the entire event. The winner dogs were now being placed by their handlers to present the best stacking. Legs were moved a little this way, a little that way to obtain the desired effect. Combs were busy getting hair into the best possible coiffure. Hands smoothed and gently shifted hair from one position to another, then carefully brushed the coats to ensure that everything was just right.

Peggy had not been paying much attention, distracted by the oohing and aahing of an immaculately dressed lady in the adjacent Committee box who seemed fixed on one of the dogs, a spaniel. Squeally said, "That's Mrs. Spriggs. She owns that dog."

Then Peggy noticed that only six dogs had come onto the floor, and the space by the cube which read Hound was empty. That should have been Trevor's spot. She was overwhelmed by the sadness, and tears came. Haley and Mrs. Heights were also trying to keep from crying, but none of them were doing it very well.

Squeally behind them blubbered, "It's not fair. Why did that have to happen?"

Peggy then realized, and said, "There should be another cube, too. Where is the one for Scamp? He won his group. He should have a cube."

Mrs. Haughty probably would have said, "We don't do a cube for the mixed breed group!"

But Mrs. Heights said, "You're right. There's no cube."

She turned toward Haley and said, "Honey, would you find Mr. Oldsmith and tell him someone must have made a mistake? We need a cube for the mixed breed group winner. Do you feel well enough to do that?"

Haley had some red scrapes on her hands and somewhat of a black eye from being thrown from Caleb, her wolf spider, but she said, cheerfully. "Of course, Mom."

That may have been the first time she had called her anything but Mother.

Peggy chimed in, "I'll go with her." Squeally added, "Me too."

The three of them made off, searching. "Do you know what he looks like?" asked Peggy.

"Sure," said Haley. "I've seen him with my mom many times, talking dog breeding, judging, and especially preparation for this show. He's tall, silver-haired, very distinguished looking--sometimes maybe a little too much."

They had no trouble finding him--or rather finding the group around him. At the moment, several elegantly dressed ladies and handsome gentlemen were respectfully listening to his views on breeding, how to reach the Standard for a breed: "Careful selection, meticulous attention to breed improvement."

There was more as the girls tried discreetly to make their way to him. They got as close as a woman at his elbow, a person Haley knew as an owner of a cute dog in the Toy group. "Mrs. Shireland, she whispered. "My mother, Mrs. Heights, has a message I need to give to Mr. Oldsmith."

At mention of Mrs. Heights, the lady raised her finger tentatively, and when the judge seemed to pay no attention, she more forcefully raised it, leaned toward him and whispered, "Mrs. Heights is sending you a message."

That got his attention. A dog show judge--any dog show judge--paid attention when Mrs. Heights sent a message.

The judge was spectacularly dressed in Club colors: handsome sapphire blue dress coat with tails and two gold buttons on either side of the open front, black waistcoat with small cave pearl studs, high-necked white shirt with cave pearl studs and cuff links, narrow white bow tie with pointed ends.

"Yes," he said, bending magisterially at the waist from his considerable height, "and you are?"

"Haley Heights," she said.

"Of course, Haley. Everyone was dreadfully concerned about you. You're all right?"

"Just some scrapes and bruises." She didn't mention that she was also sore just about all over. "My mother said to tell you someone must have made a mistake. We need a cube for the mixed breed group winner."

Had lightning struck him on the spot, the judge could not have been more shocked. With tight lips he said, "A cube? For the-----" He was having a hard time getting his mouth to say the words "-----*mixed breed*-----?"

"Yes, for Scamp," Peggy volunteered.

"For-----?" That word stuck in his craw even more than 'mixed breed.'

Some of the people around him had raised their hands to their mouths in astonishment. Squeally heard one of them titter softly the stuck word, "*Scamp*."

But the judge heard it. Mindful of how a message from the chairwoman of the Highville Kennel Club related to his career as a show dog judge, Mr. Oldsmith scowled, then smiled at Haley.

"A cube? For Scamp?" This time the word flowed easily off his tongue. And he didn't even question of what use was a cube with Mixed Breed in large letters when there was no dog to stand beside it. "Of course," he said. He turned to an elegantly dressed man beside him and expressed his wish, "A cube for Scamp," which, to the man, was a command.

A cube had to be made, and this would take some time. In the meantime, on with the show.

The announcer was also elegantly dressed in Club colors. Next to him was a young-looking man in black evening wear. "A celebrity," explained Mrs. Heights to Henry. "He will add comments to the announcements. He's a philosopher."

"A philosopher!" replied Henry in surprise. "Not a rock star or politician?"

Mrs. Heights had no idea what a rock star was other than, perhaps, an expert in examining rocks, of which there were plenty in In. Politicians she knew. How could anybody not know who politicians were?

"His theories on behavior are fascinating. Some of them, if I understand them correctly, relate to us and dogs," she said.

"I see," said Henry, although of course he was speaking metaphorically. At one point he had lifted his moonglasses and instead of seeing a dog show he was looking into utter darkness. One more reason for him and Peggy to keep In to themselves and not share it with Laurel and Melanie. How could they understand enjoying a dog show that was held in absolute, impenetrable darkness?

"Look, they're about to start," Squeally said excitedly. "I just wish that Trevor and Mugs were in it."

The announcer lifted his megaphone in Club colors with the dog emblem on it. "This evening-----" Henry fleetingly and ironically considered how the announcer or anyone else could tell it was evening in a place eternally dark. "We are privileged to be participants in The First Annual Dog Show!"

Thunderous applause, shouts, stomping of feet.

"Welcome honored guests (he looked at the Box of Honor), welcome The Committee (he looked at the adjacent box filled with ten members of the Executive Committee, those who had the final say among the much larger Committee as a whole), welcome dog breeders, dog owners, trainers, handlers, dog lovers everywhere!"

Long applause. Announcer's hand up. Still long applause, still hand up. Finally quiet enough for him to say, "Introducing our judge, a man who has long devoted himself to assisting in setting the Breed Standard for each of our seven breeds, a man who has advised an untold number of breeders on improving the breed, a man who is a consultant and friend of owners, trainers, and handlers and--yes--one who has been a breeder and owner himself, the distinguished Judge Ormund Oldsmith of Smithville !"

The judge stood tall and proud, a pleasant smile on his face as the audience applauded.

The announcer continued with an introduction of Mrs. Heights, chair of the Highville Kennel Club, chair of the Executive Committee, chair of the event itself, The First Annual Dog Show.

She stood and acknowledged the applause. Next to be introduced was the head of the Science Committee in recognition of the work done in the complex Cloning and Hermaphroditism program which propagated the pedigreed dog population of In. Squatty clapped excitedly. Henry wondered if the announcer would say anything about the many accidents of breeding which resulted in the much larger number of mutts. He didn't.

Finally the announcer called out, "Ladies and gentlemen, I have the unexpected and distinct pleasure of formally recognizing and welcoming the distinguished gentleman from Out who made all of this possible by his enormous generosity of giving us The Gift, and with him, Mugs himself! Henry nudged Mugs to wake him up to stand beside him and acknowledge the introduction. Mugs stood and grinned to enormous applause from the tens of thousands who packed the arena.

Then a hush.

"And now, the judging for Best in Show begins."

With that, Judge Oldsmith slowly walked the line of pedigreed winners of breed, six of the seven. Trevor was absent. The judge looked intently at each as he passed by. Then he went back along the line and at the end of it nodded.

The announcer said, "With one dog absent from the lineup due to injury, first, in the Working Group, the Flowstone Mastiff, Number Seventeen, Flowstone Mastiff!"

The group and breed fans shouted loudly and clapped as the handler in evening jacket with an armband in Club colors took the dog to a position in front of Judge Oldsmith and deftly stacked him. The judge bent, ran his hand over this very large dog, mostly black with long hair and a dark gray tail curled up over his backside, a dog nearly as heavy as his handler. He opened the dog's mouth and examined his teeth, ran his hands along the sides of his skull, felt his ears, looked into his eyes. Then the judge straightened and motioned. The handler and dog set off at a fast pace to make a circle.

The announcer called out, "Winner of Best in Breed at eight regional shows."

The celebrity philosopher quipped through his megaphone, "Shaggy enough to make a good warm bedfellow, an impressive companion." Some laughs and lots of applause.

Mr. Oldsmith with hand on his chin watched studiously, appearing every bit the careful, experienced judge that he was.

When the mastiff was back at his cube, the announcer called, "Next, in the Non-Sporting Group, the Rimstone Poodle, Number Thirty-Seven, Rimstone Poodle!"

Peggy said, "Grandpa, why do they do that? This would be a pretty dog, but look what they have done to her."

Henry quietly acknowledged that Peggy had a point. The dog had long, beautiful white hair, but she had been styled in such a way that she looked like a collection of pompoms, a large one surrounding her head that went to her ears, then chest, shoulders and half of her back. Then there was a short distance along the back and stomach in which the hair was entirely shaved off, meeting a smaller pompom on top of the back, then a bigger pompom sticking up on the tail, and finally pompoms for each of the lower legs and feet.

Peggy said, "I'm trying to look through the pompoms as if they weren't there, and she's a beautiful dog."

"She is. Sad, isn't it," Henry agreed.

The celebrity must have had much the same opinion. "She would make quite a powder puff," he said to loud laughing, which the announcer ignored, or tried to.

After the judge's examination, the Rimstone Poodle made her circle as the judge watched her movement and the audience applauded.

"Next, in the Herding Group, the Stalagmite Collie."

"What a beautiful, sweet dog he is!" said Peggy. "Yes, except for Trevor and Scamp, he's my favorite," Squeally pronounced. Henry saw what looked like an approving glint in the slits of the ancient man's eyes, and Mrs. Heights said, "Very sweet, gentle." The black and white collie got hearty applause, louder than that for the preceding dogs.

Henry didn't want to say what he was thinking. Aren't collies supposed to be great herding dogs, like all others in the herding group? But where was consideration for what should have been at the core of the judging process--the dog's herding *performance*? Looking great, he thought, was one thing. Performing the function for which the dog was bred was another.

Because of Henry's furrowed brow Mrs. Heights seemed to know what Henry was thinking.

"Mr. Henry, today has given me a lot to think about. Trevor found Haley. Maybe we do need to include performance in breed standards."

The announcer called out, "Next, we have in the Terrier Group our winner, Stalactite Terrier Number Forty-Two, Stalactite Terrier." He was a gorgeous white dog with long, wiry hair.

Peggy complained, "Doesn't these dogs have names? Why is he just a group name and a number? That sounds like a prison guard calling roll, 'Cell Block D, Number Forty-Two.'"

Mrs. Heights heard her. "Peggy, that may be something The Committee needs to think about too."

After strong applause Number Forty-Two was back at his cube, and Number Six in the Toy Group, a little Soda Straw Papillon, made her circuit to loud applause.

"Next is the Sporting Group winner, Helictite Spaniel Number Eleven. Number Eleven." Clearly the crowd favorite, the nameless dog--so far as the announcing format was concerned--received a rapturous welcome by the crowd.

"His name is something or other, but my friends and I call him Stubby," Squeally squeaked above the noise."I like him because he looks a lot like Scamp except he has only two colors. And he acts just like Scamp except for the silliness."

Stubby was a gorgeous, symmetric orange-brown and dazzling white whereas Scamp had an odd mixture of four or five colors that went helter-skelter, inherited from the scrambled breeds of his mutt parents and grandparents. And Stubby was larger than Scamp. But both had that same spunky attitude toward life. No opponent would be too big for a good-natured tussle or, in the case of a huge poison spider, a fierce fight.

In the absence of Trevor and Scamp from the competition, Peggy, full of spunk herself, wanted Stubby to win. She reached behind her and gave Squeally a high five.

Judge Oldsmith thoughtfully surveyed the six dogs and paced once more up and down the line. Then he sent them all together once more around in a circle, dogs and handlers performing superbly. Stubby had a mischievous, endearing prance in his stride and when he got back to his cubicle he had a wide grin showing perfect teeth, telling everyone that this was a lot of fun.

When the applause died down, the judge then went down the line, examining each, hands moving over them, his eyes studying every detail. Then he stepped back, hand again on chin, silent.

Just then two people on the dog show staff came hurrying out, carrying the cube for Mixed Breed, set it down and carefully aligned it with the other seven cubes. There were now eight cubes, six for the group winners who had made their circle around the arena and been so carefully hand- and eye-examined by Judge Oldsmith. Six spaces with dogs in them, and two empty spaces. No Trevor. No Scamp.

Judge Oldsmith had made his decision.

He pointed at three of the six dogs and motioned for the handlers to take them around one more time. The fans of those three clapped and shouted their approval while those of the other three were either silent or groaned their disappointment but then, as good sports, joined in smiling and clapping for the three dogs in the center of the arena. Circling now were the Stalagmite Collie, Toy Soda Straw Papillon, and Helictite Spaniel. Everybody in the Honor box applauded loudly, and Peggy turned to Squeally and shouted, "Look at Stubby out there. He's having the time of his life!"

He certainly was, smiling left and right at the crowd, strutting his pleasure at their applause.

The three dogs who had not made the cut were led away to great applause. They all were, as the announcer said, winners. That left the remaining three facing the judge.

The judge's hand was again on his chin. His eyes looked over the three dogs one by one. He strode to the trophy table and picked up the winner's ribbon. Two stewards on either side picked up the second and third place ribbons and trophies. They walked to the cube in the center of the area, labeled 'Best in Show,' turned and faced the three dogs and handlers.

Total silence in the huge arena. The judge opened his mouth to speak. "I am pleased to announce that the winner of Best in Show is-----

Eleven

Winners All

J ust then a uniformed man rapidly strode across the carpet directly toward the judge, holding up his hand. He stopped in front of the judge. Judge Oldsmith, startled, said, "Yes?"

The uniformed man was the captain of the Squat Squad which had ridden to find a bruised and scratched Haley, and the fallen Trevor.

The captain softly said so no one else could hear, "Sir, I realize this is most unusual, but I must speak with you."

Henry saw them conferring but could not hear what was being said. He saw the judge listening intently, apparently asking questions, nodding his head. Then the judge and the two stewards walked back to the judge's stand and put down the ribbons. The judge went to The Committee box, the captain following him. Judge Oldsmith was so close to the Honor box that Henry heard him say to The Committee members, "We need to confer." He then spoke softly to Mrs. Heights who stood up. The judge said that although she was chairperson of The Committee, he respectfully requested she not accompany The Committee. "Of course, judge," she replied and sat back down next to Henry. They looked quizzically at one another as the judge led The Committee to a conference room, accompanied by the captain.

The arena was abuzz with wonder. Thankfully they didn't have long to wait. Within a fairly short time the judge was back and The Committee members resumed their seats. The judge took the announcer's megaphone and walked to the Best in Show cube at the center.

Slowly and distinctly, Judge Oldsmith called out, "Ladies and gentlemen. The Committee and I have heard firsthand the testimony of the captain of the Squat Squad who has confirmed what we earlier today had heard only second hand. We have two hero dogs and their handlers here tonight. These two dogs won their group competition and would have been out here competing. One, Trevor de la Grand Duchy du Balmont, is a trailhound who tracked down Haley Heights in the Labyrinth of Horrors and was bitten by a poisonous spider. The other is a mixed breed named Scamp." (This time the judge said the name with pride.) The judge continued, "Scamp stuck right by Trevor and together they fought the monster spider. The skill and courage of these two dogs is so singular and commendable that The Committee voted unanimously that they should be considered in this competition."

A huge roar of approval ripped through the arena, and it continued until finally the judge was able to continue. "I am told that although Trevor is not fully recovered, his handler, Heston Heights, has said he is well enough to appear so you can see him. And Squiggly Squires, Scamp's handler, says that Scamp will not leave Trevor's side, so-----here they are, heroes all, boys and dogs!"

Out walked Heston, and on a leash, a limping Trevor beside him. Trevor had a large bandage on the split in his ear, a defect which presumably would disqualify him from further competition. Heston, realizing this, did not care. He was just glad to have his dog alive and on the way to recovery.

Beside them was Scamp on a leash held by a beaming Squiggly. The old Scamp would have been nuts, jumping, barking, showing off in joy. The new Scamp had lost none of his playfulness but some of what might have been called foolishness.

The arena was exploding with clapping, shouts, whistling, stomping of feet. A wave among the spectators started at one end, washed along the purebred side, around the end, up the mixed breed side, and back again.

Over the noise, Judge Oldsmith asked the boys, "Heston, can Trevor walk the circle so I can judge him?"

"Yes, Sir. He'll be a little slow."

"And Squiggly, what about Scamp?"

"Yes, Mr. Oldsmith. He's ready!"

To which Scamp looked up at the judge and gave an emphatic 'whoof! and a grin.

Trevor and Heston went slowly, Trevor limping but head held high-- like a knight returning to King Arthur's court, wounded but proud after furious battle to rescue the queen.

Beside Trevor, Scamp pranced and grinned. The audience loved the show. Then Scamp reached up near Squiggly's hand and tugged at the leash in it.

"You want to go free? Will you behave?" Squiggly asked.

Scamp yipped and Squiggly unhooked the leash. Scamp was now free, and he took position beside Trevor as his handler. Heston took the cue and dropped Trevor's leash so Scamp could pick it up.

Thus began a show unlike any ever seen in dog shows, whether in In or in Out. Scamp held his head high with Trevor's leash in his mouth while Trevor lifted his head and picked up the pace a bit in an approximation of the style he used in making the circle when he won Best in Breed. Here were Scamp and Trevor, dog showing dog to the best of their abilities.

Over the thunderous noise of approval, Henry said to Mrs. Heights, "Can you believe this?"

"Yes, I can. What wonderful boys! What marvelous dogs!"

Judge Oldsmith took his eyes away from the performance, went over to the Honor box, leaned and said to Henry, "You are responsible for all this with your Gift. Would you like to join them?" He pointed at the dogs and boys.

Henry said, "Would I ever!" He turned and said, "Mrs. Heights, would you care to join me?"

She replied with a big smile, "Mr. Henry, I would have been crushed if you hadn't asked!"

"And you, Mugs. How about it?"

Mugs, grinning his crooked-tooth grin, was ready to go.

Henry took Peggy's hand, and Mrs. Heights took Haley's, then Mrs. Heights put her arm through the arm Henry offered, and they all walked forward to join the boys and dogs.

First Annual Dog Show

The horrendous noise of approval rose even louder. Mugs licked Trevor's face, then Scamp's. Trevor looked handsome, Scamp mischievous, and all of them proud in what amounted to a parade which led back to the cubes, the one for Trevor and the one for Scamp. Henry, Mrs. Heights, Peggy, Haley, and Mugs returned to the Honor box.

Judge Oldsmith, raising his hand and repetitively calling through his megaphone for silence, finally got it and said, "Ladies and Gentlemen. I have a duty to perform."

With that, he put down his megaphone, went to Trevor, knelt, opened his mouth to reveal his teeth, ran his hands over him, careful not to touch his swelled shoulder or bandaged ear, stood, looked him over thought-fully, then went to Scamp.

Needless to say Scamp thought it a wonderful game and nipped playfully at the judge's hand, and yipped a couple times in joy. For Scamp, that was exceedingly good behavior. The judge stood back, looked both dogs over, put his hand to his chin in a studious pose, and said, "Hmm."

He said to Heston, "Can you get Trevor to howl?"

Heston, surprised, said, "Easy."

He raised his hand and Trevor flipped his head back and let out the howlingest howl anyone was likely ever to hear, HOWOOOO, HAWOOOOO! It was the excitement of the hunt, the desperate need to find the person hunted.

Scamp, needing no cue, accompanied his friend by barking loud-er and better than any time other than during the hunt for Haley, AHROO, AHROOAH!

The audience was astounded, and broke into laughter and applause. The judge, eventually quieting them, then called authoritatively through his megaphone, "*That*, my friends, is how great dogs *perform!*"

He walked over to the Committee box, said something and, except for Mrs. Heights, the members followed him to the conference room. The arena resorted to a buzzing, the spectators wondering among one another what was going on.

Soon the judge returned, walked to the judge's table, and with megaphone in one hand, took the winner's ribbon in the other as the arena hushed. He then strode to the Best in Show cube at the center of the arena. Next to it was a low stand, only ankle high, the surface of which was the emblem of the show's sponsor, the Highville Kennel Club. It was an outline of a dog which bore some resemblance to Mugs, but an idealized Mugs with perfect teeth.

The judge called through the megaphone, "Please bring forward Spaniel Stubby; and Hound Trevor; and Mutt Scamp."

No numbers, no pedigreed names. Just names.

After the enormous applause, he called, "And will the following come forward: Stubby's owner, Mrs. Spriggs; Trevor's owner, Mrs. Heights. Scamp's owner, still a baby, is not here. His brother Squiggly, the handler of Scamp, is already here, so will Mr. and Mrs. Squires also come forward?"

For perhaps the first time in her life Mrs. Squires could not say anything. No gush of words, just an astonished look on her face at the honor as she and S.Q. strode toward the group.

With all in place at the Best in Show cube, the judge quietly asked a question of Mrs. Spriggs, Mrs. Heights, and Mr. and Mrs. Squires. They all nodded their heads yes. "Do you agree, Mr. Henry?"

"I certainly do."

"Ladies and gentlemen," called the judge through the megaphone. "The owners of these three winners of breed, and Mr. Henry, have agreed with my decision. All of us here tonight, and I daresay all the people of In--all of us are first and foremost dog lovers, and we want what is best for our dogs and for our children. With concurrence of the Committee, Mrs. Heights, and Mr. Henry, my decision is that the Best in Show winner is -----

Not a sound in the huge arena.

"The Best in Show winner is not one dog but *three*, the one I would have chosen just as the captain of the Squat Squad spoke to me, Stubby! Great applause.

"And the one who tracked and found Haley Heights in the Labyrinth of Horrors, Trevor! Even louder applause.

"And the one who stuck with his friend Trevor to the end in rescuing Haley, Scamp! The First Annual Dog Show has resulted in a tie among three wonderful, magnificent dogs! The two other winner ribbons will be made up and presented later."

The applause went on and on and on.

Finally the judge was able to get the audience quiet, and he announced, "Mrs. Heights has asked if she could have the megaphone."

As she lifted it to her lips, Henry smiled at the thought of such a fine-looking lady using a megaphone.

"Ladies and gentlemen," she called out. "This has been an extraordinary day for me. A day in which Trevor and Scamp and Mr. Henry and his granddaughter Peggy and three Squires children and my son Heston, and finally a Squat Squad medic and captain rescued my daughter and treated my dog. I love them all, and I love all of you and all our dogs, pedigreed and mutt."

Huge applause, and finally quiet.

Mrs. Heights continued, "I believe we need to examine the question of standards in judging. As Judge Oldsmith said, we may need to include *performance* among the standards."

Another roar, followed after some time by quiet.

"As chair of the Committee, I will ask them to consider this as well as the question of health of the succeeding generations of dogs. Health needs to be foremost in our thoughts as we breed pedigreed dogs.

"And mixed breed? Mutts? They deserve and should get truly equal consideration and respect during judging in future shows at all levels. We will consider all this and more.

"My sincere thanks to all of you, to the captain of The Squad and his men and women, to the Committee, to Judge Oldsmith and all the show judges for making such a success of our First Annual Dog Show, and to Mr. Henry for his gift of Mugs. Thank you, and good night."

Henry, feeling frisky, briefly lifted his moonglasses and experienced again the darkness. He knew, but could not see, that it was in fact filled with people and dogs, vibrant, pulsating life. He said to himself that it had indeed been a good night.

Mrs. Heights asked if she might give him a hug.

Henry replied, "Mrs. Heights, I would have been crushed if you hadn't asked!"

Twelve

Scientific Explanations

The next morning after breakfast in the Squires home, Henry asked Great Great Grandfather if he could clarify some things about In before he and Peggy departed for Out. The ancient man smiled his tiny smile, made an almost imperceptible beckoning motion with his finger, and went the few steps onto the back patio. Henry asked if Peggy and Squeally, Squiggly and Squatty could come too. The answer was a miniscule nod, yes.

The patio, Henry thought, was the perfect place for a discussion on the profound matters he had in mind. It lay right at the edge of a sheer drop into the vast darkness, down to the lake below, so far down that Henry could not see the lake through his moonglasses. Could answers be plucked out of what seemed an infinite dark void?

After all were seated, "Sir," asked Henry, "How did life come into being in this darkness?"

Silence. Thinking. Then the ancient man said, "I certainly do not have all the answers. Far from it. Do your scientists and philosophers have them? No. We all do our best in applying to curiosity our investigation, experimentation, analysis. Quite likely, in the beginning the heat of the interior of Earth supplied the energy which acted on inorganic minerals to create organic matter-- microbes which are living matter."

Squatty interjected, "Simple."

The ancient man looked at Squatty and said, "Ah, the glorious naïveté of youth. Adulthood comes too soon."

"And at great cost," Henry added.

The elder Squires went on, "Through processes we still are tussling with, microbial life reached the advanced stages you have seen in In. That is, our people and our fauna--which are our animal life. Some animals we domesticate and utilize, primarily for food and transportation. Then there is our flora--plant life--which provide such things as our clothing and our salads. And there is the beauty which fauna and flora bring us."

Peggy had eaten both their fauna and flora and thought some were awful and some not bad, and she had experience with domestic and wild animal life. She smiled, thinking of Koala and Cephus, but then shuddered, remembering Skelton and the Labyrinth of Horrors.

"Life is very efficient in our dark zone because it has to be. For example, some blind salamanders can exist for what you would call months, maybe even years on just one edible bit of prey."

Peggy asked, "And blind creatures? How come they move so well? The blind centipede and spider almost got us."

"Simple," interjected Squatty. "In the dark, what good are eyes? They would just waste energy. Better to have antennae or sensors."

That didn't make entire sense to her, but the old man did not correct Squatty. She could have said, "Why can you see in the dark, and you hate light?" But by now this fact had become natural to her, and might even relate to the strangeness of their eyes, very light gray, almost pink.

Henry asked, "And your incredible ages, millions of years you live?"

"Simple," said Squatty.

"Hardly!" he was corrected. "We frankly don't know definitively, and there certainly will be things we will never know. Science can't explain everything although we try."

Peggy said, "What about your old-fashioned clothes?" She recalled when she and Squeally first met and she had made fun of Squeally's pantalettes.

The ancient man replied, "That is a matter of choice. Perhaps we choose not to adopt all the styles and customs of your more modern times."

That prompted Henry to say, "Sir, you people know a good deal more about Out than can be explained by just sending a Chosen One such as Squiggly on a quest for The Gift. You have solved the problems of cloning and hermaphroditism which is way beyond what our scientists have been able to do so why-----

The old man interrupted, "There are some areas of inquiry into which it is better, perhaps, not to go."

Henry thought. Could it be possible that people from In had regularly gone among those from Out? Had they picked and chosen what they wanted to adopt or further improve for themselves?

Preposterous.

Wasn't it?

The ancient man seemed more tired than usual. He said, "We do what we do."

"Simple," said Squatty.

His great great grandfather did not correct him. He rose and extended his hand. Henry stood and carefully took it.

"Young man, please come again."

Henry said, "Thank you," and the archaic man shuffled back into the kitchen.

Henry looked at Peggy and said, "At least we have some things to think about. I can't imagine living without being curious. But honey, I think we need to get going."

Squatty said, "Mr. Henry, please come again. I'll explain some more things to you."

Squeally squeaked, "He's got lots more lectures he can give you," and poked at her brother as he went past her, ducking his return poke.

Squiggly objected, "He knows a lot. More than I do by far."

Thirteen

A Girl and a Boy

The good-bys were difficult. Henry and Peggy looked in on Squishy who was sleeping, and gave him light kisses. "He smells so good," said Peggy.

"For once," agreed Squeally as she bent and kissed him too.

Great Great Grandfather Squires and Squatty sadly shook hands and asked them to return soon.

S.Q., too, asked them to come back. Squeezy cried, buried them both in her warm hug, held each out at arm's length and blubbered, "Promise you'll come back soon."

"We'll see," said Henry. "That would be nice."

Mugs looked up at Peggy and she smiled a little at how funny he looked in his moonglasses. "Goofy guy," she said and jiggled his head back and forth. "But I guess I look funny in mine too. Want to take a ride with us." A big grin was his answer.

Koloa was waiting outside. Peggy had a strange feeling as she climbed up to seat herself beside her grandfather and Mugs. "Are you all right?" asked Squeally.

"Yes, I-----I'm fine." But the feeling didn't go away. She had lain awake half the night, thinking, feeling. Images had come into her mind. The danger. The thrill when they had survived, Trevor and Scamp.

And Heston.

She had finally dropped off to sleep.

They went down the hill slowly, looking back at Scenic Heights, then going through Middle Manor, and then Low Meadows. "You're quiet," said her grandfather.

"Just-----just a little tired I guess."

"That's no wonder. We've had a busy time."

Squiggly, looking sad, was quiet too.

Slowly they went down the hill toward the river, and as they started to pass the pool where she found her big, beautiful pearl, Squeally asked if she wanted to stop.

"No," said Peggy softly. "I would never find a pearl so wonderful, and wouldn't want to."

They proceeded downhill until they came to the dock where Silver, the alabaster-like blind cave fish was waiting. Squiggly clucked and the huge fish swished its tail. Squiggly said for Peggy and Henry's benefit, "Silver, good boy we'll be right with you." His voice sounded flat.

Everybody climbed down from Koloa, Peggy and Squeally helping Henry whose knees had begun hurting again. They said their good-bys to Koloa. Faithful Koloa looked sad as he turned and started slow-ly back up the path.

Then Peggy saw another wolf spider hurrying down toward them. A rider jumped off and dashed forward.

"Would you have room for me?" he called.

"Heston!" exclaimed Peggy. Last night she had wondered if she would ever see him again. And here he was again!

Squiggly said that of course they had plenty of room for him.

Heston called, "Hello Mr. Henry. Hi Mugs, Hi Squiggly, Hi Squeally, Hi Peggy." His greeting was for all of them, but he was looking at Peggy. "I'd like to go downriver with you if that's okay."

Henry had not missed the exchange of looks and he smiled and said, "Are you sure you want to go. It's a kind of long trip."

"Oh, I've done it several times, sometimes with Squiggly and Silver."

"What do you think, Peggy? Should we welcome him aboard?"

"Oh, Grandpa, stop teasing."

"And how about you, Mugs? What do you think?" asked Henry.

Mugs looked up, grinned and wagged his tail.

"Well, Peggy and Mugs thinks it's a good idea, so let's go."

Everybody climbed aboard Silver, Henry with some difficulty because he didn't want to take another pill which would make him tipsy. For a moment Peggy feared her grandfather was going to sit with her, but he and Mugs sat up front beside Squiggly. Squeally sat down on one side of her and Heston on the other. They all strapped on life preservers and helmets.

As Silver moved out into the lake there was a period of awkward silence in the rear seats, finally broken by Heston saying, "Trevor is better. He even ate something for breakfast."

"That's good. I was worried," Peggy replied quietly.

The rest joined in with comments on Trevor and the surprise of him being able to appear on the floor of the arena in time to be judged. In short order a dog show song came from the kids in the rear, soft and tentative at first, then growing louder

We went to see a dog show
A wonderful show of dogs,
Trevor won and Scamp did too
Trevor howled, Scamp went ah-roo
We went to see a dog show
That wonderful show of dogs.

Heston was a little off key but Peggy in her mind gave him high marks for trying. The three in the rear seat were now laughing and talking about school and other things, having such a good time that Peggy didn't notice they had almost gone past the grotto where on her first trip upriver she was angry at Squeally, but where, on the way back down they realized they had become lifetime friends.

"Remember, Squeally?" Peggy asked.

"I remember," Squeally replied. "I will never forget. Do you want to visit it again?"

Peggy thought, and said, "No. It was perfect. Let's leave it that way." She squeezed her friend's hand.

As the lake became river, Squiggly called out, "Get set. Big Falls ahead." He clucked and Silver accelerated.

When they heard the roar, Squeally squeezed Peggy's hand. "Here we go!" she squeaked as they launched out into the air. In the few seconds before splashdown below the falls, Peggy and Heston's hands came together, and stayed that way through the next series of small falls.

Henry called over his shoulder, "How are you kids doing back there?"

"We're doing fine," Squeally responded, "aren't we Peggy?" giving Peggy a knowing nudge of the elbow.

Peggy gave Heston's hand a little squeeze and said, "We're fine."

Quite soon they were at the dock downriver, and they climbed off. Squiggly clucked their thanks and Silver sank into the current and disappeared. They walked the pathway, Peggy now with her grandfather and Mugs, all of them mostly chatting about the dog show. Heston to their rear answered questions but didn't contribute much else. He seemed off somewhere.

"Halt!"

It was the challenge from a sheriff's deputy, this time a man. He and Henry and Squiggly went through the routine. When the guard asked how many travelers, Henry held up six fingers, including one for Mugs. The deputy, tilting his head way back, trying to see under his bearskin hat said, "Oh, twelve. Destination?"

Henry grinned and responded, "Out."

Ahh-choo! The deputy got sneezing so hard he must not have realized what Henry said, and he gasped, "Pass."

They walked on in the dark. Peggy drifted back and walked beside Heston. "You're not saying much," she said.

"Well, I-----sometimes I don't know what to say so I just keep quiet."

"Well, I usually talk too much, but sometimes it's nice just to be quiet."

"And enjoy the dark," Heston added.

"Uh, sure-----enjoy the dark." Peggy took his hand and they walked along quietly in the dark.

Soon they turned a bend and saw dim light ahead. As they walked on, the cave grew lighter. Peggy pulled off her moonglasses and handed them to Squeally. At the same time, Heston pulled his dark sunglasses from his pocket. There was a brief moment when neither was wearing glasses.

Peggy said, "I like your eyes." They were the same very light gray, almost translucent eyes as those of Squeally and Squiggly--indeed, of everyone Peggy had seen in In. But she especially liked Heston's eyes.

He said, "I like yours too. They're-----different. And nice."

As they walked, the cave became lighter and lighter, and Heston put on his glasses. He didn't understand how Peggy could stand the light but said nothing about it.

Henry was talking to Mugs and reaching down frequently to pat him. "You'll be a good boy, won't you." Mugs must have felt the change in Henry's attitude because he looked up, not smiling now, but with a mournful look on his face.

Squiggly said, fighting back tears, "I'll take good care of him."

Henry replied, "I know you will," and hugged the boy he had come to love so much. "I know you will."

They were now in what seemed to be twilight, and the cave exit was right ahead. The river noise beside them made hearing more difficult. Henry and Squiggly stopped. Squiggly was crying, but he blubbered out, "Now Mr. Henry, be sure you and Peggy are outside the cave before you say 'Form.'"

Peggy and Squeally hugged, tears in their eyes.

Peggy gave Heston's hand a squeeze, and he squeezed back. She ran her hand up to his elbow and looked into his face. He was crying. He said, "Please come back. Will you?"

Tearfully she said, "I-----I'll try. Goodbye." She stood on her tiptoes and kissed him quickly.

Then she kissed Squeally, turned away, joined her grandfather in one last hug of Mugs, and the two of them walked out into twilight.

They said, 'Form,' and were dazed.

⤳⟶⟵

Beside them was the huge rock and small hole with a trickle of water coming out of it. For a moment Henry held her in his arms and they hugged in a confused mixture of sadness of parting and the feeling one gets when returning home after a long absence.

"Dad, Peggy, where are you? Supper!"

"We're up here," Henry called back to Melanie. "Be with you in a minute." They walked down out of the woods, up onto the back deck and into the kitchen.

"Go wash up. Did you have a nice walk?" Peggy's mother asked.

"It was-----quite nice," Henry replied.

Peggy said, "It was-----" She couldn't find the right words but said, "Nice."

Laurel asked Henry, "Why are you limping?"

He said, "It's these old knees again. I'll take some Tylenol."

That night for some time Peggy lay awake, tossing and turning. In that stage between awareness and sleep she thought she heard barking and young voices faintly, coming from a great distance in the woods. She wondered about Heston. She was confused. And sad.

⌘

The next morning on their walk she asked her grandfather, "Did you hear anything last night?"

His knees still bothered him. For a time he just kept walking slowly. Then he stopped and said, "You mean the barks and children's voices."

He hugged her and said, "I love you Peggy."

She hugged back, and in a jumbled mixture of sadness and joy, said, "And I love you, Grandpa."

Caves 'n Kids Books

Our picks for

Beginning readers, or for reading to them

Caves and Caverns, by Gail Gibbons
   32 pages, color illustrations. How caves are formed, types of caves, exploring them, how cave formations are created, vegetation and animals in caves, cave paintings.

Discovery in the Cave, by Mark Dubowski, illustrated by Bryn Barnard
   48 pages, color illustrations. The exciting discovery of Lascaux Cave by a teenage boy and his dog. A trip inside a hole with friends reveals walls covered with amazing paintings 17,000 years old.

For 8-12 years

The Hidden World of Caves: A Children's Guide to the Underground Wilderness by Ronald C. Kerbo
   48 pages, color photos of cave formations, creatures. Famous caves of the world. Caves you can visit, and more.

Looking Inside Caves and Caverns (X-Ray Vision) by Ron Schultz
  46 pages in color, great photos, wonderful drawings. How various
  types of caves form, many beautiful cave formations, exciting cave
  creatures, and much more.

One Small Square, Cave by Donald M. Silver, illustrated by Patricia J.
  Wynne
  48 pages in color, marvelous illustrations. One small square reveals
  an amazing world as you enter, and inside the cave you meet wondrous animals and cave formations.

Cave Animals by Francine Galko
  32 pages in color photos. Animals you may find at the entrance,
  deeper in the twilight zone, and very deep in total darkness.

Cave Sleuths by Laurie Lindop
  80 pages, color photos. All about exploring caves and what you find
  in them. Dry caves and cave diving.

Great Caves of the World by Tony Waltham
  112 pages, color photos. 28 famous caves in Africa, Americas, Asia,
  Australasia, and Europe.

And for older children and adults

Neil Miller, Kartchner Caverns: How Two Cavers Discovered and Saved
  One of the Wonders of the Natural World
  216 pages, color photos, sketch map of the cave. A real-life thriller.
  In 1974, two young cavers in Arizona struggle into a hole in the
  ground which upon further wiggling reveals a fantastic cavern never
  before seen by human eyes.

In order to preserve its pristine nature they kept the secret for years until the State of Arizona could develop a responsible, scientific way for the cave to be viewed by other eyes. Magnificent cave formations.

Michael Ray Taylor, Caves: Exploring Hidden Realms
   216 pages of oversize book, color photos. Caves in ice, earth, water. Explorations by experienced cavers.

David W. Wolfe, Tales from the Underground: A Natural History of Subterranean Life
   221 pages, black and white photos, sketches. A biochemist's investigation, from shallow subsurface to deep life in extreme conditions.

About Bill,
the author

As a farm kid I loved reading and writing, devouring books about cowboys, Indians, frontiersmen, and of course The Royal Canadian Mounted Police. Oh, to be a Mountie!--Red tunic with leather belt around my waist, blue riding breeches, broad-brimmed hat! All kinds of ideas raced through my head. When I was about 12, for some reason long forgotten I wrote an anecdote about an owl and sent it to *Open Road for Boys*. Miracle of miracles, it was published!

I became not a writer, but a career soldier, and on my first tour on the faculty at West Point the kids who played with our daughter wanted stories, so I made them up, inserting her and her friends into them as I went along. One day a little girl came to the back door and asked my wife if her "boy" could come out and play. When my wife said, "Not now, he's taking a nap," wide-eyed, the child responded, "You mean you make him take a nap?"

I've always loved kids, and I made up all kinds of stories for them and my daughter, but my professional writings were for adults--books on higher education, articles on a variety of topics, books on the war in Vietnam. Then, having more than enough of war, I finally turned to what I love best--writing for children. Somehow the characters pop into my head, and I write until I founder for a day or two, and then suddenly one of them will show me the way forward. Those kids of my stories are my great friends. Among them I feel young again.

What a joy it was to find

Mary, the illustrator

Peope always ask me how long I've been drawing, and I never know how to respond. I have no clear memory of when I first picked up a pencil and set it down on paper to draw my first picture, much like you don't remember taking your first breath. I've just always been doing it. Growing up, I was always in competition with my other brother to be the better artist. This drove me to improve my skill as often as I could at a young age. Most children, as soon as they're old enough to hold a crayon will attempt to draw a picture. This was the same for me, except, unlike most people, I never stopped.

I've always been drawing, but it wasn't until a few years ago that I got into illustration. Spurred on by the encouragement of some good friends, and a gentle nudge from God to leave my old job, I began illustration full time in the fall of 2014 and haven't looked back. Since then I've been blessed to be able to work with some incredible authors with some pretty awesome books in need of illustrations, one of these books being *The Cave of Healing*.

Working on this book has been interesting because it's one of the first chapter books I've ever illustrated, something I've wanted to do since I started this illustrating journey, but haven't really had the opportunity to do until now. Also, I've always been somewhat fascinated with caves, so it was fun to be able to illustrate them and the children in them for this story.

I've really enjoyed working on this project, and I hope you find as much enjoyment reading the story as I had drawing the pictures for it.

Made in the USA
Charleston, SC
02 March 2016